IVORY ROSE

KATHLEEN McCALL

ZEBRA BOOKS
KENSINGTON PUBLISHING CORP.

ZEBRA BOOKS

are published by

Kensington Publishing Corp.
475 Park Avenue South
New York, NY 10016

First printing: January 1988

Printed in the United States of America

In loving memory of my father
Charles William McCall

Though destiny's steps may separate us,
My heart shall always beat with remembrance.

Prologue

Shallow, gasping screams echoed through the ornately decorated bedchamber, as the small, pale-featured woman upon the large canopied bed clutched the silk sheets with slim hands, her frame contorted by the horrible pain that had been brought about by the birthing of her child.

"I surely do be a-thanking ye, Madge, for braving this fierce-cold night with me. I don't be a-knowing what I would be a-doing if'n I had to come and face this here birthing by meself." The tiny, angular midwife spoke to a woman of larger girth, as they both sat by the hearth watching their patient's struggles.

"Why are you standing over there and gaping at me?" the small woman about to give birth screeched at the pair across the room. Then, her brown, shimmering eyes enlarged to twice their normal size, she rose up on her elbows, trying to find some form of release from the agonizing pain that was attacking her body.

The midwife hurried to the bedside, heaving a large sigh of impatience at this woman's outrageous behavior. Ye would be a-thinking that no other had ever gone through this ordeal before, she thought to herself, knowing of Priscilla Buchanan's monumental selfishness and haughty manners.

When Amy Little had been asked to assist Priscilla Buchanan with her birthing she had thought that the coin she would be receiving would be exactly what she needed to buy her own small child a winter coat, but now, after the long hours of being locked in the same room with this demanding woman, she desired nothing more than to return to her own cottage and to the cozy bed she shared with her husband, Tom.

"Don't just stand about daydreaming you old hag!" Again the strident voice berated the midwife. "Fix me some more of those herbs that you gave me earlier this morn. They seemed to have helped lessen the pain somewhat."

"We can't be having any of that now, ma'am." Amy looked worriedly upon the young woman. "It would surely be too dangerous for the babe. Your time should be only moments away now."

"Do as you are told," Priscilla Buchanan screeched, and letting out another burst of abuse, she once again doubled over upon the bed, but this time there was no release from her agony and Amy, seeing that the time was at hand for the babe to make its way into the world, took full control of the situation.

"It be time now for this foolishness to come to

a stop," Amy declared. "You have to be a-pushing down hard with them pains. It is time for the babe to make its way out of your body."

The woman upon the bed quickly did as she was told and, with a mighty grunt, bore down with all of her slight strength, her body rising upon the bed as though a new plague of pain had just assaulted her.

"Now push hard!" Amy ordered, readying herself to receive the child and help it take its first sweet breath of life.

Smiling, she took hold of the babe, right away noticing that the child was a tiny girl, but as her mother let out another scream, the midwife looked back to see the head of another babe being pushed from its mother's body. "Madge, quickly," the small woman called to her companion who was still sitting near the hearth and warming herself. "It be two wee beings. Come and help me with this first babe."

After Madge had cleansed the first baby's mouth and nose, the infant girl, as if in imitation of her mother, let out a screech.

Moments passed as the mother struggled to rid herself of the babe still caught within her body. And in time, with the help of Madge who gently pulled upon the small babe, another small wail filled the chamber, though this one was much fainter than the first.

"Another tiny girl," Amy exclaimed, gently taking this babe up into her arms.

The woman upon the bed did not bother to respond to the midwife's words. She was too exhausted to do aught but fall back and shut her brown eyes, willing herself to find some peace and rest and to put from her mind the terrible ordeal she had just suffered.

It was not until late in the morning of the next day that Priscilla Buchanan awoke to see the sun shining brightly through the white-and-peach lace curtains at the windows. With a small sigh of contentment she stretched, but her body's soreness chased away her contented feeling of well-being, and all that she had endured the eve before came flooding back. What had that dreadful midwife said? Two tiny girls? She must have been mistaken. Priscilla tried to sit up against her silk pillows, and as she did this she began to tug harshly upon the bell at her bedside table. Where is that miserable creature, Mrs. Daily? she wondered impatiently.

Within moments the housekeeper came through the oaken portal and walked to the bed. "You called for me, madam?"

"Yes, blast it! I did call for you. Tell me exactly what happened last eve!"

"Yes, madam. You gave birth to twin girls. I sent the midwife and her friend home with the promise that they would be paid this very day," the woman replied in an emotionless voice.

"Twins?" Priscilla fell back against the pillows as though she had been wounded. "What on earth will I ever do with two children?"

"I truly could not be telling you, madam," Mrs.

Daily responded, though she knew that her mistress was actually talking to herself.

"My sister Mary was to take the child, but surely she will never consent to taking the pair. Her husband Jonathon would certainly object, he had to be coaxed into agreeing upon the one child." With her husband dead only five months, Priscilla did not intend to care for a child herself. She was still young and pretty, and there was much of life that she had not as yet tasted. She could not be burdened with thoughts of a child waiting in a nursery for her.

That same evening before the sun set in the sky Priscilla Buchanan ordered Mrs. Daily to bring her daughters to her bedside, and as she looked down into the identical features of the tiny girls, she named the first-born Sylvia, and the second babe, Sabrina. "Send the first-born to my sister, Mrs. Daily, the other child shall go to the nuns at Roundtree Convent. Are both men I sent for downstairs and ready to carry out their orders?" At a nod of the older woman's dark head, Priscilla cast one last glance toward the little girls, and then, taking up her hand mirror she began to brush out her long, blond curls. "Oh . . . make sure that both men are paid well for this eve's work."

Mrs. Daily nodded quietly and, taking the babes up in her arms, went out of the chamber. Handing the younger of the pair to the wet nurse, she instructed her to take it to the car-

11

riage waiting by the front steps, she carried the other child down the stairs and handed to the man who would see her safely to the house of Priscilla Buchanan's sister.

When both babes had left the Buchanan townhouse, the housekeeper sighed, satisfied to be rid of the extra burden of infants. They would surely be better off where they were going than staying in this house where they were not wanted.

Chapter One

"I shall not be forced in this outrageous manner! What do I care if the woman is my mother? She has little right to tell me to do anything."

Mary Walters sadly looked upon her niece as that young woman paced about her bedchamber. Priscilla had been adamant about her decision to wed Sylvia to a young man she had met in London over two months past. The discovery that he owned a castle of some sort near the border of England and Scotland had only further encouraged Priscilla to make the match. Perhaps this move sprang from her fear that one day her daughter would overshadow her, for Sylvia was now a stunning young woman and there was much of the mother in the daughter.

"You certainly could have tried to sway Priscilla in this matter, Aunt Mary. She is your sister and would surely listen to you of all people!"

The girl's demanding tone chilled Mary, but did not surprise her. She had seen this girl into a beauty, but she had also seen her act in the same careless and cruel manner as her mother. With a sigh, Mary looked upon the girl and found that she had little feeling for her. "I certainly did talk to Priscilla, my dear. But you know her well, and I am afraid that I could not daunt her in the least. She is, after all, your only true parent, and though I have seen to your care, she has always made the final decisions on your well-being."

"A parent who has had little time for me suddenly wishes to determine my whole life?" Sylvia flounced her skirts wide and knocked the contents of her delicately carved lap desk upon the carpet, a large, dark ink stain quickly appearing upon its light blue pattern.

Irritated by the girl's total lack of concern for the mess that she had just made, Mary reached for a cloth and patted at the dark ink. Seeing the stain only worsen, she rose and faced her niece. "You have ever had your way here in my home, Sylvia, and if your mother had not made these plans for your future you would, of course, be welcome here until you did marry. I am afraid, though, that you are taking this too much to heart. All young women must marry and start their own families, no matter that they are not that willing at the start of the venture. I myself married your uncle Jonathon as my father had planned. I did not know him, but as you can see the match was well suited and we are both extremely happy with our lives."

Sylvia thought of her heavy, rather gruff uncle,

and vowed with a shudder that she would not be forced to wed in a like manner. Aunt Mary and Uncle Jonathon rarely even spoke to each other; they lived separate, barren lives. Sylvia thought of the man whom she kept secretly in her heart. She knew that she desired only what Zaloe Tolliver could give her, though she did admit that if she had never met Zaloe she might have been satisfied with money and position and all that those allowed. After knowing Zaloe, however, she had to have him and no other. He had taught her about passion, about love, and she could not live without the tender yearnings he aroused in her.

"Priscilla has planned that in one month's time you will travel by carriage to the outskirts of England," her aunt stated firmly, "to meet the man you shall then wed. Of course there shall be a grand ceremony. I am not sure, though, if Priscilla herself will be able to attend the wedding—you know that the ball at court will be held very soon. I also shall not be able to miss the ball, for Jonathon insists that we go together. But do not fret. I am certain Priscilla will be sending someone of some importance along with you to ensure that all will go properly."

Sylvia looked at the older woman with astonishment. Did her mother and aunt really think that she would willingly comply with what they proposed? Her thoughts were not of honoring a parent's desire but of her love. Zaloe would rescue her from this horror that was threatening to engulf her. He would never allow these plans to come to fruition. He would help her to flee from her kin.

As Mary went on about the plans for the trousseau and the wedding gown, Sylvia remained quiet, thinking her own thoughts. She knew arguing with her aunt would accomplish nothing. This woman was but her mother's puppet; she was not the one Sylvia would have to confront. Priscilla would determine her fate and Sylvia knew she must stand before her mother soon and plead her own case, though she doubted the woman would relent.

"I am quite tired, Aunt Mary," she suddenly declared. "Do you mind if I rest for a time now?" She had interrupted her aunt, who was talking about the plans already made for the wedding.

With an exasperated sigh, Mary nodded her head. She would be rid of the girl soon enough, and would no longer have to contend with her flighty ways. "I shall leave you to your bed. I have some appointments to keep this afternoon. The ladies are meeting for tea at Mrs. Valroy's home."

Sylvia barely waited for her aunt to leave before she began to pull the constricting gown from her shapely body. Clad only in her chemise, she then lay full-length upon the large, mahogany, fourposter, her mind weary and filled with thoughts of freedom.

The darkness of the deep, still night enveloped the large, mansion set back upon the London street, as a tall, thin man softly walked around to the steep staircase at the back, used mostly by the servants. Deep in shadow, he disappeared through the door at the top of the stairs.

With a racing heart, Sylvia stood near the portal, at the end of the long hallway. When the door was slowly pulled open and the man stepped into the darkness of the large house, she flung herself upon his chest and, with a moan of anticipation, felt his lips bear down upon her own demandingly.

"Let us go to your chambers where we can talk without fear of someone coming upon us," a deep, rasping voice said close to her ear. And without speaking a word, Sylvia took his hand and started down the hallway toward the chambers, stepping softly upon the gleaming, dark wood of the floor so as not to awaken the entire household and reveal her duplicity.

The door to her chamber locked, the man spoke again. "Your note said that you were in some terrible trouble. This had best be good. There was an important game at my club tonight. I can still make it if you would please be quick with the telling of this disaster that has so suddenly befallen you." Irritation at having been called to this house at this time of the eve was plainly visible upon the man's dark, hawklike features, and for a moment Sylvia felt the quick sting of tears in her large brown, eyes.

"My mother plans to send me to some far-off place to marry a strange man, within the month." She let the words fall harshly upon the chamber and settle upon the man before her.

Without a word he looked the beautiful young woman over from head to toe, his thoughts turning to harsh reality upon learning of her parent's plan. He had hoped that it would be he who would one day claim her hand, not that he particularly cared to marry Sylvia Buchanan, at times her demanding ways rather unnerved him and caused a hard anger to settle in his chest, but she was the only heir of two rich families and he knew that one day, with her mother's and uncle's wealth, Sylvia would be in a prominent position here in England. "When were you told of these plans for your marriage?" he demanded, realizing that he had waited too long to put forth his suit.

He had not thought that her mother would approach the subject of marriage for her only child for another year or two, and he had wanted to wait as long as possible before declaring his intentions since another might at any day take her place. But now it dawned upon him that he had waited entirely too long.

"Today I was told all by my Aunt Mary," she answered, tears brimming in her eyes. "We must confront my mother with our feelings. She will surely relent when she hears of our love." Zaloe had doubt about this. He could offer little for Sylvia's hand, being a man who lived by his wits and his skill at cards, gaining what coin he could from the schemes he set into motion. But Priscilla Buchanan, he was sure, knew full well his position. Before he could say this to Sylvia, she shook her honey gold head.

The young girl knew that it would not be easy,

his trying to claim her. "My mother's plans are already made. My wedding gown has been ordered. I think she will not easily relent in this matter. This man must have a title of some sort, for my aunt claims that he has a castle near the border of Scotland."

"Then if she will not relent and favor me, we shall have to take other action, my little silky flower," Zaloe whispered. He then placed his thin lips over Sylvia's, hoping to silence her grating, demanding voice. If her mother would not relent, Zaloe knew that he would not let Sylvia go. He would steal her away if need be, then marry her. Given time, her mother and uncle would surely forget their anger—what other choice was open to them—she was, after all, their only heir.

Sylvia did not think while in his arms. Knowledgeable about women and what they desired, he caressed her with lips and hands as he led her toward the large, mahogany bed and eased her back upon silken sheets, his eyes greedily taking in the perfect form her satin robe revealed.

Though Zaloe could easily be daunted by this woman's nagging ways, he never grew tired of the treasures that lay beneath her clothing. Aye, he would marry her, for he knew the control he had over her. She would do as he bid, and when he had her funds in his hands, he would settle her somewhere out of the way if she became too demanding. The joys her body offered could easily be replaced if the need arose. Abandoning these thoughts, he pulled his clothing from his slim form and joined Sylvia upon the soft cover-

19

let, her soft, throaty cries of passion soon filling the chamber and his own ears.

Zaloe gave little thought to Sylvia's needs or desires. He had the honor of being the first man to know her, so he knew she was dependent upon him. He drew her soft, pale legs up into the air and settled his long, hard body against hers, not bothering to spend time with preparing her. His mind was already gone from this bedchamber to his club, where there were riches to be found.

Chapter Two

The interview was not going at all as Sylvia had hoped. She had but pleaded with her mother to relent and allow her to wed the man she loved, Zaloe Tolliver, but Priscilla though had been adamant. Indeed, she was outraged at hearing her daughter confess to loving such a disreputable man as Tolliver.

"I cannot imagine where on earth you have come up with such a ridiculous idea as this, Sylvia. To even suggest that you know this horrible man is shocking enough. Why, the stories I have heard about him! Surely your aunt has not been allowing you to receive such visitors, has she? Zaloe Tolliver is not for you, my dear, indeed not. You are worthy of an earl or a lord, not a gentleman who uses any means to gain coin. Let us hear no more about this man." Rising to her feet, Priscilla motioned for her daughter to do the same. "Come up to my chambers, dear. I am expecting a guest at any moment, and I must make sure that I look my best."

And as they left the small parlor and headed for her bedchamber, Priscilla glimpsed unsettled fury on Sylvia's flawless features. But she had no regrets. She would do her duty and see her daughter wed to Garrison McBride; then she would be able to breathe easier for this was her last obligation to her child.

Sylvia realized that she had little choice but to go along with Priscilla, for her aunt's driver expected her to be at her mother's home all morning, and would not return for some longer. Entering the bedchamber decorated in peach and cream, she took a seat near a small table.

Priscilla smoothed her hair, then turned about to face her daughter. "Would you care to join me and Anthony?" she asked. Noting that Sylvia was looking through her favorite book of sonnets, she hoped the girl would prefer to stay in these chambers and read, despite her offer of company.

"No thank you. I shall stay here and wait until you are finished with your guest," Sylvia responded, her brown eyes lingering over the pages of the book though her mind was on the man her mother was about to entertain.

Without another glance or word, Priscilla Buchanan floated from the chamber and entered the small upstairs parlor, there to find her latest gentleman friend.

Alone, Sylvia threw the book back upon the table. How could she change her mother's mind? Zaloe had insisted that she state her plea, but adamant as Priscilla was, she knew that there would be no changing her. She and Zaloe would have to run away and marry, and as Zaloe had already told her, it would only be a short time before all would turn out for the best. How long could her mother and uncle stay mad at her? Of course, for the first few months they might remain angry, but given time, they would see how happy she and her new husband were and surely they would relent.

Suddenly enraged, Sylvia rose to her feet and started to pace about the chamber. But her eyes fell upon an old family Bible, and something about it was arresting. Why on earth would a woman such as Priscilla Buchanan have such a book laying about, she wondered. Her fingers lightly traced the gold binding, and without a second thought she opened the Bible to the first page, her eyes falling upon scrawled names — her Buchanan lineage.

Perhaps this book had belonged to her father,

23

she thought; and this realization led her to sit back down on the chair, the Bible in her lap. She had been told little of her father, had only bits and pieces of knowledge about the man that had sired her and then died. Now she let her brown eyes fill with the names of long-dead Buchanans, and at the end of the list she espied her own name, but next to it was another. Sabrina. Sylvia frowned.

"Sabrina." She lightly whispered the name, and then, reading on, she saw that she and the one named Sabrina had been born the same day. Her heart began to pound. "Twins, I had a twin sister," she murmured, thinking at that moment that her twin must have died during childbirth. But at the bottom of the page, in her mother's flowery scrawl were the words "Sylvia, first-born, placed with my sister Mary. Sabrina, second-born, sent to Roundtree Convent."

"Roundtree Convent?" Sylvia questioned softly, her eyes widening as though she did not believe what she saw. But she knew these words were real. She had a sister whose name was Sabrina, if her sister still lived. As though feeling doom encircling her, Sylvia quickly realized it had been chance that had decreed she be placed in the care of her aunt. Surely Priscilla had handed over her children with little thought.

A convent. Sylvia could not quite believe it.

A dark wall encircled a convent, making it a prison that one could never get out of. And her own sister was held in one.

Looking down at the Bible once more, Sylvia thoughtfully shut the book and placed it back upon the table, not wishing Priscilla to know she had learned her darkest secret. She would tell only Zaloe, for deep within her, she knew that her discovery would provide a way out of her terrible plight.

"I think that we should go out to this convent and glimpse this twin sister of yours. Perhaps we can work her into our plans somehow. And if not, I, for one, would like to see another as beautiful as my silky flower." Zaloe looked thoughtfully at Sylvia, who had just told him all what had transpired that morning.

"Do not count upon finding too much beauty in a convent. I am sure that years behind those cold, stone walls have taken a horrible toll upon the one called Sabrina." Sylvia began to feel a burning resentment of the twin sister she had never met. She would not allow anyone to come between her and this man, not even her sister. Zaloe was hers and she would do all within her power to keep him. She knew nothing of his life away from her, supposing him to live only with thoughts of her.

"I shall meet you outside the convent in the

morning. Tell your aunt that you wish to take a long ride to clear your troubled thoughts. And instruct the driver to go to Roundtree Convent. The convent is located near your mother's country estate, and is only an hour's ride from London. I shall meet you at the front gate. Be sure that you wear a dark cloak and keep the hood about your honey gold hair. We would not wish to create suspicion since your sister will be similar to you in appearance."

Sylvia nodded her lovely head. As though she had no will of her own, she agreed to all that this man she loved was planning, not caring where it led, only knowing that he was determining her destiny and she was powerless to do anything other than what he wished. She felt safe as his long, slim arms went about her, driving away any thought of caution. He cared about their future, she told herself as the hardness of his mouth claimed her lips and he pulled her soft, yielding body down onto the bed. In that moment she was lost to all thought, responding only to the feeling he was evoking in her. He was her life, her very breath, and as was her way when she desired something, she would do anything to get what she wanted.

Its look of dismal seclusion belying any need for contact with the outside world, Roundtree

Convent sat at the end of the long dusty drive. A stone wall towered about the building to insure the privacy of those within the large, foreboding fortress.

Sylvia's carriage pulled up in front of the tall gates, and as it did, she spied Zaloe standing outside those imposing portals. He seems to be impatiently awaiting me, she reflected as she witnessed him silently strike his small, leather riding crop against his thigh.

"I had thought that perhaps you would not keep our appointed rondezvous," he stated baldly, anger plainly visible in his dark eyes as he glared at her.

An hour late for their appointed meeting, Sylvia tried to appease him by explaining that she could not get away from her aunt's home any sooner. But Zaloe clamped a hand about her arm, and wincing at the sharp pain caused by his forceful grip, Sylvia stood at his side as he hissed into her ear, "Draw your hood about your face." As he pulled the long bell rope to summon one of the nuns to the front gate, he added, "Do not speak unless I tell you to do so. Leave everything to me and stay at my side."

The large gate slowly swung open, and Sylvia swallowed back her hurt and fear as Zaloe spoke softly, almost kindly, to the nun clothed all in black. Then with a nod of her covered head, the nun stepped back and allowed the pair to enter her strange, quiet world.

"What did you say to her?" Sylvia whispered, but a hard jerk on her arm made her remember that he had told her to keep quiet. Zaloe kept his biting hold on her as the pair were led into the nunnery. Noting the walls of slate-gray stone, Sylvia again realized that it had been only a chance that had kept her from being the babe sent into this life of exile.

When the nun returned with the mother superior, after some persuasion a small pouch of gold coin changed hands, and then Zaloe and Sylvia were led by the tall broad-framed woman down a long corridor and around a corner, and then down still another corridor to a small, lone door at the end of a dark passageway.

"Sabrina is at her studies at this time of the morning. She was not expecting any company so she may well be surprised by your appearance." The woman slowly reached out from her robe, opened the portal, and stepped into the small chamber.

As the pair of visitors followed her into the room, its sole source of light one small window high up on the wall, all eyes went to the girl seated at a desk. And as the girl's warm, gold-flecked brown eyes went to those who had entered her cell, she turned about, set pen and parchment down, and folded her hands upon her lap, in her eyes a question for the mother superior.

"Sabrina" — the mother superior's voice was

28

gentle as she addressed the girl—"you have some guests, sent by your mother. They wish to have a few words with you, alone." As the kindly nun said this she saw fear come into Sabrina's eyes, and with a tender smile, she tried to alleviate it. "They bring news from your mother, dear child. I shall be standing just outside your door in case I can be of any further service."

This assurance that the mother superior would be close at hand seemed to bring some relief to the honey-haired girl. Quickly the woman glanced at the newcomers. Then she stepped outside, pulling the portal tightly shut behind her large girth.

Sabrina looked at the pair as they stepped farther into the chamber. "You bring me news of my mother?" Her voice was soft, gently musical. Not receiving an answer, she let her brown eyes steadily peruse her visitors, still not discerning what they wished of her.

Zaloe was the first to react, his dark eyes resting upon the young woman as though not daring to believe what they saw. Sabrina had a gentle softness that her sister lacked. The twins looked identical, but trust and warmth lit Sabrina's features. "Miss Buchanan we have not meant to disturb you in your studies," he finally got out, not quite knowing how to start a conversation with this young woman.

Sabrina smiled, without guile, sweetly tilting

her lips, and her brown eyes with the golden highlights seemed to see into Zaloe's very soul as she gazed upon him. "You have not disturbed me, sir, nor your friend. My studies will keep for a time longer. It is so very rare that a visitor wishes to see me here at the convent. Not even my mother comes to Roundtree, so if you do indeed bring news from her, I will be delighted to receive it."

Sylvia stood frozen to the spot. She might as well be looking at herself in a mirror. She studied the girl sitting at the desk. Her light brown hair, tinged with streaks of gold, was pulled back as Sylvia had envisioned, but the style was becoming to this young woman. A black ribbon held a mass of her curls together, letting only delicate featherlike tendrils escape about her perfect heart-shaped face. The gown that graced her body was plain and black, but it seemed to enhance Sabrina's coloring while lending her an air of mystery that was most intriguing. Pulling herself together somewhat, Sylvia started to Zaloe's side.

"Please be seated?" Sabrina pointed toward two chairs placed near her desk. "I have had some of the other girls in my chamber this morning. I have been helping them with their studies."

Zaloe seemed to be recovering from the initial impression Sabrina had made on him. "Why, yes. Thank you, Miss Buchanan." He helped

Sylvia to sit, then took the other chair.

As Sabrina watched the pair, Zaloe began to speak. "Miss Buchanan do you know much of your family — the Buchanans?"

With a slow shake of her head, Sabrina softly replied. "I am afraid that all I know has been told to me by the mother superior. I have been given the names of my mother and father, and have been told about the circumstances of my placement at the convent. It would seem that my mother was very ill and could not keep me after the death of my father."

Both Zaloe and Sylvia looked wide-eyed at the young woman. "This is all that you have been told of your family?" It was Sylvia who spoke out. "You did not ask for more information?"

Sabrina studied her female visitor, trying to see the woman's features, which were concealed by a hood. "Is there something else that I should know of?" she questioned, not being able to imagine anything that could possibly affect her here at the convent. She had led a sheltered life, and though she had, at times, longed to be a part of the outside world, she had adjusted her thinking, knowing that she would probably remain at the convent for the rest of her life, though in her dreams she still pictured her mother coming for her and taking her to a warm, loving home. Now she was confused by these two people who asked her questions for which she had no answers. She really knew very little about her family, only the facts the mother superior had imparted to her.

Without saying another word, Sylvia took it upon herself to pull down her hood, and as she did so, the girl across from her visibly paled.

"What is it that you want of me?" Sabrina quickly asked. Although she had no mirror here at the convent, she had seen her own image reflected in the waters of the pond in the gardens and in puddles after rainstorms. She knew that the girl across from her looked much the same as her own reflection had. This girl's hair was also a honey gold color, and on her face was a look that Sabrina had seen before as she had dreamily looked into the pond. And as she studied the pair before her, an uneasy feeling came over her. What were these two doing here? Was this girl kin to her? Perhaps something had happened to her mother. Were they bearing bad news? Though Sabrina had never met her mother, in her dreams she envisioned a kindly woman who worked her fingers to the bone to survive and who, upon the pitiful death of her husband, had been forced to give up her child. Knowing that her daughter was cared for and well fed at the convent, Sabrina imagined, she was able to live in peace.

"Are we related in some fashion?" The soft, gentle voice touched upon Sylvia's ears, bringing a look of surprise to her features.

32

"You cannot see what is before you?" Zaloe questioned, not believing that this girl who looked exactly like Sylvia would not know the truth of the relationship.

"What is it that I should know?" Sabrina looked first to the man, and then her brown eyes were drawn back to the young woman as though pulled by a gigantic magnet. Something surely is odd here, she thought as the brown eyes across from her studied her closely.

Rising from her chair, Sylvia went to Sabrina, and bending down, she looked her full in the face. "You cannot see that we are sisters? In fact, we are twins." Her voice was low and deadly cool.

The blunt statement hung in the chamber for a moment before Sabrina recovered her senses. "Are you sure that we are twins?" When her visitor's head nodded affirmatively, she whispered, "Do I look very much like you?"

"Yes," Sylvia answered.

Sabrina slowly smiled. "Then I must also be quite beautiful." From the moment her visitor had pulled the hood from her head, Sabrina had been mesmerized by her fair beauty. Now she had been told that she looked like this young woman.

"Does it not seem strange to you that you did not know about your own twin sister?" It was Zaloe who spoke up, breaking the magic of the moment for Sabrina.

33

"Why I would assume that my mother did not deem it necessary for me to know about my family." Sabrina seemed so innocent that the pair before her could only look at her in surprise.

"I have been raised by my aunt these last eighteen years, and though you have been told that our mother has been ill and could not raise you, let me assure you that this was not the case at all. Priscilla Buchanan has always been in the very best of health. Her only illness is selfishness. She did not care to raise her twin daughters, so she separated them at birth. If it were left to her, we would have never known each other," Sylvia declared bluntly.

Sabrina had been taught to quell her anger and to think before speaking, so she let these words swirl about in her mind. Slowly anger rose in her, and she did not know how to deal with it. "It is nice to finally meet you, sister," she said at last when she saw the eyes of her twin resting on her, expectancy in them.

"You do not object to our mother's deceit?" Sylvia's brown eyes, so much like Sabrina's, were now aflame with impotent fury.

"There surely must have been a good reason for our mother to act in such a manner."

"Are you planning to spend the rest of your life locked away in this convent?" Sylvia paced about the small chamber. "Do you not wish to flee this horrible place and see what life on the outside has to offer?"

A sudden spark of vibrance came to Sabrina's golden-brown eyes before they once again became almost lifeless. "I still have a year to decide whether I wish to remain at the convent. Life here is not so horrible as one might think," Sabrina added when a horror-stricken look came over her sister's lovely features.

"But you are my sister. I cannot believe that you would wish to hide your beauty behind these cold walls forever."

"Perhaps I would consider leaving Roundtree if mother . . ." Sabrina did not finish the sentence for her sister interrupted her.

"Mother will never allow you to leave if the decision is left up to her. She has not told anyone you exist." Sylvia did not care whether she hurt this silly girl or not. She thought only of her own ends, and they would not be accomplished if her sister could not be convinced to leave this convent.

"Here now, ladies, perhaps you will allow me to speak for a moment. It would seem, my dear Sabrina, that fate has held you a captive, but now is the time for you to break these chains and to help not only yourself but your sister, Sylvia." Zaloe began to tell Sabrina his plans while she listened, full of wonder and some small amount of horror.

Later, when Zaloe and Sylvia had taken their leave and had left Sabrina to the emptiness of her chamber, the girl stood next to the door, not believing what had taken place in the past hour. Though she had entertained thoughts of staying at Roundtree Convent she had to admit that she had only done so because she'd had no other choice. Now she had a means of leaving this nunnery, of leading the life she had always secretly desired. She would have a family; a sister; and she would learn at last how others lived in the outside world.

To Sabrina's innocent mind this was a dream come true. Out of nowhere complete strangers had come to rescue her. Remembering the way her sister had looked at the man she'd claimed to love, Sabrina felt herself begin to tremble. She would be the one to help them marry in secret. She would go to this Garrison McBride in her sister's stead and quietly refuse his offer of marriage. Then, returning to London, she would live with her sister and her husband. She would at last get a try at life.

As Sabrina remembered the vial of liquid she held tightly in her hand, a small knot of trepidation settled over her but keeping her thoughts upon her sister's happiness and knowing that she would be helping her twin, she hurriedly tucked the vial beneath her pillow.

Sabrina had promised the couple that she would go along with their plan and she would keep that promise. Her mother had played both twins false, but one day she felt the woman would realize her great mistake and would accept her daughters as part of a family. She released a small sigh. Sabrina Buchanan knew that the attainment of that goal was up to her.

Chapter Three

On the morning of Sylvia's departure from her aunt's house a light drizzle was falling on the streets of London, bringing a damp chill to the air and causing the young woman within the fashionable carriage to snuggle deeper into the folds of the fur lap robe.

Priscilla's attorney had planned to accompany Sylvia and to witness the marriage ceremony, but at the last moment he had sent word that he would not be able to join her for the weather had caused him to come down with a catarrh. Sylvia thought it wise that Zaloe had convinced the lawyer not to go with her.

With a leap of her heart, Sylvia reasoned that all was working out well and she would see a happy ending. The messenger the lawyer had sent to the Buchanan home should have been intercepted by now. Her future with Zaloe was beginning.

Her mood became more joyfully triumphant with each mile the carriage took her toward the destination outlined by her mother, who had arranged for her daughter to be met by her betrothed at a small town near the border of Scotland before the pair proceeded to his holdings. With a smug smile of satisfaction, the girl lightly blew upon the soft fur of the lap robe. Zaloe would be meeting her at any moment, the carriage driver having been paid well and instructed as to where to go for the appointed meeting.

At that moment she began to feel the easy braking of the carriage, and she heard the driver order the team of horses to a halt. Looking out of the carriage she spied the man she loved standing in the road. Waving the coachman toward him, Zaloe directed the carriage into a copse out of sight from the road that ran into the distance.

Jumping down from the carriage, Sylvia threw her arms about Zaloe's neck, and with an excited laugh, she glanced beyond him to the carriage sitting off by itself amidst the trees.

"All has gone well and as we planned." Zaloe saw the direction of her gaze, and knew she wondered about her twin.

"Is she still unconscious?" Sylvia spoke softly.

40

Now that the plan had been set into motion, she felt they were reenacting a dream she had fashioned in the throes of sleep. "I do not see her moving about."

Taking her arms from about his neck Zaloe started toward his carriage, his thoughts now going to the one called Sabrina. She truly had a beauty that her sister had thus far not displayed. It was her purity that seemed to draw one out, he thought, his mind going back to the moments when he had sat within the carriage opposite her and had studied her profile as she'd slept. He remembered her gentle manner on the day they had first visited her and a yearning stirred within him. Though he had, in the past, avoided silly innocents, something about this young woman called out to him.

Sylvia, with little hesitation, followed closely behind him. "Are you so sure of my aunt's driver?" She looked at the man now lounging indolently against the carriage wheel and lifting a small, silver flask to his lips.

Zaloe set aside his thoughts of the fair Sabrina, and he answered Sylvia in a brisk manner. "Aye, do not concern yourself with him. My coin has purchased him many cups of ale in the past. He would not dare to betray me, for in so doing, he would reveal that he had a part in this deed."

Sylvia did not reply but she still did not trust the carriage driver. When Zaloe opened the carriage door, she saw her twin stretched out upon

41

the cushioned seat. Sabrina truly looked dead, and like Zaloe, Sylvia was struck by the girl's unreal beauty. It is hard to believe, she thought, that this girl looks exactly like me. She could not remember ever looking quite like this. Perhaps the potion was responsible for her sister's strange appearance, Sylvia reasoned, not choosing to believe that anyone could be lovelier than she, not even her own twin. She silently fumed when her eyes rose to Zaloe's and she saw that he too, was aware of the unusual beauty of the young woman stretched out upon the seat.

"Get her into the other carriage, Zaloe," Sylvia said, wishing this girl far away from herself and the man she loved.

As though pulling himself from a spellbound stupor, Zaloe reached out and gathered Sabrina's petite form into his slender arms, his gaze still upon her.

Sylvia stood near the carriage door, her brown eyes following Zaloe as he crossed to her aunt's carriage. Her anger at his attention to her sister mounting, she watched the driver help him settle Sabrina in the other conveyance.

"You know what my orders are?" Zaloe asked the driver before turning back to his own vehicle.

As he approached, Sylvia climbed into his carriage, pulling her skirts back so he could sit next to her. But when he entered, a serious expression on his face, he sat opposite her, murmured as though to himself alone, and turned his dark gaze on the other vehicle. "Fare thee well, my fine beauty, until we met once again," he said.

Sylvia sat frozen, not letting herself respond for she knew that the man she loved was speaking to another. Soon enough the fair Sabrina would be gone, Sylvia would turn his mind once again toward her. She was certain that she was more beautiful and accomplished than her twin who'd known nothing but the pitiful life at the convent.

Suddenly shaking his dark head, Zaloe looked over to the woman across from him. He reached out then, and took hold of Sylvia's hand, drawing it from her lap. "The clergyman is waiting to hear our marriage vows."

Sylvia forced a smile. He looks at another with such a doleful gaze and then he comes to me with talk of marriage, she silently complained. But knowing that she could not allow him to get away from her, that she wanted to be Mrs. Zaloe Tolliver, Sylvia did not voice her black thoughts. Instead she resolved to see that her husband would never again be near her twin sister. In any case, Sabrina would marry Garrison McBride and then dwell far away near the border of Scotland.

The carriage pulled into the yard of the Boar's Head Inn as the morning sun beat down upon the earth, absorbing the tender droplets of dew on the shooting buds of grass. Having reached his destination the driver jerked on the reins and brought the team of horses to a halt. Quickly, he threw the reins to the yard boy that stood nearby as though awaiting him; then he shouted, "Here, young fellow. See that these beasts are rubbed down well and fed heartily."

The driver then heaved his bulk from atop the carriage and opened the door of the equipage. Looking within, he saw that the young woman under his charge was still deep in sleep. She had been so since yesterday afternoon. With a thought to her welfare and a growing fear for his own, he reached out and gently rubbed her soft wrist.

At the slight pressure of the driver's rough, work-worn hand upon her smooth skin, Sabrina began to struggle back to reality. Her long silky lashes fluttered open and her gold-flecked eyes looked about, trying to recognize her where-abouts. As she came to her senses, she realized that she was no longer within the confines of the convent walls. She tried to rise. "Where are the sisters?" she asked.

"You be at the Boar's Head Inn now, missy. There be no sisters here." Her driver thought she must be speaking about Sylvia Buchanan. As he looked her full in the face, he could not get over how much she resembled his employer's niece. But knowing Sylvia and Zaloe Tolliver, the driver looked with some sympathy upon the young woman in his carriage. She was only a pawn to that pair. "Mr. Tolliver and Miss Buchanan be long gone from here, missy."

Trying to clear her thoughts and make some sense of what was happening, Sabrina closed her eyes and tried to remember what had brought her to this destination.

The messenger had slipped a note to one of the nuns when the sun was low in the sky the past evening, and the folded piece of parchment had been placed in Sabrina's hand as she was making her way to dinner.

Knowing that the message was from her sister and the gentleman that had accompanied her to the convent, Sabrina had quickly concealed it within the folds of her gown, her nervousness such that she could hardly spoon her food into her mouth. As soon as possible, she had hurried back to her chamber, had drawn forth the parchment and had gone to the small, flickering candle upon her desk. Her brown eyes had scanned the short message.

With the first break of dawn, drink fully, for your life shall begin.

With shaking hands Sabrina crumpled the note. She had thought of this moment and nothing else for the past weeks. At times, she had feared that she could not bring herself to drink the liquid so that she would appear to be dead

and would be taken from Roundtree. She had
wondered what would happen if she were caught?
And she had pictured the disappointment on the
mother superior's face, had envisioned Sister
Gwyneth weeping. That young nun had been a
true friend to Sabrina for the past year. But
when she had looked about her small chamber
she had found no help except within her.

If she did not take this chance she might
remain at Roundtree forever. It was doubtful
that some other means of rescue would be presented to her? Had she not been told many times
in the past that she should do a deed well the
first time for there might never be a second
chance. Was this what the nuns meant? She
shook her honey-colored hair. She must brave her
fears and drink the vial of liquid, not for the
death it would seem to bring to her, but so her
life might begin.

Truly she had little choice. If not for herself,
then for her twin she must try to carry the plan
through. Could she live with herself knowing
that she could have helped her sister and she had
not.

That eve little sleep came to Sabrina. She kept
her hand wrapped around the small vial, her
mind on what she must do. And when dawn
finally broke, she slowly sat up on the bed and
gently removed the small cork top from the vial.
Deliberately, she brought the cool glass to her
soft lips, held her head back, and let the amber

46

liquid slowly trickle down her throat.

As she swallowed the last of it, she began to feel dizzy. Quickly she recorked the vial and placed it beneath her thin mattress. Then she lay back, her head falling onto her pillow as though it were too heavy for her to bear.

She remembered hearing, as in a hazy dream, voices from far away.

"Call the mother superior. I think that Sabrina is not breathing," one said. A nun had come to summon Sabrina to break the fast. She had desired to speak with her about one of the younger girls who was having trouble with her studies. When she had knocked and had received no answer, she had quickly opened the door, her eyes going to the bed where the girl lay, so still.

The nun had called softly to Sabrina, but upon receiving not so much as a flicker of a response, she had gently taken hold of Sabrina's shoulder. Feeling the limpness of her body, she then bent down to her lips. She felt no breath coming from Sabrina's mouth, and dread filled her. She shouted to one of the nuns in the corridor, and within moments the mother superior was in the chamber.

Sabrina had wanted to comfort the women at her bedside, but she was not able to move or speak. Finally a deep, gentle sleep overcame her, sending her into a limbo, into nothingness.

"But whatever am I to do?" She shook her head to clear her jumbled thoughts, and tried to remember all that the man called Zaloe Tolliver had told her to do. All must have gone as he had planned, for she was now outside the convent walls. She remembered that she was to travel to the border of Scotland, to meet the man that her mother had wanted her sister to marry. Sabrina hoped that she could remember what she was supposed to do so their plot did not go awry.

"I do not be knowing what you will be doing next, miss. I was but told to deliver you here, where you would be met by someone." The driver saw stark fear written upon this young woman's lovely face.

"Who . . . who is to meet me?" Sabrina asked softly, patting her hair and trying to smooth out her black woolen gown.

"A gentleman that be called Garrison McBride, miss. That be the name I was given by Mr. Tolliver. I'll be taking your bags into the inn now, and ordering us a bit to eat. You'll be needing a room for the rest of the day and for this night. You must rest after all your traveling."

Sabrina relaxed somewhat. Even though it was but for this day, she needed some time to settle her frayed nerves.

Taking hold of the driver's arm, she let him lead her across the dirt yard and into the large inn. Her warm brown eyes surveyed the large, common room and finally rested upon the blazing fire in the large fireplace.

The driver saw where her gaze went, and taking charge, he directed her steps toward the table nearest the hearth.

"Sit yourself down here for a time while I see to our meal," he said. Then he sought the proprietor.

Sabrina complied without hesitation, relaxing by the fire. As the driver crossed the room and began to talk to a large, buxom woman, she let her eyes roam about the interior of the large common room.

Several men were lounging about, some taking their meals and others just talking companionably. When her gaze fell on a gentleman seated in a far corner of the room, he seemed to hold her attention for a moment longer than the others.

Life in the convent had not prepared her for what she was now witnessing, and as her pulse quickened she cautioned herself about looking too long at men like that handsome gentleman. She would have to be on her guard. The nuns had often told her that she was growing up and her body could betray her at any time. A hot flush darkened her delicate features.

It was only a short time before the driver returned and sat down opposite her. "The owner's wife shall bring our meal shortly. I did not ask whether the man you are to meet has arrived. I shall speak with the good lady when she brings our food."

Sabrina nodded her head, her brown eyes still

taking in the common room. It seemed so color-ful and alive, so totally different from her sur-roundings at the convent. There everything seemed so bleak. As the driver talked about the countryside and how he had stopped at this inn on another occasion, Sabrina's gaze again re-turned to the man across the room, his masculine visage exerting some strange attraction.

When the innkeeper's wife came to their table, bearing a tray laden with food, and began to place plates and bowls before them, the driver waited for the woman to finish her work before he questioned her about Garrison McBride.

A large, toothy smile graced the woman's fea-tures at the mention of this man's name. "Why he's been here the better part of the morn. He said he was awaiting someone, and I be taking it that this be a special meeting indeed." Her in-quisitive gaze went from the driver to the young, beautiful woman across from him.

The driver turned from the innkeeper's wife, and looked about the room. Seeing him do so, the older woman shook her dark head. "He was in here a short time ago. He must be in his room. But he'll be down again shortly."

"Thank you, madam." When the driver dis-missed the kindly woman, she returned to the kitchen to supervise the cook, who was prepar-ing large quantities of food to supply the needs of her customers.

As Sabrina began to partake of the delicious

repast before her, her eyes went to the other side of the room. To her disappointment, the handsome gentleman was gone.

"I shall be leaving you, miss, as soon as I finish with me meal and see that your bags are taken to your room." The driver spoke between mouthfuls of food.

Sabrina nodded her golden head, again feeling nervous about being on her own. But she straightened her shoulders and told herself that she was acting childish. This was an adventure such as she had often dreamed about while at the convent. She had been rescued from those cold, stone walls, and she had nothing to fear, she told herself sternly. She would meet the man her sister was supposed to marry and go to his home. Then she would return to London, but this time she would not be hidden away from the world by the walls of Roundtree Convent. Now that she had fled that place she was determined never to return to it. The convent had served her as home, the sisters had always been most kind to her, and she had learned much from her hours of study; still, after only a few short hours in the outside world, she knew that the life of the convent was no longer for her. She desired a taste of what life could offer her, and she was determined, despite her shyness, to see what was before her and to live fully.

The driver ate quickly, hardly tasting the scrumptious fare, and within moments, he rose to his feet, threw down a few coins, and started toward the door of the inn. He soon returned, however, carrying the numerous trunks and bags that Sabrina's sister had had loaded into the carriage.

Sabrina finished her meal and then went to find the innkeeper's wife. The buxom woman stood near the kitchen doorway, ordering everyone about and keeping an eye on the girls serving the common room and the cooks. As Sabrina approached her, her merry eyes settled upon the young woman and she smiled, then reached into her apron pocket. Handing Sabrina a key, she told her where to find her room.

Sabrina started to turn away, but she suddenly spun about. "Would you please tell Mr. McBride that I have arrived but that I shall be needing my rest this evening? The ride from London was very tiring."

Her soft voice fell gently upon the large woman's ears, and with a tender smile she wiped her hands upon her starched apron, then nodded her large head. "I surely will tell Lord McBride, miss. You just go along to your room and later I shall be sending a girl up with a tub and some hot water for a bath." She could tell that the girl was weary, and noting her slight form she wondered about her health. This young woman was a tiny bit of a beauty, and the innkeeper's wife thought it would be a shame for any harm to come to one such as she. She could tell right away that the

52

girl had a kind and giving nature, and that she had traveled a long way to reach this inn. For her part, the woman decided that she would do all that was possible to see that the young lady was made comfortable.

Sabrina's chamber was small and tidy. As she looked at the numerous bags and trunks piled in one corner of it, amazement overcame her. Where all of these for her? Her sister had said that all the clothing she would be needing would be in the coach, but she had never expected so much. With quick steps, though she hardly dared to believe all these pieces of luggage were hers, Sabrina crossed the small room and opened a trunk. Upon seeing the abundance of gowns within, she gasped and extended a shaky hand to the luxurious materials. Then she touched the dark woolen gown she was wearing, and without a second thought pulled it over her head.

Opening another trunk, she found undercloth-ing. Soft silks and laces of every color met her gaze, and as though her fingers could not believe what they felt, they slowly traced the delicate stitchery of a petticoat. She could not help but stroke each item, finally drawing forth a cream-colored chemise and slipping it over her naked body. Going back to the first trunk and search-ing through its contents, she then found the gown that had first struck her eye, a delicate cream silk with pale rose embroidery upon the bodice and sleeves.

As she rose to her feet, she drew the gown to her, and going to the floor-length mirror hanging upon the back of the door, she stood back and looked at her reflection. The cream coloring contrasted starkly with the black she had always worn, and she had to look at herself for some moments before she noticed that the soft cream of this gown enhanced her golden curls and peach complexion.

Never had she really seen herself, and now, seeing what others saw when they looked upon her, she smiled as though experimenting with her expressions. She rather enjoyed this first glimpse of herself, and liked the golden yellow sparks that glittered in her eyes. With hands that still touched the material carefully, she removed the gown, and looking into the mirror, she slowly let her eyes travel over the reflection of her shapely form. Then, standing back for a moment, she turned about in order to view her back. Thrilled, she swept about the small room, still clutching the cream dress. So much had already happened to her since she had awakened from her deep sleep. No longer was she imprisoned behind the convent walls. She was free. She had seen many sights at the inn, and she had these wonderful clothes that her sister had given her. It seemed another world was opening for her.

At a slight knock on the chamber door, Sabrina froze in the center of the room. "Yes?" she finally got out. She clutched the dress to her bosom.

"It be the maid, miss," a voice called.

When Sabrina went to the door and slowly pulled it wide, a small-framed woman entered the chamber, pulling a large, wooden tub behind her.

"Mrs. Barker told me that you would be wishing a hot tub, miss." The woman stood back and took in the young girl's state of undress.

Feeling herself flush as this woman observed her, Sabrina hurriedly went to the trunks and searched for the dressing gown that she had glimpsed earlier. "Yes, a bath would be most welcome," she said. As she found the robe, the maid, smiling at this young girl's nervousness, began to ready her bath.

When Sabrina had bathed, instead of lying down and resting as she had planned to do earlier, she asked the maid to help her into the cream-colored gown that she had only an hour ago been holding up to her. Her eyes lit with pleasure as she caught a glimpse of herself wearing the gown.

"Ma'am, you are a beauty," the small woman exclaimed as she stepped back to look at Sabrina. She then took up the hairbrush Sabrina had found in one of the bags, and began to stroke out the young woman's waist-length golden curls. Instead of pulling Sabrina's hair back tightly into a knot, the woman found a ribbon that matched the cream gown and tied it loosely about a shimmering mass of ringlets. Finished, she sighed with her pleasure at her own handiwork. "Will you be coming down for dinner, ma'am?"

Sabrina had not intended to leave this chamber until someone came to fetch her, for she was certain that Lord McBride would sooner or later seek her out. But as she again looked into the mirror, the excitement of the moment touched off a fire in her veins. "Yes," she replied, unable to pull her gaze from the vision in the looking glass and not daring to believe that it truly was she.

"Good enough then, ma'am. I'll be telling the mistress to save you a table and to have a good, warm meal and some warm cider ready by the time you come down."

Sabrina smiled at her, and the maid added, "You just be getting yourself a moment's rest, and I'll return when it is time for your dinner."

"Thank you so much," Sabrina said earnestly. She was not used to such kindness or to such service. In the past she had tended to her own needs.

As the woman left the chamber, Sabrina cast a glance at her reflection and then sat down upon a soft, comfortable chair, her brown eyes shutting almost instantly.

It was not long, however, before she was drawn from her rest by knocking at the door. Her eyes opened, and recognizing her surroundings, she hurried to the door.

"Who is there?"

"It be only me, ma'am. The mistress sent me to tell you that your meal is ready," the maid responded.

"Thank you," Sabrina called out. Then she stepped to the mirror to make sure that in sleep she had done no damage to her hair or dress. Seeing that all was still in order, she left her chamber and started down the stairs leading to the large common room that served as lounge and dining area for the Boar's Head Inn.

Smiling, the innkeeper's wife greeted her, and quickly led her to a table near the hearth. Sabrina had no sooner seated herself than the good woman handed her a warmed mug of cider and told her that her dinner would be brought out shortly.

Sabrina thanked the kindly woman; then her brown eyes surveyed the room as though she were still amazed that the outside world could offer such a variety of people and colors. But this evening, as she looked at the people in the common room, they were looking back at her. The inn seemed full to bursting at this hour, and with some hesitation, Sabrina noticed that there were more men than women present. Most of the women in the room worked at the inn. They were busy serving meals and drink to male customers. Feeling a bit apprehensive, Sabrina tried to calm herself. She appreciated her position near the fireplace, for most of the tables were positioned toward the center of the large common room. Her own now seemed to offer some small measure of privacy, despite all the eyes turned in her direction.

As the innkeeper's wife approached, a laden tray in her large arms, she was stopped by a squat beefy-looking gentleman. Sabrina watched the pair talk, noticing that the man's eyes kept coming back to her until, with an angry huff the large woman left his side. Her anger obvious, she arrived at the young girl's table.

"You be staying put right here at this table until I send a girl to take you to your room this eve," the heavyset woman abruptly told Sabrina as she set about placing the evening meal before her.

Sabrina just looked at the large woman. Noting her lack of comprehension, Mrs. Barker went further. "I haven't the time to keep you company, but if those about you see you making your way up them stairs, alone, why a pretty little morsel like yourself would be quite a temptation for any of these lowlife rascals."

Sabrina looked up into woman's kindly face, fully understanding now. The man must have said something simply awful for her to be cautioning Sabrina in such a manner. She nodded her golden head to indicate that she would certainly do as she was bid.

The large woman smiled with relief. "That's a love then. You just enjoy this food and I'll be sending a girl to you later, to escort you up to your chamber." She started to leave Sabrina's table, but turned back and added, "I left word with my husband to tell Lord McBride that you are here at the inn."

"Why, thank you so much. You are very kind," Sabrina responded in a small voice. She then took a sip of the warmed cider.

"I am not sure that my Bill has yet seen the gentleman, but as soon as he does, rest assured that he will know you have arrived at the Boar's Head." The buxom woman smiled fondly down upon the girl, thinking her to be the prettiest child-woman she had ever seen. The young woman had been beautiful even that morn in her drab, black gown and with her hair pulled back into a tight bun, but this eve, in this stylish gown, with golden curls falling down her back, she was simply stunning, a rare natural beauty that needed little adorning. And there was a true innocence about her. The innkeeper's wife was determined that no harm would befall the girl while she was at the inn.

Alone at the table, now, Sabrina slowly began to adjust to the staring eyes. Taking tiny bites of food and small sips of cider, she soon felt somewhat at ease despite the people about her. The

59

heat of the hearth also lulled her into a sense of well-being.

When she was almost finished with the savory repast, her brown eyes were drawn to the long, wall-length bar across the room. They came to rest upon the tall, handsome gentleman she had noticed that morning, and a slight flush gave her cheeks a rosy hue.

The man was talking with the proprietor, but he seemed to be in a restless mood.

He turned at the moment Sabrina looked at him, and their gazes met and held, his light green eyes looking upon her with an almost hungry glare that sent a current along the length of her spine.

Forcing her gold-flecked orbs from his, Sabrina felt her hands begin to shake as she tried to bring the mug of cider to her lips. She scowled herself as she felt her face flame. She had been caught boldly looking upon a strange gentleman. And the eyes that had touched hers had been hot with something she had never before seen, but it had had an effect on her entire body.

Not allowing herself to look up from her plate Sabrina sensed someone approaching. Thinking it was the gentleman from the bar coming to speak with her, she kept her golden head downward, hoping that he would not embarrass her any further. But a gruff voice startled her, and unable to believe that such a handsome man would sound so hard and callous, she raised her head.

"Little lady, mind if'n I take this here seat?" It was the short fat man who had stopped the innkeeper's wife. Sabrina was terrified as she stared into his small beady black eyes.

Coming to her senses rather quickly, she began to shake her head. But her long curls seemed to attract the man and he watched each movement she made. "I am to meet—"

He did not let her finish, but taking his small eyes from her hair, he grinned slyly. "Don't ye be a-trying to fool old Rupert now. I be knowing that ye be here this eve all alone."

Sabrina glanced about the common room, intending to ask the innkeeper's wife to have one of the serving girls take her up the stairs. But she did not see the large, kindly woman.

"Ye needn't be afraid of old Rupert Briggs now girlie. I am alone also on this fine eve, and only wish to spend a short time in your company." His pudgy hand reached out to take hold of Sabrina's. Capturing it, he held it tightly as she tried, despite her mounting desperation, to pull it away. "There ain't no harm in the pair of us to being alone for the rest of this eve, now is there?"

Sabrina could not believe the boldness of this man, and in a fearful tone she tried to plead with him. Not ever having been in such a situation, she did not know how to handle it. "Sir, please, I do not desire any company. I only want to be left alone."

61

Rupert Briggs, caught in the spell of the woman opposite him, only held her hand more tightly. "Why don't ye be coming up to me room for a time? Perhaps we can be finding ye a trinket or two from me chest. Ye see, I be a salesman of ladies' trinkets and lovely little baubles."

Before Sabrina could respond to the horrible little fat man's latest affront, Rupert Briggs was hoisted from his chair, his pudgy-little hand still holding on to Sabrina's. But his hold was soon broken, and the small fat man stood face to face with the gentleman who had dared to lay hand to him. He sputtered with anger, but as he found himself facing the large man he had earlier seen at the bar, he began to calm his rage. "How dare ye!" he said.

"I dare what I please." It was a strong masculine voice. "Take yourself from this lady's presence." At this command, all in the room quieted, awaiting the outcome if the fat man did not do as he was told.

"I was but talking to her. And who be ye to order me about? The girl is alone and willing." The fat man saw that all eyes were upon him so he felt he had to make some display of courage. His eyes once again went to the young woman, and seeing her beauty, he thought that perhaps if this bloke thought she was a willing maid, he would leave them alone.

But this was not to be the case. The large man

had been watching the interplay between the pair, and he had seen the fear that had come to the young woman's face, had seen her try to free her hand from the pudgy fist that had clasped it. "I have little patience with those of your ilk." His eyes turned icy, crystal green, as though he were some fierce predator, and with a smooth movement of his arm, he took hold of the fat man's shirt front and lifted him off his feet. "I shall tell you only once more to leave this lady's presence." The words seemed to be pulled from deep within the large man's expanding chest.

Knowing that the game was now to dangerous to play, the fat man nodded his dark head, affirming that if he were let loose he would be gone.

The large gentleman then let go of him and as he made his way out of the inn, Sabrina regarded the man who had saved her from that vile, little creature with almost as much fear as she had felt earlier.

Seeing that her fear was now directed toward him, the large gentleman lowered his frame onto the chair opposite her. As his glance traveled about the large room, the eyes that had been regarding them looked away. No one dared to have this man's anger turned in his direction.

"Thank you for your help," Sabrina murmured when she saw that the man was not going to leave her table.

The soft lilt in her voice touched her protector,

but he stiffly replied, "It was certainly my pleasure, madam."

Though his manner unsettled Sabrina, she was grateful to him. "I must confess that I do not know what I would have done if you had not come to my rescue. I had thought that the innkeeper's wife would be coming from the kitchen to give me some assistance," she finally said.

As though pushing her thanks aside he responded, "A beautiful, young woman such as yourself should not be here alone and unprotected." His light green eyes fixed on her small heart-shaped face questioningly and rather coolly, bringing a quick flush to her cheeks.

"I am to meet someone." Sabrina felt the need to explain, but she feared that this gentleman, with his cold bearing, like the fat man, only wished for her favors, whatever they might be. Are all men like this? she wondered fleetingly, but as a coolly arrogant smile settled about her companion's sensual mouth, she tried to still her nerves and relax. Of course this man was not like the other. Had he not saved her from the horrible embarrassment that she had been almost forced to endure. With this thought, she allowed herself to gaze upon his handsome virile features. The brownish sun-streaked hair that lay boldly upon his shirt collar and the untamed look in his light green eyes lent a daring air to his strongly chiseled features. He was quite large, but in his perfectly tailored, dove gray suit, he did not seem so ominous. And he reached out to help himself to a mug of warmed cider, she noticed that his fingernails were neatly trimmed and his hands were large, strong. "Are you meeting someone here at the inn?" Sabrina ventured to ask, curious now, and imagining this man to have a bevy of beautiful women at his beck and call.

"Aye, I am to meet my bethrothed." His cool green eyes rose from the mug, and his penetrating glare held her golden brown gaze.

A chill swept over Sabrina, and she thought to herself, he is to wed. For a moment she tried to picture in her mind's eye the woman who had captured the heart of such a man. But her knowledge being limited, she realized she could not possibly know what the woman would be like. He seemed cool and distant, almost arogant.

"Would you care for some more cider?" His icy gaze never left her features as he reached for the pitcher.

"Nay," Sabrina shook her head, one hand going to her lips to stifle a yawn. Though the evening had been exciting and this man was intriguing, the warmth of the drink and of the fire in the hearth was making her sleepy.

The gentleman across from her smiled slowly, delighting in her beauty, but setting this feeling aside, he asked. "Would you permit me to escort you to your room?" He had noticed that her eyes were heavy and though he did not wish to feel any softness toward her, he had extended the courtesy.

Sabrina looked somewhat taken aback. Her fear again had come to the fore. "The innkeeper's wife has offered to send one of the serving girls to take me there as soon as business permits."

The gentleman heard the stiffness in her voice and attributed it to her fear of the fat man. With a thin smile, he turned his head and looked about the busy common room. Then, bringing his gaze back the young woman, he said, "You may have to count upon spending the eve down here in this chair." In response to her questioning look, he went on. "All those who work here will be busy far into the morning hours, serving and keeping the customers happy. Perhaps that gentleman was not intruding as I had thought. Some women enjoy the attentions of such as he."

Sabrina gasped aloud. Did he truly think that she had enjoyed that fat man's pawing. Her anger was beginning to kindle, but she did not see the wisdom in his invitation to escort her to her chamber door. For a second she thought of spending more hours down here when she could be upstairs, sleeping upon a soft, down bed. "Are you quite sure that you would not mind escorting me to my door? I do assure you, sir, that I did not enjoy the pawings of that man." She spoke shyly and then hesitatingly looked at the man across from her. She still had some doubts, but surely after rescuing her he did not wish her any evil. This cold, hard gentleman would not approach her, she reasoned.

"It would be an honor, madam." The gentleman rose and pulled back Sabrina's chair. His eyes seemed to devour her as her silk gown settled about her small form.

Taking hold of his offered arm, Sabrina felt the heat of his strong body through the material of his jacket and shirt, a lump rose in her throat as he started toward the staircase.

She could not speak, and her senses seeming to be shattered.

Somehow without being told, the gentleman stopped before her door. "Do you have the key?" The words were cold as ice, but without a second thought, Sabrina drew the desired object from her drawstring purse.

Only a second passed before the door was unlocked and pushed open. "It has been truly my pleasure, madam, meeting you and lending you assistance."

The voice that she had heard earlier had seemed cut from crystals of ice. Now there was a different tone to it, a husky gentling, yet Sabrina could not seem to respond to the change as she stood close to him outside her chamber door, her gold-flecked brown eyes looking up into his green ones as she seemed to drown in his gaze.

As though lost to reality, she stood quietly as his handsome face slowly descended. She could do naught but hold her breath as his mouth approached hers carefully as though he didn't want to frighten her, and took hold of her petal-soft lips.

She was lost. Never had any man made such an assault on her senses. And though she told herself that she should run, she could not move. Her mind reeled as his strong mouth claimed hers. And when his tongue touched parted her lips, spiraling silky-soft bursts of pleasure went through her, and her arms went about his neck as though she were seeking support.

The gentleman molded his body to Sabrina's, holding her tightly in an iron grasp. His mouth played a melody on hers, and he was lost in the taste of her—sweet ambrosia.

She felt light and delicate in his arms, like a bit of fluff, as her rose scent filled his nostrils and enflamed him. He caressed the soft skin of her neck and then stroked downward. Then he came to himself, and shoved her from him, his green eyes looking deep into the lovely, passion-filled features before him. Anger burned deep in him.

At the loss of his lips and hands upon her, Sabrina regained some control, and her face flamed with embarrassment. Now her only desire was to flee from this stranger and to gain the safety and privacy of her chamber. Recalling the way he had thrust her from him she felt shamed. "I . . . I . . ." she stammered.

The gentleman did not speak but stood watching her, as if aware of her dilemma. When Sabrina hurried into her chamber and quickly shut the door behind her, he remained in the hallway his own senses swimming with desire for this woman.

Finally deep breaths cooled his heated blood, and he went down the hall and through the portal at the top of the staircase. His large frame tense, he then strode about his room agitatedly.

Lord Garrison McBride had not planned to confront the woman he had come to the inn to meet until morning, and then he had planned to see that she was made comfortable in his carriage and taken to his keep. He himself had brought his horse and he'd thought to go to the village to visit with his latest lady love before riding to his keep.

But when he had seen the fat man forcing his attentions on the woman the innkeeper had said was his bethrothed, his pride had made him chase the scoundrel from her presence.

He had known that Sabrina Buchanan was beautiful from the tiny miniature that her mother had presented to him at their last meeting, but he now thought that no woman ever was so lovely as the one he had just seen to her chamber. To get a grip on himself, he recalled all that his solicitor had told him about the beautiful Miss Sylvia Buchanan. She was the pampered only daughter of Priscilla Buchanan, and had been raised by a doting aunt. Always she had been presented with whatever she desired. And his solicitor had learned that she was fond of playing the games of the court and of fawning and flirting with any gentleman that took her fancy.

If it were not for the fact that his time was nearly up—according to the terms of his father's will, he must soon marry—Garrison would never have considered Priscilla Buchanan's daughter as a future bride. But Priscilla had offered a substantial dowry—lands and money—and knowing that he had little hope for wedding a woman with a better name than Buchanan, Garrison had talked the offer over with his attorney. After discarding several other possible mates he had finally chosen Sylvia Buchanan.

His thoughts of marriage did not parallel those of the average young man's. He would be thirty years old in a few weeks, but to his thinking he was too young to find himself bound by the vows of wedlock. He had never tied himself to one woman, had always avoided the traps set by those that desired his name, fortune, and home, and he had no desire to be led about, as some men were on the strings that pulled a man behind a woman's skirts.

But to hold on to all that he now possessed, he had to comply with the terms of his father's will, and therein it was stated that he had to marry by the age of thirty. That clause was what had led him to this day.

Pulling off his jacket and shirt, Garrison threw his large frame down upon the bed. He had expected a much different woman. The reports he had been given had led him to believe that Sylvia Buchanan was a woman of the world, not the shy, delicate flower he had just left. Perhaps she thought to fool him with her innocent looks and lowered lashes. But if she intended to capture a husband with her lovely looks and then to surprise him with her willful ways, she would surely be in for a surprise. He knew all about her, and though he needed a woman to call his wife, he was not one to be led upon a merry chase, to fall head over heels in love and then, after the vows were spoken, to see the true light of his bride.

He would know from the start the type of woman he was gaining. And she would be the one to be surprised, for he needed a wife only to keep that which was his. If she stirred up his life too much, he would settle an allowance on her, establish her on the estate that was part of her dowry, and have done with her as easily as he was going to marry her.

With this thought in mind, Garrison closed his green eyes and sought to sleep, but as he did the vision of the beauty down the hall filled his mind. The response of her soft lips came back to him, the feel of her silken skin, and the sound of her gentle voice. Why did this woman that he

71

was to marry have to be so beautiful. He tried to chase thoughts of her from his brain, but when time slowly passed and her vision remained in his mind, he finally threw his long legs over the side of the bed.

"Damn her!" he shouted to the empty room, and flinging his jacket back upon his shoulders, he stomped from the room and down the stairs. He needed another woman to chase away these nagging thoughts. India would be sleeping at this hour, but if he rode hard and fast, he could be at her side in a few hours.

With slow steps Sabrina walked from the chamber door. As she began to undress, she wondered if the nuns been right in cautioning her to be wary of men. She had been warned that men would wish her to do things that were degrading and that she should only allow such acts to be committed by her husband, it being his right to possess her, and the only way to gain children.

With a sigh she shut her brown eyes tightly, what had transpired between herself and this stranger coming to her mind. She had almost let herself be put in a compromising position, and she knew she had been lucky for this man could well have done with her whatever he chose. Sabrina admitted to herself that she would have made only token resistance. With her eyes closed, she imagined those warm, seeking lips upon her own, that hard, unyielding chest tightly pressed against her breasts. Were the stranger's actions a prelude to the vile attacks the nuns had told her of? If so, she wondered fleetingly, was there something wrong with her? For at the start, when this man had held her so tightly within his embrace, she had felt a deep pleasure, one she had never before experienced. Only his shoving her away and the coolness of his regard had cooled her own fervor.

Tying the sash of her nightgown Sabrina blew out the single, tallow candle and climbed into the comfort and safety of her lone bed. Closing her eyes, she again allowed her thoughts to go to the gentleman that she had allowed to kiss her. The taste of his lips had stirred her beyond all reason. With a start, her brown eyes opened wide. This man who had held her so tightly had either forgotten or had not cared that he was to meet his bethrothed at this very inn. Was he so fickle that he could so easily be misled by another woman? At this thought, she tried to force thoughts of him from her mind, except the remembrance of his hard, cool manner and of the icy glare he directed toward her. She would think of her own future. She was at this inn for a purpose, and would then be reunited with her family.

Again she shut her eyes, but this time she forced herself to try to forget this strange man she had met. He is a part of the outside world, she told herself, and I will meet other gentlemen so I would do well to forget a man such as this, one who so easily sweeps any woman into his arms, forgetting that he is already claimed.

But putting him from her thoughts was easier contemplated than done, and Sabrina soon found that her dreams were centered upon a man with the greenest eyes and the most handsome face that she had ever seen.

Chapter Four

With the breaking of dawn, shafts of sunlight filtered through Sabrina's draperies. Accustomed to awaken at the sun's appearance, the girl stretched full length and sat up on the bed, her eyes going about the chamber and once again seeing that her life had changed greatly. She was no longer at the convent, but was at the Boar's Head Inn.

Her thoughts going back to the gentleman she had met the eve just past, Sabrina quickly began to dress for the long day ahead, choosing a pale blue traveling suit, for the day she would be going to the home of the man her sister was supposed to be meeting here at the inn. Surely this morning Garrison McBride would approach her, and then she could get on with this affair. She desired to end the matter of Mr. McBride quickly and to be again in the company of her sister. She did admit to herself that she had felt a coolness from her twin, but it was her wish to know the young woman better, and then to meet her mother. She had a yearning to be close to someone, to belong somewhere, and since she had left the convent this feeling had intensified. She recalled the promise that her sister and Zaloe Tolliver had made—that she would live with them until they all were fully accepted by her mother—and she truly believed that at the finish of this affair she would at last find happiness.

Smiling at these happy thoughts of being reunited with her family, Sabrina brushed out her golden hair, leaving it unbound. After last evening she realized that to bind her hair back, as she always had, was like binding her own new spirit. She now knew that she never again wished to be confined as she had been all those years by the cold walls of the convent. She wished to taste life and to enjoy all that it had to offer.

As she entered the large common room, Sabrina noticed that few people were about at this time of the morn. The maid who had helped her the day before approached upon silent feet.

"Your breakfast will be ready shortly," she said. "I was on my way up to your chamber."

Sabrina looked at the girl questioningly, not knowing what she would say next.

"The gentleman that you were to meet has left a carriage for you. The driver will take you where you are to go. I shall be sending him up for your things, if that is all right with you."

"Oh," Sabrina replied, not knowing what else to say. She had thought that she would at least

76

meet this Lord McBride before going to his home, perhaps she had even hoped that she could just meet the man here at the Boar's Head Inn and when he had seen her he would not wish to wed her. Then she would not have had to go to his home but could have been reunited more quickly with her own family. But as the maid stood before her, waiting, she knew this was not to be the way of things.

"The gentleman must have had some pressing business." Sabrina sought some excuse that would explain why he had left her to the care of his driver and had not bothered to meet her himself.

Breakfast was a quick affair, and when she was finished eating, Sabrina went out into the yard, her eyes soon falling upon the carriage standing near the stables. And as she began to approach it, the driver hurried up to her. A large grin on his face, he extended an arm to her.

"Lord Garrison said that I was to take you to his keep, Ma'am." He hoped that he was approaching the right woman, for the description Garrison McBride had given left the previous night, as he had hurriedly saddled his stallion, was a terse one. Though he thought the young man's words had sounded rather gruff, the driver had to admit that when he'd said she was a rare beauty with flowing honey-colored locks, he had been absolutely right. For a second the driver questioned his master's senses for leaving a woman such as this to the attentions of his driver instead of seeing to her comfort himself.

Nodding her golden head, Sabrina let herself be led to the waiting carriage and then settled within. As she settled back against the seat, the driver dutifully placed a lap robe over her legs, but Sabrina's eyes rested upon the seat across from her. There, upon the leather cushion, was a beautiful, lone white rose.

The driver hastily climbed up to his seat and then began to drive the team of horses toward their destination. But Sabrina, still looking upon the flower, barely noticed as the carriage pulled away from the inn.

Slowly reaching out, she took hold of the delicate white rose. "A winter rose," she said softly. She wondered why it would be on the seat of the carriage. Had the elusive Garrison McBride left it there to pleasure her? Or could it be an apology for his absence? She brought the flower to her nose and inhaled deeply, its heady, delicate fragrance delighting her as no other scent could.

The ride seemed interminable, the bumpy dirt roads jostling the carriage; but even though the ride was long and somewhat irritating, Sabrina felt little discomfort. She had not lived a life of luxury. She was used to hard work and the vigorous life at the convent. Even so, had she been displeased with the trip, she had but to look at the beauty of the white rose to find some peace. No other gift could have given her more enjoyment. As the light waned and darkness replaced it, still the carriage went onward.

Finally Sabrina was awakened by the gentle touch of the driver. "We are here, my lady." He spoke softly, as though hardly daring to rouse this beauty from her deep sleep.

Sabrina looked out of the carriage door and saw a towering stone fortress, ablaze with light. "I must have fallen asleep." She sighed, reaching for her purse.

After stepping down from the carriage, Sabrina turned back to it. "My rose," she whispered softly, and then hurriedly recovered her treasure.

The driver smiled kindly at her as he watched her retrieve the flower Lord Garrison had sent to the inn in the wee hours of the morn. Her pleasure in this gift, he thought, is well worth the effort it took to get it to the Boar's Head before she stepped foot into the carriage. "Come. I shall walk you to the door of the keep." He took hold of her elbow, escorted her up the winding steps, and then opened the wide double doors.

Sabrina did not know what kind of man she was to meet. But as she and the driver stepped through the doorway of the keep, her eyes enlarged to twice their normal size.

The interior walls of McBride keep had been plastered and they gleamed with lime, all smoke and dirt stains being cleaned to a shining upon each new moon. The main hall had two great hearths, wood ablaze upon them. And there was much light everywhere in spite of the cavernous size of the hall, which had towering ceilings that seemed to rise upward to the sky. Numerous rushlights and torches burned, as did oil lamps hung by thong and chain from the rafters, and everywhere one looked there were men eating and drinking. Women were serving the men. They rushed about carrying pitchers of ale, platters of meat, and bowls of fresh vegetables.

Sabrina stood for some moments, taking it all in. Never had she viewed such a sight. Even the smells of roasting meats and fresh-baked bread seemed new to her.

"I shall be right back, my lady. I shall get the lord." The driver hurried from her side, leaving her near the front portal.

Sabrina held the rose in a tighter grip as her brown eyes followed the driver. He approached a man who had one booted leg propped against the hearth, his large frame facing the blazing fire. Around him was a small group of men.

When the driver spoke to him he turned and looked across the room. As he did so, Sabrina's mouth opened in utter surprise.

Garrison McBride then strode toward her purposefully, his face breaking into a cool, calculating grin as he saw the look upon her lovely features.

"You? But what on earth are you doing here?" Sabrina finally got out as he stood before her. She could not fully comprehend what was taking place, but she now faced the gentleman who had rescued her from the evil, fat man and had then seen her to her chambers. Her mind dwelt on what had occurred when they had gained her door, but she forced herself to turn aside these thoughts. Perhaps this man was a guest of Lord McBride. Looking over his tan breeches and his lightly ruffled silk shirt, she hoped that this would not prove to be the case. The sooner this man was away from her, the better she would feel. Something about him robbed her of her very breath.

The gentleman seemed not to have heard her question, and his green eyes devoured her beauty with an icy glance.

Sabrina's cheeks were burning, and she quickly looked about to see if anyone was watching this strange interplay. She did not want Lord McBride to see the effect this man had on her. "I thought you were to meet your betrothed at the Boar's Head Inn?" She asked uneasily, for those eyes were studying her as though trying to see into her inner soul. She could only be thankful that the men in the hall were intent on their own amusements, and were ignoring the couple standing at the entrance.

As though shaking himself from a stupor the gentleman came closer to Sabrina, so close, in fact, that she was aware of the scents of masculine cologne, of tobacco and leather. "Aye. I was to meet my betrothed. But having second thoughts, I left the inn."

"And what of the woman?" Sabrina, still nervous about the situation, looked about for the carriage driver, but not seeing him in the hall, she decided that he was still in search of the master of the keep.

"Come with me." The man took hold of her arm and began to walk her through a door near the front portal.

Sabrina balked, not believing that he would

dare to grab hold of her in the house of the man she had traveled miles to meet. Though her intention was to refuse his proposal, no one else knew of this, and certainly not the men who were now watching what was going on between her and this stranger. When Sabrina saw grins upon many of their faces, she tried to pull back. Her attempt to release herself was futile, and as she was pulled into a room off the hall, and the door was closed behind her.

"How dare you drag me in here!" Sabrina protested as he let her go and looked her full in the face, his glare cold yet searing. Sabrina wondered for a moment if she had done something to offend him. Was that the reason he had forced her into this room, not caring who witnessed her embarrassment?

"Take a seat." The offer was more of a command. The stranger sat down upon a small sofa near the hearth.

The room was a small, comfortable study Sabrina realized as her eyes took it in. There was a desk in one corner, and the walls were lined with bookshelves. Near the fireplace were a sofa and two upholstered chairs. "I do not care for a seat, thank you. I have come many miles to this keep to meet Lord McBride."

"And that you have done, sweet." The man smiled up into her face coolly as he stretched out long, muscular legs and leaned back against the sofa.

"Nay, you are wrong. I have not as yet met this man. He left only his driver to escort me from the inn." Sabrina looked somewhat confused.

Thinking that she could not possibly be this innocent, the man rose to his feet, and with a small mocking bow he said. "Let me then introduce myself. Garrison McBride, at your service. And let me also add that the pleasure has certainly been mine."

Sabrina blushed at this statement and the implications of his words. "You . . . you are not Garrison McBride?" Her brown eyes widened in disbelief. "But why did you not tell me that this past eve?" Again what had taken place outside of her chamber door at the inn struck her with full force. She had thought this morning that she would never again have to face this man and be reminded of the feelings he had evoked, but here he was, telling her that he was the man her sister was supposed to marry.

"Would it have made a difference if I had told you that I was Garrison McBride?" He carefully watched her reaction to the question.

Slowly nodding her head Sabrina said, "I could have been more prepared for this meeting."

"Prepared for what? You are to be my wife within the week. There is little need for preparation. Everything shall be taken care of here at the keep." Despite himself, he, too, thought of the previous evening, of the sweet taste of her lips, of holding her close, and of storming from the inn into the cold night, her rose scent still clinging to his clothing as he rode at a hard pace to India Sterling's door.

"A week?" Sabrina repeated the words, her

voice weak, her senses reeling. She had not been told that a marriage was planned so quickly. She had intended to turn this man down and then be free to return to London to meet her sister.

Garrison caught sight of the rose she still clutched, and slowly his gaze went back to her face. "I take it that you liked my small gift?"

With a start Sabrina remembered the rose, and she slowly nodded her golden head. "Roses are my favorite flowers, but however did you know this?" She seemed to be in a daze. So much that was happening seemed to be eluding her, and she was completely befuddled.

Reaching out, Garrison momentarily seemed to soften toward her, for her confusion was evident. "No other flower would ever suit you. Your own scent reminds me of this flower, and your beauty is as perfect as a single, pure white rose." For a short time he lost himself in her beauty.

Aware that, as on the preceding eve she was losing her reason, Sabrina withdrew her hand from his grip and then crossed to the other side of the small room. She steadied herself on the oak desk. "I shall be needing more time than a week," she said in a weak, small voice, not quite knowing how to phrase her refusal of his proposal. But upon reflecting, she realized that he had not proposed to her but had told her when the marriage would take place.

"There shall be no more time. The deed must be done in haste and all has already been set into motion. In a week you shall be my bride. The banns have been posted the last month and your mother and I have signed all the papers." His words were tossed out as though he dared her to refute them.

"But how can this be? I thought I was but to come here to meet you?" Sabrina could not help but question him. Her mind was in turmoil. She had thought that her sister's plan would be so easy to follow; now she was learning that she was truly supposed to wed. And it would appear that she was being offered little chance to refuse.

Could it be that she really did not know that we were to marry within the week? Garrison wondered. Could Priscilla Buchanan have fooled her only child into coming to her betrothed with the promise that the wedding would be held sometime hence? "I can see some leeriness on your part, madam. But I assure you that your mother was fully aware of my need for the vows to be said with all haste." Seeing that she was still confused, he added, "It pleases me not at all to have to marry, but my hand is being forced in the matter. I can see that you have been left in the dark about much of this matter, but your mother is quite persistent in such affairs, and after seeing the miniature of you that she sent to me, I must confess I was impressed by your beauty. The main thing, my dear, is that I am in need of a woman for my manor, one I can call a wife."

"A miniature of me?" The words left her mouth before she realized that he had been looking at a likeness of her twin.

"Yes, your portrait. Priscilla presented it to me

at our last meeting. My need for a wife to share my life, and for children to be my heirs is great, and all must be done with haste." He was trying to explain the situation, for he realized that this girl had truly been left in the dark about the plans for her own wedding.

At the mention of children, Sabrina paled, the counseling of a nun came to her mind about what happened between a man and wife, about the dreadful pains that a woman suffered to bring a child into this world. She had planned on none of this, her only thought to escape those stone walls and to be with her family.

Seeing her pallor, Garrison lost some of his hardness toward the woman he was being forced, by his long-dead father's will, to wed. Quickly he went to Sabrina's side, his arm going about her for support. "Sit down," he said. "You are in need of food and rest. We shall discuss this at a later time." His concern was genuine, for he feared she would collapse at any moment.

"But I cannot marry you—"

Garrison did not let her finish, but brought a finger to her lips. "Not now. It is not the time for such talk. I will have Katie show you to your chambers and bring you a tray." He let a finger gently caress her lips, wondering at her innocent beauty as he looked down upon her golden head. "After a good night's rest, you will be feeling better." He had thought that the arrival of this woman would present no problem. A quick marriage, a woman to call wife. One who kept to her place and did not interfere with his life. One who would provide him with heirs. But from the moment he had set eyes upon this woman he had been totally confused. From the reports he had been given she was not supposed to be an innocent. He had expected a woman quietly knowledgeable about the way of life, but the one standing next to him was a lovely little blossom. Perhaps it was the long trip; first to the inn and then to his keep. Mayhap tomorrow she would act in the manner he had expected.

A tall gray-haired woman wearing a black dress and a white, starched apron, knocked and then opened the door. She smiled at the couple within. "Corry came to the kitchen and told me that the lady had arrived," she said to Garrison. So familiar was her tone, Sabrina thought the woman a part of his family.

"Aye, Katie, this is Sylvia." Garrison watched the housekeeper look over the young woman who was to be his bride and the mistress of his keep. Seeing a glow come to her bright eyes, he felt a small catch in his chest.

"She be right pretty, Lord Garrison. But you had best not be tiring her out with all of your talk. There be plenty of time for the likes of that tomorrow." The woman took charge in a quick, kind manner.

Sabrina swallowed nervously. "I am afraid that there has been a slight mistake." Two pairs of eyes looked at her questioningly, and she all but whispered, "My name is not Sylvia, but Sabrina."

Garrison's brow rose archly at this statement. Searching his mind, he was sure that in all of his correspondence with Priscilla Buchanan she had referred to her daughter as Sylvia. "But your mother—"

Before he could question her further, Sabrina blurted out, "Sylvia was the name of my mother's mother, it became my pet name. But my given name is Sabrina, the name given me by my father." The lie felt bitter on her tongue, but certain she was being caught in a trap, Sabrina covered her shame despite the blush that rushed to her cheeks.

"Sabrina be beautiful," Katie responded. Noting the color that came to the young girl's cheeks, that kind woman's heart went out to her. Sabrina looked so small and tired standing next to her imposing lord. "I will show you to your chambers now, my lady." The housekeeper came right to the point and then started from the room, expecting the girl to follow close behind, certain that Lord Garrison would not dispute her on this matter. If this young lady did not get some rest, she would surely become ill. She was so frail and so young.

Garrison did not say a word, but watched as his housekeeper led his betrothed from the study. Strange that he had been given the wrong name, he thought as she also went from the room. But he believed her explanation that her mother used the name Sylvia instead of Sabrina.

Sabrina . . . He let the sound of the name echo in his mind, and he had to admit that it did have a lovely ring. Remembering the sound of it on her lips, her softly lilting accent, a small smile replaced the gruff expression of the lord of the keep.

As he looked about the main hall, seeing his men relaxing about the hearths and drinking cups of ale, he found that he had little desire to spend the night in their company. His mind was plagued by thoughts of the young woman that was to be his bride. She was a mystery to him, and Garrison McBride was a man who could not let anything unresolved rest. He had to be sure of all about him and as his gaze went to the long, trailing stairway, he slowly began to head in that direction.

This girl-woman had some strange hold on his senses, he thought as he lightly ascended the stairs. At this thought, another came to his mind. When he had stood outside her chamber door the eve before, her rose scent enveloping him, her body drawn tightly into his embrace, her lips sweetly pliant beneath his own, in that moment she had not seemed the innocent young woman she seemed at other times. He remembered her silken arms about his neck, the yielding of her supple body; and he wondered how many other men she had treated so favorably. And though he scorned himself for needing to be near her, he found himself outside her chamber door.

"I expect that you will find some pleasure here in my home, Sabrina." Her name flowed easily from his lips as he stood at the portal, which was slightly ajar, and saw his bride-to-be, alone and looking about. He was certain that Katie had left her for a short time to fetch her a tray. "If there is aught that you would change, you have but to do so or to tell me what you might desire." His intention was not to treat this woman unkindly. He cared little about the furnishings of a home, and he knew that seeing to such things was the province of a woman.

"It is all quite lovely," Sabrina responded, surprised to see this man standing at her chamber door. She already knew that he was a man who did as he pleased. But truly she found her chamber beautiful. She liked the peaches and pale greens in which it had been decorated.

Garrison watched her closely as she gazed about. "This bedchamber belonged to my mother," he said. "It suited her personality."

Already a fire was chasing away the chill of evening, and resting before the hearth was a large brass tub, steam rising invitingly from it.

"It would appear that Katie has been hard at work," Garrison said thoughtfully as he glanced about the chamber, making sure that all was in order and that Sabrina would, indeed, be made comfortable. Yesterday, before meeting this woman, he had planned to leave all the details to his housekeeper, but something caused him to be concerned for this young woman's welfare, though he told himself that she meant nothing to him, that she was only the means to keep that which he already held.

"Your housekeeper seems kind," Sabrina ventured, her appreciation of Katie evident.

"Aye, she is that and more. And she has also

been impatiently awaiting your presence." In response to Sabrina's wondering gaze, he added, "for several years she has thought there has been a need for me to wed."

As a flush came to her cheeks, Sabrina turned her golden head away from him and forced herself to admire the pleasant bedchamber.

Garrison looked for a moment at her trim back before turning toward the door. This woman seemed so indecipherable, yet she exerted a pull on him. "Will you be needing any help with your bath?" he asked, though knowing her to be the spoiled daughter of a rich woman, he already knew what her answer would be.

A slight shake of her head made him look again upon her lovely visage. Never before had he viewed a woman of such beauty. Her every feature seemed to be perfect and he suddenly wanted to hold her, to taste those petal-pink lips and let go of the control he had been enforcing on himself.

Seeing heat replace the coolness of his green gaze, Sabrina became nervous. "I think I shall be able to manage quite well. Thank you, sir," she replied, thinking that this would bring him out of from whatever was plaguing him and that he would leave her to bathe in peace.

Her words did seem to have the desired effect for Garrison shook himself and started toward the door, but turning, he suddenly made his way to Sabrina's side. When she looked up at him, her fear evident, he quickly stepped behind her, pulled her mass of hair about one shoulder, and slowly began to unbutton the tiny row of blue buttons at the back of her gown. "Katie may be some time seeing to your meal," he said to explain his reason for handling her so. As she stood quietly, allowing him to ministrate to her, the delicate rose scent seemed to envelop him, and as though he were some young lad with his first love, his hands began to tremble as they completed their simple task.

Sabrina stood as still as possible, not daring to breathe with this man so close. His slightest touch evoked a spasm of delightful sparks that flowed through her entire being, but determined not to forget all that she had been taught, she forced herself to remember his cold manner. And she stood still, so as not to let this man know how he was affecting her.

When he had finished undoing the row of tiny buttons, Garrison looked at his quaking hands, muttered a curse, and quickly strode out of the chamber. What on earth was coming over him? he wondered. He had done naught but moon over this girl-woman since he had first laid eyes on her at the inn. He, who had had all kinds of women at his beck and call, now could not even unbutton her gown without shaking as though he were a green farm lad?

True enough, he told himself, this beautiful woman was to become his wife, his lifelong mate, but still where was his pride? Was he to let his body succumb in the assault that had beseiged it since yesterday? Had this brown and golden-eyed woman cast some spell upon him? Why else would he act the fool in her presence? Anger raging within him, Garrison grabbed up his jacket and went down to the main hall. As he passed through it, he called sharply to the men sitting nearest the hearth when they started to rise, ordering them not to follow him.

Last eve he had known this same anger after he had left Sabrina at her chamber door at the inn. Mounting his horse, he had pushed the beast hard until he had reached India Sterling's door. But when he had dismounted he had stood in the cold of the night. Something had stopped him from knocking. For the first time since he'd met the dark and seductive India he did not eagerly anticipate having her knowledgeable hands roam over him.

"Damn," he said aloud. Could he think of nothing but Sabrina's fair beauty. Must he only anticipate her changing from an innocent girl to the sultry woman that seemed to be a part of her.

Well, he would put her from his thoughts this very eve. India would be awaiting him, and in her arms, he could always forget Sabrina.

In the main hall the men about the hearth stared at the slammed portal. Brian Craig, a large man, who since the lord of the keep had been a small child, had been a friend and teacher to him, rocked back and forth in his chair when his lord left so abruptly, his laughter drawing the attention of the men who did not know the cause of their master's anger.

"It all be love, lads," Craig had said. "The wee lass surely has Lord Garrison on the run."

Seeing now what had caused the anger of the lord of the keep, those within the hall began to chuckle at the thought of Garrison McBride having been caught in the trap of a woman's tender smile. They knew him as a womanizer and a fighter, so it amused them to see a woman make Garrison storm from his own home.

As Garrison had hurried from Sabrina's chambers she had watched his retreating back, wondering what she had done to make him so angry. The word he had muttered had been one she had never heard before, but she knew it was a curse. A few moments later, when she had heard the loud slamming of the door below, she had known that her estimate of Garrison McBride's fury had been accurate.

Sinking her body into the warming depths of the crystal-clear bath Sabrina tried to pull her thoughts together. Surely some underhandness had been involved in these arrangements. Either her mother had not told Sylvia the timing of her wedding, or Sylvia and Zaloe Tolliver had not told Sabrina the truth. She had no idea of what to do, except to refuse to wed this Garrison McBride, but deep inside she was beginning to doubt whether this powerful lord would allow anyone to thwart his plans. He seemed intent upon having the marriage vows spoken in a week's time, and he was not the sort that could easily be put off. Perhaps the best thing would be to flee while she still had the chance, but she was weary from the long trip. She needed rest. Perhaps in the next few days she would be able to find a way out of this predicament. If not, she would have to escape. She would never go through with this farce of a wedding.

Stepping out of the tub, Sabrina dried herself off and donned a nightgown. Without delay she then pulled down the coverlet on the large bed and snuggled in to the soft mattress. Her brown eyes closed, and for a moment she allowed herself the luxury of envisioning Garrison McBride. Her hand reached out to the opposite pillow and touched a delicate white rose.

India Sterling answered the hard knocking on her door. Knowing it could only be her lover at this time of night, she did not bother to draw her satin robe about her to conceal her full, ripe breasts. As she stood in the doorway, the soft light in her front hallway cast a glow upon the visage of Garrison McBride.

Without speaking a word, he pulled the luscious India Sterling into his hard embrace, and his lips descended to plunder her willing mouth.

Wrapping her arms about the man at her door, India admitted to herself that his overpowering ways were much to her liking. Yes, Garrison McBride's manliness kept her wanting more from him. He had a strength and power that few men possessed. Indeed, he was much like herself, he lived behind a hard shell that could not be penetrated unless he chose. And as his lips slowly relented in their compelling devouring of her, India's husky voice beckoned him into the small house. "The neighbors will be enjoying the view, my love. Come within," she murmured between panting breaths.

Garrison needed no further invitation from this warm-blooded woman, and easing open the door, he swept her up into his arms. He would need more of her to chase away thoughts of Sabrina Buchanan, for even with India's sweet lips upon his own he had imagined he held his future wife. So with long strides he started up the stairs and kicked open India's bedroom door, knowing from past visits exactly what he and and this woman desired.

India did not hold back, but purred at this harsh treatment. She had never seen Garrison in quite such a mood before. He seemed not to want to talk or waste time on any amenities, and this suited her. She enjoyed the roughness of his touch when he was angered, no matter the cause.

With a smooth movement Garrison put her on her feet next to the bed, and at the same instant he tore her robe from her shapely body.

India stopped breathing momentarily, and in the next second she felt his mouth tracing an inviting path down her slim neck to the tips of her abundant breasts. His hands quickly removed his own clothing as she stood in a daze, allowing his ministrations.

Losing himself within the folds of her soft

giving body, Garrison's lips caressed her bosom, his tongue making small circling patterns around the rose-tipped mounds, and as she caught his head within her hands, holding him tightly against her, of a sudden her musky scent seemed to penetrate his brain, filling him with revulsion.

India was a woman wise to the desires of men, and the moment Garrison was assaulted by her perfume she sensed that something was troubling him. She slowly stepped from his grasp and went to the small table next to the bed. Taking the bottle of brandy that she kept there for him, she poured a snifter of the amber liquid. "Drink this my lord. The ride from the keep is quite long," she said. When he had taken the potent drink she went to her wardrobe, pulled out another robe—like all the others she owned, made for a man's eye—and donned it.

"Did your day go well, Garrison?" she asked as she went to her dressing table. Sitting down upon a softly cushioned stool, she picked up a hairbrush and began to stroke out her long, straight black hair, her dark eyes holding him, his every movement captured in her mirror.

Garrison did not respond. He swallowed the brandy right down, and then, as though plagued by evil, he put both hands to his head and rubbed forcefully.

"Did your future bride arrive as planned?" India could not help but ask this question, for she suspected that this woman was the cause of the pain that was pressing down upon her lover.

Garrison took up the bottle of brandy, and

poured himself another drink. "Aye," he said curtly.

"Does the woman not please you?" India had often entertained thoughts of becoming this man's wife, of sharing in his wealth, but all that he had ever offered her was the honor of sharing his bed. Now, seeing his dark looks and strange behavior, she thought that perhaps she could press her suit further. Certainly it was not too late. He could always send this little milksop of a girl back to London.

She rose to her feet, and with a walk that would have made any other man desire her, she approached the man across from her. "Send the bitch back where she came from, Garrison. You and I are one and the same. We understand each other, and would make a wonderful match. Send her away; then say the word and I will stand at your side willingly."

Garrison raised his gaze to hers as she knelt down next to his chair. Never had he considered this woman as his wife. He enjoyed her body as she did his, and he had also enjoyed her undemanding company. But take her to wife? He knew her past, knew of the others she had taken to bed when he was not about. No, she was not the woman to be mistress of the McBride keep. The image of his mother came to his mind and he slowly shook his head. "Nay. Sabrina Buchanan shall become my wife."

His words struck India like a slap, and rising to her full height, she spoke with some control. "I have decided then that I shall be leaving this village. There is little here for me, and I have an offer from Lord Denvey to stay for a time at his country estate while his wife travels in France."

Garrison's green eyes looked her up and down before he nodded his tawny head. "I wish you the best then," he said coolly. He rose and reached for his shirt.

India had thought only to taunt him with Lord Denvey's offer, believing that it would make him say the words that she wished to hear. She had hoped he would offer to make her the lady of McBride keep, but instead he was looking at her as though he had never seen her before. His cool regard told her of his true feelings.

"I wish you well in your endeavors," Garrison said as he started from the chamber, slowly buttoning his shirt. He had thought that all would remain the same between himself and India, but now he saw that this had been folly. He could not afford to have a demanding woman draped about his neck. It would be bad enough to have a wife to answer to, let alone a mistress who did not know her place.

"But you cannot just turn your back to me and leave like this," India cried out, forgetting her demeanor. She had never begged or pleaded, thinking to reach Garrison with coolness and her body, but when he had started to walk through the door, the full realization that he would never return hit India and she hurried to his side. "Is this all? You can so easily walk away from what we shared?" She had felt that there was something between the two of them, and though he

99

had never spoken of love or sharing, she had always thought in the end he would see that he could not go on without her.

"What else is there?" he looked at her, his eyes icy emerald chips. "We enjoyed what we both wanted, and now it is time to go our separate ways." He desired no nagging wife or mistress pulling at him.

"You cannot treat me like this," India shouted at his retreating back as he started down the stairs. Never had she been thrown over by any of her lovers. It had always been she who had gone on to better things.

Garrison sighed aloud, but did not turn about to face his mistress. It was over. And perhaps that was for the better. He was seeing a side to India that he had previously been blind to, and when she started to follow him, cursing and shouting accusations, he determinedly walked out the front door.

"You'll pay for this you blackguard. You and your lady love will both pay dearly." Sobbing out her hurt and anger, India reached the bottom of the stairs as Garrison closed the door behind him.

In the early hours of the morn Garrison followed closely by several of his men, rode his stallion back to the manor. Now that he had put a halt to his relationship with India, he was plagued by visions of Sabrina Buchanan. After leaving India's home he had gone to the tavern, and had tried to dull his mind with strong drink in order to purge Sabrina from his brain, but she had been in the forefront of his drunken thoughts. He felt free now to think of her beauty; her creamy complexion, golden hair, and warm brown eyes, even the delicate rose scent that clung to her, could not be driven from his thoughts. He speculated on their wedding night. Perhaps after that he would be able to drink his fill of his new bride, and so find release from his plaguing, haunting thoughts. Even the girls from the tavern had not been able to hold his interest for he had compared each woman he saw to the lovely Sabrina and his thoughts had strayed to the beauty at McBride keep.

With quiet, ambling steps Garrison started down the hallway toward his chambers, but as he passed Sabrina's door his hand lingered for a moment, reaching out as though of its own accord and gently easing the portal open. His red-rimmed eyes sought her beauty one last time before he put his head on his lone pillow.

Holding his breath, he quietly went to the side of the bed and gazed down at the beauty lying in its folds. Her soft visage was in repose, and one delicate hand was tucked under her chin, the other held tightly to the white rose. She seemed so different from the women he had known, and for the life of him he could not understand her strange hold over him. "An innocent, pure beauty," he whispered aloud. "Yet you have turned my insides upside down." His green eyes lingered on her face and then slowly descended

101

to note that she had, in sleep, pushed the covers away from her body. The sheerness of her gown drew him to her loveliness, for it left little to the imagination.

He marveled, at her perfection, his eyes lingering upon the fullness of her woman's curves and then going back to her heart-shaped face.

He envisioned her as she stood before him that night at the inn, her sparkling golden eyes seeking his own. She had drawn him to her, had sparked something within him that he had never felt before. Even in India's arms he had not felt what he had during those few minutes with Sabrina.

As a gentle smile came to her delicate lips, Garrison thought to smile in return, but gave her a drunken leer. Was she dreaming about him? With a jolt, he realized that she did not desire to wed him and there might have been another man in her life. Was this why her mother had wished the ceremony to be arranged with dispatch. Had Priscilla Buchanan known that her daughter cared about another? Was this why she had sent Sabrina so far from London and had told her so little of what was to take place here at the keep.

Thoughts of Sabrina in the arms of another seemed to tear Garrison's chest asunder. But even as he looked down upon her, he desired her more than he had any other, and without thinking, he leaned down and gently placed a light kiss upon her brow, tasting her softness. His lips went to the hand that held the white rose so tightly. "Sleep well, my beauty. If there be another, I shall chase him from your mind—at least until I have had my fill of your beauty." This decision made, Garrison turned and left the room, thinking that he would win her over with a gentle hand and when he was tired of her he would walk away from her as easily as on this night he had walked away from his mistress. Oh, he knew it would be different with this woman, for she would be his wife; but when he was able to chase her from his thoughts he would then go on to livelier pursuits.

Chapter Five

The next morning when Katie came up to help Sabrina dress, she told the young woman that Lord Garrison would like her to break the fast with him in the rose garden. "The weather this morning is warm indeed for this time of the year, my lady," she added as she brushed out golden curls that dutifully fell into place.

"That sounds quite pleasant," Sabrina softly replied, but within she quaked at having to face this man that her sister was supposed to wed. Each moment that she posed as her twin it seemed doom hung over her. For at any time she might be caught out, and she could not even imagine what would be done with her then. Her toilet completed, she followed Katie down the stairs. The main hall was quiet at this early hour, and the older woman led her through French doors and into a beautiful garden.

The table on the patio was already set, and as Sabrina approached it, she noticed that Garrison McBride was impatiently striding about the gardens. When as she neared him he greeted her cheerfully, however. "Good morning, madam." His jovial tone belied his haggard appearance. "I do trust that you slept well."

"Indeed, quite well," Sabrina responded, her eyes going over his drawn features and wondering what had caused his pallor and his bloodshot eyes. He looked as though he had not slept a moment this past night.

"I hope that you do not mind eating out here this morning." Garrison pulled back her chair and allowed her to sit down. "I have always loved the gardens at this time of the day. I am afraid that the weather has done some damage this year, but farther to the back of the gardens Mikey has a hothouse that flourishes in all seasons. That is where I got your white rose." His light green eyes studied her as she looked about the gardens. She seemed as lovely in the morning as she had in the evening.

"All is very lovely here, sir, and I wish to thank you once again for the rose. To think that you have these beautiful flowers all the year through." She said this with a touch of wonder in her voice, and her mind went back to the gardens at the convent. She had loved to work in the gardens with the other sisters. The smells of earth and flowers had given her a vitality that she seemed not to find anywhere else. But the gardens at the keep were lavish with blooms.

Katie set to serving the couple, quietly delighting in the pair. She had longed for the time when her master would bring a bride to the keep, and now that she had met Sabrina Buchanan, she knew that she would be the perfect wife for Lord Garrison. She had a gentle quality that was rare, yet her heart seemed true, her manners sound. "I shall be leaving you two to yourselves for now. If you require anything else, just ring." She looked to Garrison before going back into the main hall to see to the running of the large stone mansion.

"You look unusually lovely this morn," Garrison ventured, and he could not help but cast his eyes on her winsome good looks. Her golden curls fell freely to the shoulders of her wine velvet gown, and she wore no adornments.

Flushing at the compliment from this man who for two days been so cool to her, Sabrina tried to concentrate upon the food on her plate, but she softly murmured, "Thank you." She did not wish Garrison McBride to see how he affected her, but she knew that he would have to be blind not to notice her reactions to the slightest remark he made. She felt like a ninny, tongue-tied and stumbling, her features turning to flame at his slightest glance. Nothing at the nunnery had prepared her for an arrogant, handsome man such as Garrison McBride.

"Do you ride?" He asked, so suddenly that Sabrina started.

"Why I . . ." She had never ridden a horse, but she could well imagine that her beautiful twin sister sat a mount with ease. And not knowing what this man had been told about her by her mother, she slowly nodded her golden head. "I am afraid that I am not a good horsewoman though." She hoped that he did have the impression that she could ride but did not want to be boastful. If he had not been told of her sister's riding abilities, he would indeed reason that she had been given little training in this area, when he saw her upon the back of a horse.

"Fine then. After breakfast, if you would care to join me, we shall go for a ride. Some matters in the village have need of my attention and I am loath to set forth this day and leave you at the keep by yourself." Garrison spoke smoothly, thinking that he was courting her well. He only hoped that he would reap the benefits of his efforts.

Again Sabrina blushed. She was confused by his manner this morning. The last evening she had thought his cold treatment of her was his rightful manner, but his tone did not hold the hardness that she had become used to. She turned her gaze to her plate, not knowing how to regard the man across from her.

Garrison, too, was confused. He did not understand why his future bride blushed and turned her head away from him whenever he spoke to her. She played the sweet innocent to perfection, but was this truly the way she had spent her days at court instead of flirting and preening with all manner of gentlemen? Surely a woman of her beauty would have had a number of admirers begging for her favors and the reports given him had indicated that Sabrina Buchanan was certainly not one to turn her gaze from a gentleman. Why is she playing the innocent for me? he wondered. Does she think as my wife she can forever play this role. His light green eyes went over her pink cheeks and soft gentle features and he decided that there was little reason why he could not enjoy her beauty. Soon enough, he would have his fill of her, and he would become bored with her.

At the completion of their meal, the dishes were cleared away and Garrison walked Sabrina back into the main hall, which was now crowded with men eating breakfast. But as Garrison walked Sabrina to the stairway, his gaze remained on her, and when she started to leave his side, her thoughts on what she would wear to go riding with him, he gently reached out and took hold of her hand, bringing it to his lips. "Do not keep me waiting long, my sweet." He planted a soft, searing kiss upon the back of her wrist, then gently let it slip back to her side. He smiled as she turned to the stairs and hurriedly made her way to her chambers.

Sabrina's limbs trembled when she had gained the safety of her chamber. What strange power did this man have over her? she wondered, as she went to the wardrobe and took out a dark green velvet riding habit.

His mere presence evoked strange feelings in her. Sabrina wasn't certain that only he could make her feel this way. Would many men have this strange effect on her? She knew very little about men. She had been around only a few in her life. A doctor was called to the convent at times, and a messenger was, on occasion, allowed past the outer stone walls. The only truly horrible man Sabrina had met thus far was the short, fat man at the Boar's Head Inn, and Garrison had cast him away in short order.

Yet despite these thoughts, Sabrina suspected that Garrison McBride was the one man that could make her feel she was melting within, the only man who could make shivers of delight tingle along her spine. His merest touch set her aflame, and left her weak and trembling. She again considered fleeing before it was too late.

But where would she go and how would she leave? If she could not to put this man off without a terrible scene, how would she ever return to her family and live in peace. She was here so that her sister and the Zaloe Tolliver could be together. If she were to flee now, would not Garrison McBride give chase and wouldn't he go to her mother? If so, it would only be a short time before her sister's trickery would be out in the open.

Sabrina stood back to make sure that she looked her best in the riding apparel, her more sensible side cautioning her that playing with peoples lives was dangerous. Then, with a sigh of exasperation, she thought of Garrison McBride. What did this man see when he looked at her? Did he not see a woman who was taking her sister's place here in his household, one whose whole personality was based upon lies? But she knew this was not the case. He had no idea that she was not the one he was supposed to wed. He thought her to be Sylvia when he looked upon her, he knew only that she was the woman who was to be his bride.

Perhaps she would be able to reason with this man today while riding. She would have to try to gain her freedom quickly before it was too late. She pulled her tiny, green hat to a jaunty angle, letting the long feather point down toward her back. The deep green of the habit and hat set off her golden curls and gold-flecked eyes to perfection.

After one more glance into the mirror Sabrina started from the chamber, reason telling her that if she could not sway this man about the wedding, she would have to run from his keep. She could not possibly marry Garrison McBride.

Garrison was awaiting her near the hearth in the main hall. He was talking with a group of his men. "Aye, Brian, perhaps you are right on that score, but keep all to yourself or I shall take the hide off your old back," he laughingly declared, but when his eyes caught sight of Sabrina making her way down the stairs, he quieted and let his emerald gaze feast upon the vision gliding toward him. Though his purpose was to court this woman, he now knew it was going to be a pleasure.

The talk of the others about him also stilled, and their eyes followed his glance. Seeing the reason for his sudden quietness, some of his men

111

grinned.

"Shut yer mouth, lad, before ye be catching yeself a fly." Brian Craig rose to his imposing height, vacating the chair in which he'd been lounging near the warm fire. Turning about, he strode across the room to Sabrina's side. "I am afraid that the lad is quite smitten by yer fair beauty, my lady, and he can't grab hold of his senses long enough to greet ye. But I, Brian Craig, will be telling ye at this moment that ye be the fairest lass to ever be gracing this dark keep. Now let me introduce ye to the others hereabout."

Sabrina smiled into the time-worn face grinning down upon her, grateful not to be too near Garrison, and Brian took her about the huge room. As he introduced her to each man and woman present, she could feel light green eyes upon her.

Finally Brian led her to the small party near the hearth, and Sabrina looked up at the imposing man she was supposed to wed. Once again his nearness made a flush come over her body.

"Ye be minding yer manners now, boyos, in the presence of a lady," Brian instructed the men who had not risen upon Sabrina's entrance into the hall. In short order, all, in turn, bowed over her hand and smiled into her warm, brown eyes.

A young man, with a gaze more bold than the others, was overwhelmed by the beauty before him and forgot that she was to become the bride of Lord Garrison. He lingered over Sabrina's hand a moment longer than necessary, loath to release it. "My eyes are truly blinded by the sheer beauty that stands before me," he declared. "Ah, fair lass—"

But Sabrina did not get to hear the end of his flowery praise of her, for Brian Craig harshly pushed the young man aside and, with an angry glare, rebuked him. "Pauly get yerself away from the wee lass, she be not fer the likes of ye. Take yer mooning ways out of doors and see that the horses are readied for the day's ride."

The one called Pauly at once saw his mistake in being too forward with the woman who would soon be Lord Garrison's bride. And stammering out a hurried apology first to the lady and then to Brian and Garrison, the youth, who to Sabrina seemed no more than an overgrown boy, turned and fled from the main hall.

Brian's bold laughter and that of several other men followed upon his heels and then Garrison, seeing that Sabrina also had been embarrassed by this encounter, quickly went to her side, aware that when he had seen the youth holding tightly to her hand, a stirring had happened in the pit of his belly. What did it matter that the lad was infatuated with Sabrina? He was sure there had been many like him in her past. But, even at this thought, he still felt jealous. Suppressing that feeling, he smiled down at Sabrina and slipped his arm about her waist. "Are you ready?" he asked. When she nodded, he said, "Let us be about the day then."

Sabrina needed no further encouragement than these words, and she and Garrison started to leave, his arm still about her as though he were lending her some much-needed protection.

Brian, quickly noticing how Sabrina had stilled and quieted after the youth Pauly's embarrassment, stopped laughing and waving to the men about the room, he started after Lord Garrison.

As Garrison stepped out into the morning sunlight, he took his arm from about Sabrina's small waist and grasped her hand. "You truly blind these eyes of mine, fair Sabrina." Tucking her hand in the crook of his arm, he did not give her a chance to be embarrassed by his words. "The horses should be at the ready and awaiting us," he said and then started toward the back of the towering stone fortress. Sabrina had to hurry to keep up with him.

As the boy called Pauly led two horses toward Garrison and Sabrina, his dark eyes watched his master's face to see if the master had truly been angered by his lack of good manners moments ago. But only a stern look was sent in his direction, to tell the youth to be on guard now in his actions around the lady. Then Garrison smiled down at Pauly before turning his smile on Sabrina. Instantly, a large-wide grin appeared on the lad's face, for he knew from past days that Garrison McBride was not one to let his anger fester or to hold a grudge. And Pauly himself was one who learned a lesson and learned it well. Perhaps the lady was a stunning beauty, but in the future he would only admire her from afar. He would not be so bold again.

"Come, sweet, let me help you up." Garrison

took the reins from the boy, not wanting any other to have the honor of assisting his lady onto the mare. He gently took hold of her waist and, with ease, placed her in the saddle.

Sabrina sat upon the sidesaddle with some trepidation, her brown eyes worriedly watching the beast she was to ride. But quickly noting the steady mein of the animal, she soon relaxed and, with a bit of nervousness, brought her leg about the sidesaddle before arranging her habit to make sure that her legs were completely covered.

"Some of my men will be accompanying us, love." Garrison brought his large black stallion near her smaller mare and lightly placed his hand over the one she was resting upon the saddle horn. Green eyes held brown ones for a moment. "You truly are a beauty, sitting there so prim and serene," he declared, but before Sabrina could respond, a group of riders, headed by Brian, reined up their horses near the couple.

"Are we off to the village, Lord Garrison?" With a hefty hand Brian pulled off his hat, revealing a mop of reddish blond hair. The twinkle in his eyes was for the woman at Garrison's side.

"Aye, to the village, Brian." Garrison grinned at the large man, then directed a more gentle smile toward Sabrina, nodded his head, and kicked at his horse's sides.

Nervously, Sabrina softly kicked her own mount, setting the mare into motion. Then she and Garrison and his men slowly rode toward the village that was situated upon the McBride lands.

"Who is this man, Brian?" As Sabrina shyly questioned Garrison she wondered about this man's familiarity her with her husband-to-be, and about why he was leading the other riders.

"Brian has been at McBride keep since I was a child. He and I were best friends during my youth, though he is ten years my senior. He taught me much in those days, when I was in need of a man's hand. And he has helped to protect my holdings and my people with his very life. Aye, he has been a friend and much more."

Something in his voice touched Sabrina, for his tone was masculine but gentle. Her mount was walking at a steady pace, and she began to relax as Garrison told her of his friendship with Brian Craig. "Did you not have a father then, while you were growing up?" she questioned, being unable to imagine a man such as this not having had someone strong and forceful to pattern himself after. He seemed so self-assured and reliant, almost arrogant, and able to handle any situation.

"My father died when I was but an infant, and my mother would have no other." He looked over at this woman who was soon to share his life, and realizing that this was one of the first times that he had let himself share any portion of his past with a woman, he quickly told himself that was of little matter. This woman would share his name, and would know all about him within the week anyway.

"I did not know of my father either." Sabrina spoke quietly, but having done so, she was struck by the realization that she had known none of her family. She had been shut away from the world, and unlike this man, she had not been allowed a mother's love or a friend like this Brian Craig that was riding behind them. "It is good that you had one such as your friend, Brian." She spoke a bit louder now, because of the noise of the horses, her brown eyes holding Garrison's gaze in their first truly understanding moment.

The talk of the men behind the couple was coarse and jovial. The riders were laughing and joking about the past night's revelries, and they brought a quick flush to Sabrina's delicate cheeks as they bandied words about the delights of a tavern girl called Maggy.

Having himself enjoyed nothing more than such rough friendly talk with his men, Garrison nonetheless felt some sympathy for Sabrina, and casting a heated look back toward Brian, he motioned to her to bring up her pace a bit in order that they might proceed without his men so close upon their heels.

Brian, knowing well that Garrison wished to be alone for a time with his lady slowed his own pace and his men followed suit, thereby permitting Garrison to ride at a goodly distance from the group.

"This land is truly beautiful." Sabrina was much more relaxed now in Garrison's presence, because of his kinder manner toward her and because they were no longer within the confines of his home. At the keep she was reminded of the forthcoming wedding at every moment, and of why she was in this man's home. Her presence was the result of deceit and trickery.

"Aye, 'tis beautiful, but at this time of year, when the cold is just starting to be felt, all turns dull and brownish. Garrison looked to Sabrina, sensing that she was more able to talk now, and there was a tightening in his chest. He suddenly wanted to tell her everything that he knew, all about the land, his people, and his inner feelings. "My father brought my mother here from London, the city from which you have come, and she fell in love with this wild land about McBride manor."

Sabrina listened with quiet interest as he went on.

"Her name was Euphemia and she had a mystical, shy way that suited that name. My father, Charles McBride, met her one day while in London, and fell in love with her upon first setting eyes upon her. And my mother claimed that the moment my father introduced himself to her, she knew he would be her husband."

"She must have been a very special woman." Sabrina could sense by his gentle tone when he talked about his mother, that he had held Euphemia in high esteem.

"She was a rare woman, indeed. She was like the sunshine after a pouring rain, like the sheerest wind blowing off the Irish Sea on a warm, gentle day. All about her loved her, and if she were alive this day, you would agree. And I think that she would find pleasure in your being here at the keep."

Sabrina instantly saw that this conversation was becoming more personal, and wishing to make her position clear, she cleared her throat and ventured to say, "Mr. McBride, I truly did not expect to come here to wed. I was under the impression that this visit was one in which we would only meet and get to know one another, with a future match in mind." She wanted him to understand that his plans were being put into motion far too quickly.

As Garrison looked upon her, a gentle smile played about his lips. "It matters little now. We have met, and our vows will be spoken before the priest at the ending of the week. For, you see, my need to take a wife is great, and all must be done with haste."

"But you truly do not understand. I need more time to get to know you. I cannot simply be rushed into a marriage that will last for the rest of my life, not with a man I do not even know." Sabrina was trying to reason with him, hoping that he would relent in his decisions to hurry the wedding and would allow her to return to London.

Only a slight movement of the muscle near his jaw belied Garrison's fast-mounting anger at thinking of why this woman wished to postpone the wedding. He pictured her within the arms of another. That had to be reason why she did not wish this match, and why Priscilla Buchanan had taken it upon herself not to tell her daughter all of the arrangements that had been made. But remembering what he had promised himself while in her room the past eve, he spoke softly trying to woo her to him. "I have known many women in my life, Sabrina. I will not try to make you think that I have ever been a perfect man. But I can tell you this. I have never before asked another to share my name for I did not deem any worthy of it. And to be truthful I was reluctant to meet you. If it were not for matters I have no control over or for your own mother's persistence in this matter, I am sure that you would still be living your a sheltered life in London. I had thought I'd find you lacking, but this has not been the way of it. From the moment I first set eyes on you at the Boar's Head Inn, I have been of a different mind. You are the woman I wish to share my name, the one I want to bear my children."

Sabrina cringed at his words. At the mention of children, once again black dread settled deep within her, bringing a pallor to her face. What am I to do? she wondered. Do I have no option but to flee from this man? He seemed so intent upon wedding her she did not know how to change his mind. But she would never go through with this farce of a marriage when it should be her sister who was wedding Garrison McBride.

Seeing her become pale and frightened, Garrison went back over his words, and thinking to the eve before when she had acted in a like manner, he realized that her fear must surely be based upon the mention of children. Was she so frightened of the marriage bed then? How could this be? The reports he had gathered on her had indicated the opposite. But if this were the case, he would put her fright to rest in short order. He was no novice, and well knew how to please a woman, to bring only joy with little pain. "Sabrina, if you fear the night of our union, lay that fear aside." Seeing her scarlet flush he knew he had struck home, but he was now even more confused about this young woman. He had not thought to be gaining an innocent virgin, but her actions and manner would indicate that this was what she was. How had his solicitor been duped into bringing him such a false report? Noting that she was still embarrassed, he went on. "I will only bring you happiness. As my wife you shall be a part of myself. I would never allow any harm to befall you." Glancing in her direction, Garrison noticed tears in her brown eyes, and for a moment he wondered if there was more to her fear than she was allowing him to see. If a fear of men kept her at a distance from him, surely she would know that she could not forever put off marriage. If not, he that would enjoy bringing her to complete womanliness, after which another would take his stead. But at this thought anger began to build in him. Now that he had met this woman and had seen her beauty, he knew that he would never allow another to take her in his stead. He would be the first to show her the joys of love, and when he had tired of her, perhaps another would be allowed to attend her, but only if he allowed it.

Suddenly, another thought struck him. All this

might be a ruse if she feared he would discover something on their wedding eve, something that she would prefer to keep secret. Again thoughts of another man came swiftly to his mind, and with a muffled curse he tried to get a hold on himself. If this were the case, he had already decided the night before that he would win her and make all thoughts of another flee from her mind, at least for the time he wanted her at his side. Why now did such thoughts compel him to unreasonable anger?

"I cannot marry you." The soft, flowing words came from the woman riding beside him, but with a tight smile, Garrison reached out a large hand and put it upon hers. As he did so, he felt a wet tear lightly hit the back of his hand.

Glancing behind and seeing that his men were nowhere in sight, Garrison took hold of Sabrina's reins and guided her horse into a thicket of tall trees. Halting his mount, he jumped from its back, and as though it were the most natural thing in the world, he reached up and took hold of Sabrina. Pulling her graceful form into his arms, he silently kissed the crystal tears coursing down her cheeks. "Hold tight to me, sweet. Let me be your strength. All shall turn out for the best. It shall be but a simple thing, this joining of two people."

As he soothed her tenderly, suddenly Sabrina let herself go, her tears now came freely, her breath came in short heart-rending gasps, and she clung tightly to the man standing over her.

Sabrina's tears were only for herself at this

moment. She had known no release since that day her sister and Zaloe Tolliver had come to her with their plan. Since that day her life seemed to have turned into a horrible nightmare, and now she did not know which way to turn.

As Garrison's lips came away from her eyes, he glanced down into her pain-filled features, then his mouth slanted across her own, drinking of the sweet, life-giving substance of her being.

As though he were a life line, Sabrina clung to Garrison with all the strength that she could draw on. And Garrison McBride, feeling her momentarily relent, drew her ever closer into his grasp, hoping that she would lean on him, forget her reasons for not allowing him to claim her as his wife, and put her future in his safekeeping.

For a time Sabrina lost herself in the arms of this man who seemed so strong and caring, her past rising up before her and then dissipating into unreality. Nothing matters, her inner self declared. Nothing but this man and this moment.

Garrison's heart lurched, and he strove harder to gain Sabrina's trust. His mouth and tongue plundered hers, gently urging her to respond freely to the honey feasting of their senses.

Sabrina soared, feeling total rapture as she let herself be led where he would take her, her only care that he not release her and leave her alone once again. There was no evil in his hold upon her, none of the fear or horror that the nuns had told her would greet her in the arms of a man. There was only a sense of belonging, of being cared for, of being held tenderly.

When he began to undo the tiny pearl buttons of her blouse, she did not stop him. It was meant that she should be his, no matter what had brought them together. Though her sister should be in the arms of this man, Sabrina did not care, she cared only that she and he were sheltered from the outside world, hidden within this copse of trees, secluded from life's storms.

It was Garrison who pulled back when he felt her soft, yielding flesh against his palm, his tender strokes over the top of her chemise bringing a heat to his body that was hard to quiet. But as his light green eyes looked into her stunning passion-absorbed features, he knew that he dare not touch further. This woman would be his, he had decided to make her his wife. Yet he would be the gentle lover, would slowly teach her the joys of being man and wife. He would not introduce her to lovemaking in this copse of trees. She deserved much more than this, much, much more.

So with a tender hand he slowly began to button her blouse and to straighten her clothing, his eyes resting upon her face. Then his lips taking the moist, soft petals that were hers alone. "Your beauty astounds me, Sabrina," he whispered as he finished dressing her.

Sabrina could not reply. Shattered by his touch, she wished only for his hand upon her, his gentle voice next to her ear.

Pulling her into his arms once again, Garrison spoke. "Say not that we shall not wed, for nothing shall stop me from wedding you. You belong to me from this moment forth and nothing can change this."

Sabrina could do naught but nod her golden head as his full lips once more descended upon her own, leaving her shaking and unsteady upon her feet as he began to lead her back to her mount, which was standing close to Garrison's large stallion and munching on the first growth of winter grass. Deep within, Sabrina knew marrying him would not be right. She would have to flee now for certain, for she would be trapped. Garrison McBride had strange seductive powers that she must get away from. Now she was not only prepared to flee from her lies, but also from her own body's awakening needs.

"The others shall be wondering where we are. At times they follow me as though they fear some great harm shall befall me. I am sure that they are at this very moment scouring the countryside for the pair of us." His warm eyes held hers and his handsome smile stilled her thoughts of freedom for the moment. She decided to think it all out when she was alone in her chamber at the keep.

"Let us go to the village." After helping her to seat herself upon the mare, he mounted his stallion and taking her hand within his own, he rode with her from the stand of trees. As they reached the dirt road, Brian and his men hurried toward them.

"We thought some grave harm had befallen you." Brian looked somewhat embarrassed to

125

find Lord Garrison and his lady coming from the woods and looking like satisfied lovers. Sabrina's face was flushed and Garrison's expression fitted a man lucky with love.

"We had thought to rest for a moment," Garrison responded, not caring what his men thought. Only Sabrina mattered to him, and he was very glad that he had led her horse into that copse. Their short time together had been sufficient to wear down the barrier that she had built about herself, and he was determined to allow no further hindrance to his careful courting of her. Now that he no longer had India's companionship he could well spend his time on the project at hand, wooing this lovely lady. A small, thin smile touched his lips. He had never heard of a man putting such an effort into winning his bride's affection, but he had ever been one to prefer a willing woman to a cold unyielding one. And in those few moments in the trees, he had learned that the shyly innocent Sabrina Buchanan was neither cold nor unyielding.

Garrison and Sabrina passed the afternoon in a most companionable fashion, their eyes often seeking each other out and revealing their inner thoughts. Even the townspeople responded favorably to Garrison McBride and his lovely lady, seeing a side to their lord that they had never viewed before. He had held himself in reserve about them, and had often seemed fierce and hard, giving them only the knowledge that they were well protected.

After some hours had passed, the group went

126

to the only tavern within the small village to satisfy their hunger and slake their thirst. While they were seated at a large table a dirty young lad was dragged before Garrison, who had just started to fork up a mouthful of food.

"What is his crime?" Garrison said to the man who held the boy's shirt collar, his eyes going from him to the youth.

Sabrina studied the small boy, not understanding how a mere child such as he could have done anything to merit being dragged about by his shirt collar. Noting Garrison's cool manner with the man, she held her peace, however, and waited for him to mete out justice in this village.

"He was caught early this morning, my lord, trying to steal a loaf from the baker." The large man's voice resounded through the tavern, and he grasped the lad's collar and shook him.

Garrison's voice was hard as he addressed the lad, who could have been no more than twelve years old. "What have you to say to these charges, Johnny?" His green eyes studied the small face before him.

"Me dad is laid up sick, sire, with the fever. Me and mum is trying, but there be not enough food to go around, what with two babes to be feeding."

"Why did your mother not send word to me about your father?" Garrison asked, his interest aroused by the boy's tale of sickness and hardship.

"She told me that I weren't to be bothering ye with our troubles—ye be having plenty to be

127

doing without having to be plagued with the likes of us. We thought that me dad would be up and back on his feet by now, but the fever seems to come upon him quick and then it be gone just as fast."

Garrison looked at the man who still held the lad tightly. "You can release him into my care, Gerald." The man did so, then turned and left the tavern. As he did so, Garrison called for the owner to bring the lad a plate of food. "You do understand that you will have to pay for what you did, Johnny?" He said as the proprietor set a heaping plate of roast beef and potatoes before the lad.

"Yes, sir. I be knowing full well the punishment." The boy's thoughts went to the whipping post.

"I have a different punishment in mind for you, Johnny." As Garrison spoke, the boy's eyes rose from the food before him. "You shall report to the keep every day for the next month and help my stableboy. If I deem your work satisfactory, I shall pay the baker for your loaf and you will have served out your punishment."

The lad's dark eyes came alight at Garrison's description of his punishment. "Yes, sir. I shall come each morning before sunup. I will work hard, sir," he added as he finished the food on his plate.

Turning to Sabrina, Garrison smiled into her sparkling eyes. Then, to the boy, he added, "Don't be coming for the rest of this week, I am sure that your mother will be needing you at home until your father returns to his health."

"Yes, sir." The lad said, and then he rushed from the tavern. He raced toward home to tell his mother the outcome of the day, for he knew that by now the neighbors had already reported his offense to her and she was beside herself with worry.

"You were most kind to the boy, my lord." Sabrina declared. She seemed to see more in Garrison with each hour that passed.

"Brian, go to the lad's cabin and see to his father. Send the doctor and see that they have food upon the table." Garrison delighted in feeling Sabrina's warm eyes upon him, and his heart was bursting with the desire to do as many good deeds as possible. Taking her hand from her lap, he held it in his own under the table, feeling a delightful peace settle about them.

Sabrina did not pull away. The feel of his hand encircling hers and of the hard, large thigh on which her palm rested gave her a security that she had known infrequently in the past.

When Garrison and Sabrina finished their meal a young, slim, full-busted woman came up to their table and began to clear away the dishes, her creamy, smooth bosom brushing boldly against Garrison's arm as she leaned across the table. "Ye be needing anything else, Lord McBride?" she questioned in an all too familiar tone of voice.

"Nay. The lady and I are both quite finished," Garrison responded, finding Maggy a bit much this afternoon as he wished for nothing else to upset Sabrina and to turn her from his company.

"Then perhaps this eve you shall return?" Maggy looked full into the handsome face of Garrison McBride, ignoring the woman at his side as she displayed her abundant wares to him in the hope that she could win him before he wed.

Garrison scowled darkly at the girl, then his glance went to Sabrina. But seeing her expression had not changed, he only shook his head in the negative. "Nay. There is more to content me at the keep these days than in the past. Do not count upon me this eve or any other." He rose to his feet, all but upsetting the load of dishes that the girl had piled upon her large tray, in such haste was he to gather up Sabrina and make his exit.

"Are you ready, Sabrina?" he asked. When the woman he was lavishing attention on nodded her head, he led her out of the tavern, feeling Maggy's piercing glare upon him.

"I believe that girl is smitten with you, Mr. McBride." Sabrina gently chided, as Garrison helped her to mount her horse. With a grin, he nodded, relieved that she was not going to pout and storm about such a one as Maggy.

"She is a part of my past that shall never come up again," he promised, letting his hand rest easily upon hers while his green eyes looked deeply into her brown depths. Seeing no anger there, he grinned and mounted his own steed. Then the small group started their way homeward, Garrison thinking that Sabrina, having grown up around the court, was accustomed to gentlemen's slight indiscretions. Certainly this was the type of wife that would well suit his needs — or was it? he fleetingly wondered, not quite sure anymore of what he wanted.

Chapter Six

In the days that followed Sabrina tried to put from her mind her reason for being at McBride Keep. It was as though a dream had come true for her while she was in the company of Garrison McBride. His gentle eyes now regarded her tenderly, and she had changed toward him since that day in the copse.

She had even considered telling him that she was not the one he was supposed to wed—her twin sister was—and to let him then decide for himself where his true feelings lay, but she feared that she would lose all by doing so. Garrison McBride was a man of honor, and at times when she caught him looking upon her, she felt he was estimating her worth. If she revealed her deceit, what other course would she leave him except to cast her aside for her duplicity.

She truly wished for nothing except the love he

was lavishing upon her day and night, but what if he learned the truth, he might feel the need to confront Priscilla Buchanan and to bring all out within the open. And when light was shed upon all that she and her sister had set out to do, Sabrina feared it would be Sylvia who would stand beside this man and repeat the wedding vows.

As she dressed for dinner, it came to her that she had but two more days before she would become Mrs. Garrison McBride. With a small smile, she let this thought settle about her and envelope her in blissful thoughts of the man who would be her husband.

She had but to make sure that the marriage contract read Sabrina instead of Sylvia and she would be forever Garrison's wife.

Patting the last curl into place in her coiffure Sabrina started from the room, her pink taffeta evening gown floating about her like a cloud as she went down the stairway and entered the main hall. Indeed, Sabrina was more than pleased with the reaction provoked in the lord of the keep.

She had never in the past thought much about her own looks, but seeing the pleasure in Garrison's eyes as he hurried toward her from across the large main hall, she knew that she would forever go out of her way to ensure this same reaction.

Gaining her side, he reached out and took her

hand. "You look lovely sweet." Noting her slight blush, he knew that again he had struck the inner core that instantly made her shy and innocent.

"Would you care to relax within my study before dinner is ready?" he asked her softly.

Sabrina took in the bustle and noise of the large, main hall, then eagerly nodded her head, wishing for some privacy with him.

As soon as they reached the small study Garrison closed the door behind them, and leading Sabrina to the small settee he murmured lightly, though with ill-concealed relish, "It shall only be two more days, love, and then you shall be mine." He lightly rubbed the back of her hand, his green eyes resting upon her features and delighting in the gentle turn of her shoulders in the low-cut dress that seemed to cling to her perfect form.

"Are you so sure that you wish to be tied down to a wife, my lord?" Sabrina asked, still at war within herself and regretting her duplicity because of and her new-found feelings toward this man.

With a small grin, Garrison pulled her tightly into his embrace. "Could ever a man wish to be so delightfully tied, madam?" His lips caught hers and held them, bringing to life in her the overwhelming feelings of desire that he inevitably evoked when she was in his arms.

Finally he released her with a sigh. "Have you any doubt about my desire for you?" He was patient as he probed her eyes to find the truth, and seeing the dawning of her acceptance of him, his face broke into a smile.

"Never try to frighten me again, madam, with words about not wishing to be my bride. Never have I wanted anything more than I want you." As he said these words, he realized the full truth of them. This woman was not at all what he had expected, nor was she like the women in his past, of whom he had tired in a short time. No. Sabrina Buchanan had some sort of strange hold upon him. As the days had passed he had only become more enamored of her, and he was now eagerly awaiting the day when he would claim her.

"I pray that all will turn out well and that you will not be disappointed," Sabrina said aloud. She was still uneasy about this whole affair, and was not able to keep back these words.

Garrison thought this moment would be a good time to question her about her past, for he felt that he had gained her confidence. After all she had not denied that the marriage would take place shortly. "Sabrina has there been another that you were fond of in the past?" His light green eyes watched her carefully.

At her startled look, Garrison looked sharply down upon her.

"Why, of course there have been others I have cared for." She had almost spoken the mother superior's name, but warning herself to be careful, she had remembered that Sylvia had lived with her aunt. "I was quite fond of my aunt."

Could any woman be as innocent as this? "I did not mean that kind of fondness, sweet. I was thinking of a gentleman."

When his meaning dawned on her, Sabrina stared hard at him. "Whyever would you question me about another man? Have I given you reason?" Sabrina searched her memory, trying to recall what could have provoked his questioning. Had he somehow heard about Zaloe Tolliver, her sister's gentleman friend. She did not know how to respond, thinking that she would soon find herself within a trap of her own making if she were to say the wrong thing.

Garrison saw the flush come over her features, and taking this to be her true answer to his question, he said, "I did not mean to pry. I, for one, can certainly well understand the need for companionship." Both he and Sabrina were remembering when, only a few day past, Maggy had approached him at the tavern. But in his mind were visions of other women, including India Sterling. "I myself have been no angel. I shall not pry into your past, for I would not wish another to pry into mine. I but wish for a beginning between the two of us. I would see us happy."

Sabrina felt the swift sting of tears as she looked into his handsome face, reading for herself the truth of his words and at that same

137

moment vowing silently to expose the deception that had been played on him. As soon as the vows were safely spoken she would tell him the truth, when she was at last truly his. She could not chance that upon knowing of her part in this ruse to change his bride's identity, he would turn from her, and would not go on with the marriage until all was set aright. She felt that his sense of honor would compel him to make sure that they had a fair start if he truly did care about her. But if she said nothing until after the vows were spoken, she would have a certain hold upon him that would forever bind them, and perhaps, in time, he would learn to forgive her.

Not willing to cast a pall over the evening ahead Garrison swiftly wrapped his arms about Sabrina, and gently kissed her forehead. "Let us not speak again on this matter. It is sufficient that in two days you shall be my wife and we shall begin our life together."

Sabrina could only smile her agreement, her heart aching at the deceit she was practicing upon this man that she was growing to care more about with each passing day she spent at the keep.

But before any more words could be exchanged, Katie entered the small study, a slight frown upon her kindly features. "I am afraid there is a visitor, Lord Garrison." She looked to the pair, noting their closeness.

"Who is it, Katie?" Garrison asked when he

saw her concern. He knew the eve was not a fit one — a storm was pelting the countryside — for anyone to be coming to the keep at such a late hour.

Katie looked first to Sabrina and then to Garrison, but seeing no way out of a reply with his questioning eyes upon her, she softly murmured, as though hoping that neither would hear, "It be Miss India Sterling." Katie did not approve of this young woman, having met several times in the past when she had come to the keep to visit Lord Garrison. And since Lord Garrison was soon to wed she was certain nothing but trouble could come of this visit.

Garrison quickly rose to his feet, a quick anger come over him. What did India want? He had made it clear to her that all was over between them, and he had thought that by now she would be on her way to a country estate with her new gentleman friend.

Sabrina, seeing the fury that settled on Garrison's features and Katie's worried look, wondered who this visitor could be.

But before Garrison or Katie left the study to confront this visitor, a tall, darkly beautiful woman entered the study. To Sabrina she seemed to sweep into the room as though carried by a whirlwind.

As the dark gaze of India Sterling took in all before her, first the housekeeper, her black orbs finally settled on Sabrina, who was sitting upon

139

the settee, hands folded primly her lap. As though discounting the girl-woman, India glided past her to stand directly in front of Garrison. "I hope you do not mind my stopping by, darling. But it has been some days since your last visit to my house and I was wondering what was keeping you." Before Garrison could respond she wrapped her arms about his tall frame and kissed him fully upon the mouth.

Sabrina was painfully embarrassed as she witnessed this intimate moment between the man she was supposed to marry and the woman with whom he apparently had some form of romantic entanglement.

And Katie was outraged by what was taking place right before Sabrina's eyes. But before she could respond Garrison, and with a light movement, removed India's arms from him.

"What is it that you are here for, India? I thought all was said that other eve?" His voice held an icy tone that was not lost upon the others in the chamber.

But as though his tone did not affect her at all, India smiled fully into Garrison's face, and her hands again rose, this time to fondly caress his chest, covered by the satin doublet he was wearing. "You sound so gruff this eve, my love. I hope that you have not been ill and that has been the reason for your absence?" Then, before Garrison could say a word, she twirled about and stood before Sabrina. "This must be the girl who is to

140

become your bride. I do hope that you have told her about our arrangement, my darling." India's dark eyes went from Sabrina to the man who was now fuming with rage over her daring to come to his home to confront the woman who would be his wife.

"India, I think it is time for you to leave. Katie, please see her to the door." Garrison started toward his former mistress, and taking hold of her forearm, prepared to drag her from his study. But something in Sabrina's glance stopped him.

Sabrina could not believe her own ears. This woman was Garrison's mistress. She had come to his keep to see why he had not been visiting her. How horrible! He had thought he could wed her and still have a mistress in town. Perhaps many men did the same, but there had seemed to be something special between the two of them. Now she knew that Garrison McBride had been only been treating her with tender kindness to get her to wed him according to his plan. And to think she had been willing to go along with it. Her senses had been so misled by this man that she had forgotten all in her eagerness to become his bride. But with this woman looking down upon her, Sabrina knew that she was no more than a gullible fool. She had been raised within the shelter of a convent. She was not wise to the world, or to the things that men could do and say. But now, with the reality of what was taking place here in this chamber, she knew that she had but one option. She must leave this keep and this man, and find her sister. Sylvia would help her to start a new life once she heard what had taken place. Tiny droplets of tears formed within the brown eyes that looked up into Garrison's as he stood next to his lover, and without saying a word Sabrina ran from the study. India Sterling's laughter followed her out of the room and up the stairway.

Garrison could easily have struck the woman with whom he had enjoyed so many pleasant hours. "Get yourself from my home, India. And if you return I shall set the dogs upon you." He was furious, for he was well aware of the hurt that had been inflicted upon Sabrina. It had taken him days to build up her trust and now that had all been shattered by this vengeful woman.

India was lost to laughter as she witnessed Sabrina's flight from the study. "Don't worry, my love. I shall be leaving for London this very night." Her laughter stopped as quickly as it had come upon her when she noted Garrisons fierce anger. "I told you that I would not easily let you get away with treating me so cruelly. Let your little friend now lovingly take you within her embrace. But she will always wonder where your heart is—here at the keep with her or in the village with another?"

Garrison, losing reason for a moment, took hold of her as though he would throttle her.

142

But India pulled herself free. "I know my way out of this keep, and shall see myself to the door." Turning from him, she hurriedly made her way to the front portal. Having seen the extent of Garrison's fury, she knew that it would be wise not to linger any longer. She had done the deed that she had set out to do; she had realized that when she had watched the beautiful young woman flee from the study. Perhaps this was a small price for Garrison to pay for turning from her charms, but it was all that she could do. So thinking, India hurried out of the keep to her carriage. Her friend would be awaiting her by the time she reached her home.

Katie stood looking at Garrison, and seeing the anger coursing over his features, she was glad that India Sterling had left the keep so speedily. She had never known Lord Garrison to harm a woman, but by the look on his face, he would have delighted in wringing India Sterling's neck.

"See that she is never again allowed within this keep, Katie," Garrison called out as he swiftly made his way through the main hall and up the staircase, his thoughts black with worry over what Sabrina would be thinking at this very moment.

All had seemed to be going so well these past few days as he had wooed her into desiring their wedding, which was to take place in two days. But now all of his efforts had been in vain. He had thought to have Sabrina willing in his bed, at least until he tired of her. But now he could well imagine her reluctance to become his wife.

Standing outside her portal, he gently knocked upon it. When no reply was forthcoming, he called softly, "Sabrina, let me explain. India was but trying to get even with me for my refusal to see her again."

Sabrina did not respond. Hot tears of shame, at being so confronted by his mistress and at her own deceit, washed over her. She had thought that all would be well, that she could wed this man and live happily ever after as heroines died in the pages of the romance novels she had read at the convent, but the appearance of the beautiful India Sterling had pulled her to her senses. She could no more live a lie than she could live with a man who was living a life apart from her. How had she ever let things get so out of hand?

As she heard Garrison calling to her, she sniffed back her tears. For some strange reason she believe what he had said, but her tears were caused by more than what had happened in the study. She now knew that she had to leave this keep. She had let the situation get too far out of hand.

Garrison's appeals quieted after a moment. He had decided to leave Sabrina to herself for a while, to give her some moments to settle her thoughts.

Sabrina dashed the tears from her cheeks as

she heard him head down the hallway, toward his own chamber. She had made up her mind. She would leave this eve when all at the keep was still. Time was running out, and she had no other option. She would try to make her way back to London and find her twin. Surely her sister would not turn her away, even though the situation at the keep had not turned out as Sylvia and Zaloe had expected.

Sabrina had fallen asleep after Katie had come to her chamber door. The housekeeper receiving no response to her knocks had shaken her head and slowly left.

It was far into the night when Sabrina awakened, and all was quiet. Realizing she had fallen asleep, she hurriedly pulled herself from the large oak bed, went to the wardrobe, and pulled out a riding outfit. She hoped its dark coloring would help to conceal her from prying eyes in the darkness of the night.

On silent feet she then went into the hall, and looking both ways along it to make sure there were no servants about, she quickly started down the long, winding staircase, holding her breath as she grasped the banister.

No light greeted her in the main hall, only the dim glow from the glowing coals in the two hearths.

Sabrina's brown eyes were ever watchful as she

started toward the door, but it was the low snarling of a dog that brought her to a quick halt. The animal arose from a corner, and gave another warning growl. Sabrina halted her steps, her hand clutching her throat as her eyes sought out the beast.

It seemed to her that she stood frozen to that same spot for hours when in fact it was only moments before a great, hairy mastiff approached her at the foot of the stairway. After sniffing her leather boots and recognizing the odor of one that had on occasion thrown him a morsel during mealtime, his large tail began to waggle in a greeting.

Sabrina let out her breath as she recognized that the dog's warning was for a stranger and it had known her scent. "Good dog," she lightly murmured, and she bent down and patted the mastiff's head before starting once again for the door.

As she turned the knob, the huge portal swung open, and Sabrina sighed with relief. Hurrying through it, she went down the stone steps, gazing about her.

She had not planned her leave-taking while in her chamber, yet had known she had no option except to flee on this very eve. Now, standing out in the cold, dark night, she wondered what she should do next. She would have to hurry. Her escape might soon be discovered. She started to the back of the keep, hoping that she could find the stables and the mare she had ridden the other day.

Finding the stables was not as difficult as she had anticipated, and within a few moments she was standing within that structure, her brown eyes seeking the horse that she desired.

A small lantern had been left alight near the front door, so with cautious steps, Sabrina went farther into the stables.

She found the mare near the back, and the gentle horse, as though expecting her, whinnied lightly.

Not daring to speak to her, Sabrina hurriedly placed the bridle about the mare's mouth, then led her from the stall and out of the stable. Standing upon a small bucket, she mounted the unsaddled mare.

Feeling desperate and fearing she would be caught stealing this horse, Sabrina patted the mare to quiet her, knowing that any noise could awake the entire keep. And at an unhurried walk she led the horse away from the stables and down the long lane that led to the great stone keep.

Letting out a long, deep breath Sabrina at last kicked the sides of the animal. She held tightly to the reins as the mare started off at a gallop.

She planned to try to reach the Boar's Head Inn and once there to secure passage to London, and she reasoned that she had only borrowed Garrison's horse. She would leave the beast with

147

the innkeeper's wife to make sure it was returned to the master of McBride keep.

Sabrina had gone only a short way upon the back of the mare when she heard another rider behind her. Kicking harder at the mare's flanks, she shouted for her to increase her pace. But as she glanced behind her, out of nowhere a large apparition swooped down upon her.

Sabrina screamed as this phantom grabbed her and pulled her from the back of her mount, then grasped her in its dark clutches.

Numbed by fear, Sabrina fought her captor, hitting out with arms and feet, but to no avail. Then she heard loud, deep rumbling laughter. The man's dark cloak covered his face, but his laughter left her with a feeling of dread.

Had she left the keep only to meet a worse fate? she thought as she felt the breath being squeezed from her.

"Where were you fleeing to, my lovely beauty?" The cold, hard voice of Garrison McBride plundered her brain and left her quaking.

Garrison had gotten little sleep during the early hours of the eve, so he'd decided to go to Sabrina's chambers. For some reason that he could not explain, he desired to look upon her as she slept, as he had that other eve.

But when he had gone to her chamber he had found the door slightly ajar and the large bed empty. Thinking that she perhaps could not sleep either, he had gone down the stairway, expecting to find her in his study, seated near the hearth and reading one of his books.

Not finding her in the study or anywhere on the lower floor of his keep, and all being dark and quiet, he suddenly thought that she had flown from him.

Unreasonable anger filled him at this thought, but it was quickly replaced by a growing fear for her safety. He had no idea how long she had been gone from the keep, and in the wild country about it, he knew a woman alone could run into harm. There were those about doing mischief at all hours, some poaching and others with a more deadly intent such as highwaymen.

Without a second thought Garrison donned the cloak placed near the front portal, and headed for the stables. As he saddled his stallion he imagined all manner of horrible things happening to a young and beautiful woman traveling by herself, and he feared for more than her safety. What if she did escape him and he could not find her? What would he do?

At this thought he swung his large frame upon his stallion and urged the beast forward. He took the main road, and prayed that she had gone that way. He had little time to wed, and he might be forced to find another to take Sabrina's place. But this truly did not worry him. There were plenty of young women whose mothers were eager to make a good match. What bothered him was something more, something that he did not want to think upon at the moment.

As he pushed his mount harder, he thought of Sabrina's tender beauty, her gentle manner, and her silken tone. And again he could have throttled India Sterling. But for her, Sabrina would still be safe and well protected within his keep. He promised himself that India would pay if any harm came to Sabrina this night.

Only a short way down the road Garrison saw the dark form of a horse in the distance. Praying that this was the one he sought he urged his stallion to a faster pace.

And indeed it was Sabrina. The moon lit her beautiful features for a moment as she turned in his direction, her fear evident when she saw that she was being fast approached from behind. Knowing that she was within his reach made his chest swell jubilantly. He had thought that the chase would be much harder, had even feared that she would be harmed; but she was before him and all he had to do was reach out and grab hold of her. That was exactly what he did, telling himself that he would not again let her escape him.

The moment that Sabrina heard the cold words and the deep-throated laughter she knew who her dark abductor was. Garrison McBride had given pursuit and had caught her. What can I do now? she asked herself, but at the same time she felt the security of his arms about her and laid her cheek against his strong chest. She had not

150

realized how much she had feared what she was doing. His capture of her meant that she did not have to find her own way to London and seek her sister. She had never in her life been on her own, and though she had thought to flee this man, she now knew a deep sense of happiness in his embrace. Nothing else mattered, not that she was not the one he was supposed to wed, not all the lies she had spoken since knowing him, not the fact that his mistress had paid them a call. At this moment all that was real was his strong body so close to her own, and as he looked down into her face and his lips descended on hers, Sabrina knew that this was where she was meant to be. Nothing else seemed real at this moment but his touch.

The exhilaration of the chase and the victory at hand had Garrison's blood pumping as he looked down at the vision in his arms, watching her fear be replaced with something else when she realized who her attacker was. And losing himself in her eyes as she was lost in his gaze, he lowered his mouth to hers. Wishing at first to remain hard and teach her that she could not flee from him with ease, his lips took hers, but tasting the sweet ambrosia of her, he was swept into a sphere of loving that was totally new to him. This woman was doing something to his senses, something that he did not understand. From the first moment that he had looked upon her he had wanted her, but had declared to himself that he would soon grow tired of her, that all he desired was the pleasure he could gain from her luscious body. Yet this night when he had discovered that she had disappeared from her chambers he had known there was more to it. He was often torn asunder by her merest smile, and though he had tried to ignore these feelings he was incapable of hiding these facts from himself any longer. She was a burning fever in his blood, and until he indeed became immune to her bewitching hold upon him, he was not about to let her go from him.

He would figure it all out at another time, he told himself, and he let himself just enjoy holding her in his arms.

Neither spoke as Garrison turned his horse about and started toward the keep. The moon cast its light on the young lovers, and it seemed short time until Garrison halted his stallion and lowered his frame to the ground. With a gentle ease, he took Sabrina in his arms and started up the steps to the keep. Then as they stood before the wide, double portals, he once again captured her mouth with his own, seeming to devour her sweetness.

"Do not try to flee me again, love," he huskily whispered, his mouth still next to hers.

Sabrina did not answer but nodded, knowing that she would not be so foolish again. She could only hope that all would turn out for the best.

Opening the door Garrison entered the main

hall, and hearing the barking of the large mastiff that had stopped Sabrina on her way out, he ordered the beast to quiet down. Then he started up the stairs, Sabrina still in his arms.

Sabrina did not speak. She just relaxed against him as he made his way into her room, allowing him to set her down before her dressing table and then to turn her about with a gentle hand. As he easily undid the row of buttons at the back of her habit, she saw nothing wrong with him being in her chambers and acting the part of lady's maid.

With deft hands Garrison helped Sabrina pull the outfit from her, his gaze feasting upon the delicate creaminess of her curves when she stood in her chemise. But exerting his will, he went to the foot of her bed and brought her the dressing robe Katie had placed there.

Sabrina had not known what to expect, but when Garrison handed her the robe she smiled upon him, knowing that if he had desired her, she would have been powerless to put up a struggle.

After a last fleeting kiss, Garrison murmured low, "Sleep well, my love. Tomorrow will be a beautiful day."

Smiling in agreement Sabrina walked him to the door, and then as he made his way out of her chambers she leaned against the portal, a large sigh escaping her.

No matter what was to come, she had tried to flee and to put a stop to this wedding. Was it her fault that Garrison McBride had caught up with her and had forced her back to his keep? As she walked to the bed she admitted to herself that she had put up little argument.

Lying upon the soft coverlet, she smiled. She knew little of the ways of the world, but she did know that this man had stolen his way into her heart. He was all that mattered to her now, though it seemed impossible that she could so quickly feel the way that she did. She was caught in a quandary and could see but one way out of it. She would marry Garrison and then explain all to him later.

The morning of the wedding day Sabrina slept late for the first time that she could remember, the draperies having been drawn tight the eve before by Katie. The housekeeper thought that on a girl's wedding day she needed to look her best, and for such a long drawn-out affair as this would be, Sabrina would need all of the rest she could get.

So it was with some surprise that Sabrina awoke to the humming of Katie's soft voice as a breakfast tray was set beside her. The housekeeper then arranged the articles needed for a long, leisurely bath.

"Good morning, my lady." Katie saw Sabrina's brown eyes flutter open, and she went to the window and drew back the draperies.

"Why good morning to you, Katie. But it is not awfully late?" Sabrina saw that the sun was now high in the sky.

"It is not all that late in the morn. Just a touch past your usual time of getting up." The housekeeper admired this girl for not being lazy and staying abed like so many would if given the chance. "I brought your breakfast to your chambers on this special morn."

"But what of Lord McBride? Has he eaten alone?" Sabrina quickly remembered what day this was and thought of the man she was to marry. Yesterday she had seen him for only a short time during dinner, which they had shared with his men at the long table in the main hall.

Garrison had been most polite and considerate during the meal, yet when his eyes had touched upon hers she had felt the heat of his gaze.

He had left shortly after dinner, excusing himself to help one of his men in the stables, and Sabrina, not daring to question him, had nodded her head as he had helped her out of her chair. But as he had started from her side he had bent and lightly whispered. "Only one more day, my sweet. I pray that time flies."

Sabrina had not known what to think due to his quiet manner during the meal. She had even begun to fear that he was having second thoughts about making her his bride, perhaps because of the past night when she had run from his home. But at his tender words, her whole being had

155

come alive and she had gone to her chambers to ready herself for bed, hoping that time would pass swiftly.

Now her wedding morning was upon her, she realized as she questioned Katie about the whereabouts of Garrison McBride.

"Aye, that one ate early and went to the village. I think he was in need of some action to make time move at a faster pace. Most of the men rose early and rode off with him, and I am sure that they'll find some enjoyable sport on which to release their pent-up steam." Katie knew how much her lord was enthralled by this lovely, young woman, even if he was not yet aware of it. And it had surely done her old heart good to watch him dote upon Sabrina's every mood these last few days, though Katie had thought some horrible disaster would befall them when India Sterling had paid a visit. But she had been right in her estimation of this young woman, and this morning, only hours away from the marriage, she had sensed in Garrison an impatience to speak the vows and to be alone with his young bride.

Sabrina smiled, imagining Garrison's desire to make all ready for the afternoon ahead. More than likely, he was bringing the priest from the village, and the villagers would be at his heels. "I hope that I can make him happy," she said aloud.

"Aye, lass. I can see it written in the depths of

your eyes. Real love cannot be hid from any, and when the two of you are alone together there will be a rare quality to your union."

Sabrina felt reassured by this woman's kind words and for a moment peace came over her.

"You had best hurry with your breakfast now, child. Your hot water will be brought up shortly and then we shall dress and arrange your hair. I had your wedding gown taken downstairs to be steamed and hung out to prevent wrinkling. That was done the day of your arrival at the keep."

"My wedding gown?" Sabrina looked to the woman, her expression incredulous as though she had not heard her aright.

"Why yes, child, the gown that was packed in your largest trunk. It is the loveliest creation that I have ever seen, and each time that I see it hanging in the room off the kitchens I can envision you walking down the aisle in the chapel."

My wedding gown, Sabrina thought. If a wedding gown had been packed along with her other gowns, then her sister had known that the wedding was to take place as soon as she arrived at the McBride keep. Had this whole affair been a plot created by Sylvia and Zaloe, to ensure that Sylvia would be free to wed Tolliver? Had Sabrina really been expected to meet them in London and live with them until Priscilla Buchanan came around and accepted both of her children? Or had Sylvia known that Sabrina would be forced into marriage and would remain so far away from her family and London that no one would ever recognize her and think she was her twin?

While these thoughts plagued Sabrina, Katie left the chamber to order the servants to bring water for her bath.

Upon hearing that her wedding gown had been in one of her trunks, Sabrina had been forced to look at this whole affair in a new way. She no longer felt any guilt about her part in this plan, not when whole affair had turned out as it had. Was it her fault that all had been set into motion before she had ever arrived at the McBride keep? Had she not tried her hardest to convince Garrison that she could not marry him? Had she not even fled him? Surely it was not her fault that she had fallen in love with the lord of the keep. She could no more have helped these feelings than she could change who she truly was. And if somehow in the future Garrison were to find out that she was truly his betrothed's sister and that he had wed the wrong woman, she would say that the plan had been Sylvia's and that she had only been a pawn in the game of deceit.

With a loud sigh, as though a weight had been taken from her chest, Sabrina sat up and began to lightly nibble at the sweet roll upon her tray. Today is my wedding day, she thought, a thrill going through her. But when she remembered a nun telling her that men only wanted of a woman's body, to abuse and to use in all manner of sordid ways. Then, left with child, the woman had to bear the horrible pain of bringing an infant into this world – all for the pleasure of being named wife.

As this thought came to her mind, a cold chill swept over Sabrina. Was this truly going to be her fate as wife? she wondered. Could Garrison be so inhumane? Were all men alike and was his kindness only an act to lull her into trusting him.

Putting the roll from her, Sabrina rose from her bed, her mind in a whirl. Should she somehow at this late moment try to sway Garrison from the marriage, and beg to be returned to London? But he would never agree ... and if he did it would mean that she would never see him again.

"Nay," she said aloud to the walls of the chamber. She would not lose Garrison McBride so easily. She knew he was a man that would never deliberately bring her pain or harm, and if the act of bearing a child entailed the horrors the sister had outlined, so be it. Would not anything be worth her being able to hold in her arms a tiny being that came to be because of their special joining?

The chamber door was opened wide, and a number of servants brought in buckets of steaming water, driving all thoughts of running away from Sabrina's mind. The marriage would take place that very afternoon.

Katie hurried the servants about their work and then helped Sabrina into the tub, handing her a delicious rose scent to place upon her sponge.

"Have you ever been married, Katie?" Sabrina ventured as the woman began to rub foamy lather across her slim back.

Something in the young woman's tone brought a smile to Katie's sharp face. She knew the girl was an innocent, and was sure that Sabrina knew little of the things of a man and wife did. "Why yes, child, I was married long years ago. It was truly the most wonderful time of my life – especially my wedding night."

Sabrina turned her head, her honey-colored hair swinging about as she did so. Was the older woman mocking her? she wondered. But seeing Katie's kindly expression, she knew her to be speaking the truth. "Your wedding night was wonderful?" Sabrina finally ventured, not seeing how any woman could say such a thing if she had endured excruciating pain.

"Why, lass, my man was so kind and loving, his every thought was only to please me." With a loud laugh the older woman threw back her head and added, "And please me he surely did."

Sabrina could not believe her ears. What was this woman telling her, that she had enjoyed what had taken place? "But, Katie, I thought there was horrible pain?" She had to ask this question, though she felt her cheeks flush as she

160

did so.

Katie had been right in thinking that someone had told this young girl naught but what to fear upon her marriage bed. "Nay, child, there is but a second's pain when first you are joined, but after this you will find only pleasure in the union with your husband."

Not being able to fathom what she was hearing Sabrina again turned about to see if Katie were jesting with her, but as before the housekeeper's eyes, kindly and concerned, held Sabrina's gold and brown gaze.

"Lord McBride is an unusual man, child. He would never do anything that would cause you any great hurt. I have seen his eyes upon you as you have approached him, and there is something in their depths that reveals his caring and devotion. He would never bring you pain. You will find only happiness in his arms, my lady."

Tears came to Sabrina's brown eyes, and she dashed them away with the back of her wrist. Then she turned in the tub and tightly hugged the housekeeper's neck. "Thank you so much Katie. You cannot fully imagine what I was anticipating in the night to come." A happy smile broke out upon her lovely features before she looked with some guilt at the housekeeper's black dress and starched white apron, now both sopping wet with bath water. "I am so sorry, Katie," she added but the glint of joy remained in the depths of her brown eyes.

Katie broke out into a large grin, well knowing the horrible fears this young girl must have been holding within her, and glad that she had dispelled her terror by telling of her own joy in the arms of her husband. "Never forget, child, that Garrison is a man that can carry many burdens upon his shoulders, a man that can tend to his lands and his people with a fierce, possessive pride, but alas he is but human and vulnerable. He needs love as much, if not more, than most."

"I will not forget, Katie." Sabrina's spirits soared now, and her desire to be a good wife to Garrison grew ever stronger. To evoke this kind of trust and love from a servant, Sabrina knew he was a special man, and she considered it lucky that fate had brought her to his arms.

At the completion of her bath, Sabrina was told to lie abed while Katie rubbed some fragrant rose-scented ointment over her limbs. The rub left the girl with a delightful feeling of satisfaction in her entire body, and she felt she could face any dilemma that arose.

After these languorous ministrations, Katie helped Sabrina into her chemise, this garment being made of white transparent lace that clung to the young woman's form.

"Come over here, child, to the dressing table so I can brush out your beautiful hair. I will send Molly up later to arrange it for you. She is the best one at the keep at dressing a woman's hair, and this day you will be needing only the best." The

162

older woman stroked Sabrina's honey curls until they fairly gleamed.

Next she lightly dusted Sabrina's cheeks with a touch of powder and then rouge, wishing only to bring out her natural coloring. She brightened her mouth with a hint of lip rouge and then stood back to admire her handiwork. "You are truly a beauty, my lady." She sighed as Sabrina rose, and then she began to help her don her stockings and petticoats.

"When I go to fetch Molly, I shall bring up a tray for your lunch. We surely would not wish you to be fainting from hunger while walking down the aisle," Katie joked, bringing a smile of pleasure to the younger woman's lips.

"Oh yes, and your gown. I will bring that along also, though we wish to put this on last, to ensure that all shall be just perfect."

Sabrina had never had so much attention lavished upon her, and not knowing how to thank this woman, she could but smile in gratitude. "I don't know how to thank you enough, Katie," she finally whispered.

"You already have, child." At Sabrina's look of wonder, she added, "By being here at the keep you have given me all the thanks that I will ever be needing." This said, she started from the chamber in order to fetch Molly, the gown, and a tray for her mistress.

As though caught in a dream, Garrison McBride stood next to the priest and watched as Sabrina came down the aisle on the arm of his best friend Brian Craig. And as his light, green eyes beheld her beauty he felt his breath catch. Never have I seen such loveliness, he thought.

Sabrina's gown of pure white lace flowed about her tiny form, billowing like a fleecy cloud of thistledown, and her long white train whispered at each tiny step her slippered feet took.

Stitched into the bodice of the gown were tiny, perfect seed pearls, sprinkled among them glittering bits of diamonds and rhinestones. At Sabrina's shoulders, the sleeves rose up in a billow of puffed lace, and from the elbow down they were skin tight and ornamented with the same embellishments as the bodice. Her golden hair was piled atop her head, and in the midst of each perfect curl was a tiny pearl hairpin. The effect was breathtaking.

Her beauty is unequaled, Garrison silently declared as Sabrina gained his side. He reached out and took her hand from Brian's arm, gently tucking it into the crook of his elbow, his eyes devouring her face.

The small chapel was filled to capacity with friends of Garrison and any villagers that could squeeze within. The priest first looked to those attending the wedding, and then to the young couple standing before him. Having known Garrison McBride for many years, he smiled toward the young woman who had finally captured his heart.

As Garrison began to repeat after the priest the vows that would forever bind him to Sabrina, he turned his green gaze upon her face, his every word holding a promise that touched her heart.

At the completion of her own vows, Sabrina smiled radiantly, her spirit seeming to soar under his watchful gaze. And when the priest pronounced them man and wife, Garrison bent his tall frame in order to claim his wife's mouth, and Sabrina felt a thrill of anticipation as her senses reeled.

It was a moment before Garrison came to himself and remembered that he and Sabrina were not alone in the chapel. Then he drew back from his wife and stood erect once more as the loud shouts of well-wishers assailed the pair, villagers and McBride's friends alike rushing forward to offer loud congratulations.

Then the reception began to get underway, the villagers and the keep's servants joining in the celebration of the union of their lord and his lady. Shouts and laughter filled the yard, where long tables stood, heaped with food, and toasts were offered to the bride and the groom as they were ushered out into the yard.

Garrison smiled fondly at everyone about him, his own laughter resounding often as he joked with friends. But always his hand held his wife's. He did not allow her from his side, not even late in the afternoon when she smiled up at him and told him of her need for a private moment. He just escorted her into the keep and waited impatiently outside her chamber door.

He gazed at her lovingly as she returned to his side, and arm in arm, they went back to the wedding party. Before going into the yard, however, his lips captured hers in a searing kiss that set their senses to reeling and their bodies to trembling. "I have not told you this fine day how beautiful you are. Let me do so now." He gazed boldly into her gold-brown orbs, and when she smiled he proceeded to tell her what was in his heart.

"These words do not come easy for me. I have never spoken them before, and am not sure that I have ever felt them. You have come into my life and my heart with the swiftness of a breeze, so suddenly that when I am not near you, at times I doubt that these past days have been real. Life has lost all meaning except where you are concerned; I hold only those moments I spend with you as meaningful. I did not fully realize this until I almost lost you. You are my heart, my breath, my song. I never lived until I beheld you."

"Oh, Garrison," Sabrina responded, melting against him. "I wish only to please you—to be a good and faithful wife, and to love you more with each passing day." A lone tear slipped from her brown eyes and, he lightly reached out a long masculine finger and wiped it away.

"You can do naught but please me, sweet. If you but stand beside me, I wish for no more."

At this moment the door was pulled wide, and Brian spied the newly wedded couple, close together at the entrance of the main hall of the keep. "Time enough for this later, you two," he shouted and bid them join the others in the yard.

Time seemed suspended for Garrison and Sabrina on this special afternoon. Though they were surrounded at all times by their guests, they were in a world of their own. Each time their glances met, their eyes spoke the words that could not be said aloud, and the smallest touch of their hands or legs infused them with feeling. Finally as darkness was beginning to descend upon the keep and lanterns were being placed about the yard, Garrison found his wife and softly whispered, "Follow me, love, and we shall escape this horde of merrymakers and have a moment to ourselves."

Without a word, Sabrina clasped his hand, and began to follow him toward the back of the keep, intent upon not being seen and quietly gaining their own chambers.

But as the pair rounded the corner a group of Garrison's men spied the newly wedded couple, and seeing their intent, they quickly rushed over to detain them, heartily clapping Garrison upon the back and shouting praises of Sabrina's beauty.

"What is this, Lord Garrison? Do you mean to hide away from your guests?" It was Brian. Knowing his master sought to be secluded with his beautiful, young bride as quickly as possible, he stoutly pulled Garrison off to the side while other men drew Sabrina in the other direction.

Garrison tried with to see over the heads of the men circled about him, not wishing to lose sight of his wife, but within moments he knew he had failed. For as the men pulled him back toward the partyers he found that Sabrina was nowhere in sight. Sighing, he took hold of the mug of ale that one of his men pushed into his empty hand.

"To the bride and the groom," another shouted at the top of his voice, bringing the attention of all to the master of McBride keep. "May their days be many, their children be blessed, and their pains be few." A round of cheers and similar statements followed. Then Garrison's men gulped down their drinks and again clapped their master on the back.

Almost an hour had gone by before Brian turned to Garrison, a slanted grin on his face. "Why are you standing out here in the yard while your young bride awaits you in your chambers?" he asked, then laughed loudly at Garrison's surprise. "Where did you think the lass had flown?" He shouted after his lord, as Garrison raced up the steps of the castle.

Where indeed? Garrison thought. That sly, old fox had planned this, dragging Sabrina from his side in order to let Katie and the other women ready her for her husband. As Garrison hurriedly approached his chamber door, he suddenly stopped. Taking a deep breath he let his hand rest upon the knob, his pulse rising alarmingly at the thought of what lay ahead for him this eve.

Would he find a willing bride or would Sabrina be reluctant and shy? He had no idea, but he gently turned the knob and then stepped through the doorway, his green eyes swiftly going about the room, until they rested upon his bride.

Her form was outlined as she turned from the window at which she had been watching the goings-on of their guests, but her gaze now rested upon her husband, her warm brown eyes beheld only his manly visage. Slowly, she started toward him.

Garrison stood frozen, and when his wife gained his side she gently held out her small hand, her beauty astounding him, her gown of gossamer blue lace holding nothing from his heated gaze.

"Come, husband. Let me help you take off your jacket, and perhaps you would care for some warmed wine?" Sabrina took hold of Garrison's arm and steered him toward the hearth, thinking to delay their union by performing these small wifely duties. Though her fear was not so great after talking with Katie, a nagging anxiety lingered.

Garrison, his mind in the clouds, let his wife lead him to a comfortable chair, and sitting down, he stretched out his long, muscular legs, his green eyes going toward the woman of his heart as he awaited her next move. But noting that she stood next to his chair as though not truly knowing which way to turn, he gently reached out and took hold of her hand. "Sit with me, sweet." Gently, he brought her down upon his lap, the heat of her silken body scorching him and fully awakening his desire.

Nervously, Sabrina sat in her husband's arms. "Relax, love," Garrison soothed, feeling the tension in her small form, and he brought his hands up to cup her face and bring her lips down to meet his own, knowing that the power of a kiss had always eased the strain between them.

And as before, Sabrina responded when his tongue made tiny circling motions about her mouth until she was leaning against him, breathless and wanting.

As her arms slowly moved up to encircle his neck, Garrison felt true pleasure. But aware of her reluctance and shyness, he was determined to give her time, to wait until she was relaxed and trusting in his arms. He had no desire to rush her, knowing that their wedding night should be a loving time, a night they could both remember.

These thoughts brought another, but he quickly tried to drive it from his brain. Was his wife as innocent as she acted? Had she not shyly avoided telling him about another man? And her flying from his keep, her reluctance to wed him — was that because there was another? Had his solicitor been right about this young woman?

While these thoughts plagued Garrison, he continued to plunder Sabrina's mouth, driven by a desire to prove his suspicions wrong, a need to know that her heart was truly in his keeping. His pulse racing, he gently reached up to feel the softness of her slim neck, aware of the beating of her racing heart as he slowly began to unfasten the small satin ties of her nightgown.

Her body quaking as her own passion built Sabrina held Garrison more tightly, wanting him, rapture filling her.

Barely audible, love words came from Garrison's lips and then his mouth began to explore where his hands had roamed earlier, his warm breath touching upon her skin as he tasted of her delicious nectar. Enflamed, he nonetheless held himself in, not willing to frighten her with the all-consuming feelings that were overpowering him.

Her head held back, Sabrina lost herself to Garrison's lips, now traveling from the slim column of her throat to the firm mounds of her breasts, his tongue a fiery brand upon her soft skin as he nibbled and lightly tasted of her body's delights. Losing all sense of place and time, Sabrina held tightly to this man — her husband. Her hands could feel the manliness of his torso, even through his white silk shirt.

Sabrina's slightest touch enflamed Garrison. As her small fingers moved along his back, hot sparks fired every nerve of his body. "Ah, love, let us go to yonder bed." He brought his head up, and meeting her passion-filled orbs with his own he nodded toward the massive, fourposter bed that stood in the center of the chamber. "Let us share the delights of our union to the fullest, tasting deeply of the sweet fire and ice of our bodies." He rose, Sabrina's small form held tightly against his chest, and before she could say a word in protest his lips again covered her own.

His steps were quick, and when he had gained the magnificent bed, he gently placed his wife upon it. Her gown was now open to her waist, and the moonlight coming through the windows, the firelight from the hearth, permitted him to feast his greedy eyes upon her perfection before he began to remove his own clothing.

Sabrina watched with quiet amazement as Garrison stepped out of his trousers and then pulled his ruffled shirt from his muscular frame. Never had she seen a man fully naked before, and with bated breath she let her brown eyes roam over his hair-matted chest, then downward over his flat belly and narrow hips, and still lower until she drew back in surprise at the discovery of his male readiness.

Garrison had been watching Sabrina as her eyes left his face and traveled downward. Her knowledge now complete, a flame came over her face and neck, and she quickly pulled her brown orbs back to his green ones, her panic evident. Slowly Garrison lowered his frame onto the bed, not rushing her for fear that she would become terrified.

With gentle persuasion he cradled Sabrina in the crook of his arm, his lips seeking hers and then lightly plundering her mouth. He held back his body, not wishing her to feel his need until he knew that she, too, was ready.

The fear that had come over Sabrina was quickly dispelled by her husband's knowing hands and lips. Once again she cared only about the feel of his hard, large body.

Garrison then pulled her gown from her delicate form, and he allowed his hands and lips to travel the length of her, spiraling her heavenward until finally he again claimed her mouth with his own. His hard, virile body was pressed to hers, sharing warmth and desire, until driven to the brink of losing control he rose up, his hands caressing her everywhere and not allowing her time to think of the outcome of their play.

With a soft gentle pressure Sabrina and Garrison became one. Sabrina had little time to dwell on the sharp pain of losing her womanhood, for the slow, undulating movements of her husband soon brought her into a sphere of pleasure and then sheer rapture.

Garrison had known as he'd entered his bride that he had misjudged her. She had indeed, been chaste until that very moment. Since she knew so little of the joys of love, he was certain that he would be able to quickly drive any thoughts of another man from her mind, and with great control he moved within her, not wishing pain or discomfort to hinder her first, initial plunge into love's realm. But noting that her pain had quickly vanished and she now had a look of wonder in her brown eyes, he smiled tenderly as his body moved rhythmically, bring them both to fiery passion.

Quick as the sun bursts through a clouding they scaled the peaks of rapture, each striving ever onward toward the goal ahead, their bodies evoking new beginnings, until at last they touched the stars. Then iridescent diamonds showered all about them as they rode across the heavens upon moonbeams, to ever so gently rest on white, fleecy clouds.

In the glowing aftermath of pleasure, Garrison looked deep into Sabrina's enraptured face, his eyes misting. Never, had it been like this. "Sweet, sweet Sabrina, keeper of my heart," he whispered. "How did I exist until this moment? My senses, my feelings, my very breath were not yet in my body. You have brought me to a new beginning."

Sabrina felt somewhat the same. She had

feared the worst, but his touch had brought only happiness. Never before had her senses been so alive. In their closeness, those moments shared, she also had been made new. Garrison was the completion of her, body and soul. Fate had joined them together. They were meant to be, now and throughout all eternity. Tears came to her brown eyes, and seeing her feelings, Garrison rejoiced. His lips gently caressed hers in a gesture of completion.

"Heart's love," he whispered, wiping away the glistening droplets, "I place all that I have in your tender keeping. Do not deny me. Let this bud swell to full bloom, to unshakable love." Never before had he bared his heart to a woman but something within him had urged him to let Sabrina know the extent of his feeling for her.

With a gentle nod of her golden head, she responded. "I have known little of sharing my feelings with another, but within my chest"—her small hand went to that most delicate spot and rested there while she continued—"there beats a tender pulse that only you have touched. My heart is yours, forever as my honor would demand. I know that men speak of honor, but I, a mere woman, hold this word, perhaps, more dear. The vows I have spoken before man and God surely place me, through all of our tomorrows, beside you, my husband, my heart." She then sought his giving mouth.

Her tender words seemed branded upon Garrison's mind, and at the taste of her soft lips, he lost all hold on the present. He just let her sweetness enfold him.

As the revelers enjoyed themselves outside the McBride keep, within moonlight shimmered in the master's chamber, illuminating the happy couple as their small gasps of passions echoed about the room until far into the morning hours. The villagers had long ago sought their own warm beds by the time the newlywed pair slept.

Tenderly Garrison had partaken of the repast before him. Having first tasted of love and been fulfilled he had savored the delight of teaching his new bride the joys to be found in his large bed. He had lingeringly caressed her breasts, her throat, her face; had gently pressed her body against his large frame, letting her know his body's appetite.

Strong, probing fingers had roamed freely over Sabrina's body, bringing from her soft moans. And Garrison's lips and tongue had seemed to be devouring her own lips, lowering to take a full, ripe breast, then making delicious patterns across her engorged, rose-tipped nipples, and sending her into spasms of wantonness. But he had not relented and taken her. His mouth had roamed further down, across her flat stomach, over a hip until at last it had come to the triangle of her womanhood. Her very core had then been plundered until she'd become a pulsating, storming maelstorm of white-hot passion,

176

her body writhing against his.

Garrison drove Sabrina ever higher, his mouth and fingers playing the sweet tune of love on her body and as he swept her along to a world only they could share.

As he once again lay at her side, wishing to prolong these feelings of rapture, Sabrina reached out, for the first time, to touch a man's body. Slowly but boldly she ran her hands along the length of his frame, feeling the corded muscles of his chest the smooth hardness of his tapered hips, the flatness of his stomach. And as her small fingers roamed farther down, not quite sure of herself, she carefully encircled his throbbing maleness. In that moment her husband caught his breath, his arms enfolded her, and her hand was gently pulled back.

"I can take little more, love," Garrison panted, his body throbbing with desire for this woman as he rose above her and spread her creamy thighs, intending to plunge into her soft yielding body.

Soft, languorous words of love came from Garrison's lips as he stroked her sensuously, rhythmically, and wrapping Sabrina's legs about his waist, he drove deeper and deeper into her, making them one.

She knew an unquenchable need for fulfillment, and pulsated with pleasure. As she strained upward, sweating and reaching out for the earth-shattering pleasure so near at hand, she looked into her husband's face, seeing for herself the love so boldly exposed to her gaze.

And when her desires erupted into a shattering force, she gloried in the pulsating, spiraling culmination of pleasure.

For a moment longer, Garrison drank of her body's giving. He knew Sabrina had reached total fullfillment, and soon he, too, was swept into the eddy of pleasure. Lost to reason, he was plunged into rapture.

Suddenly Garrison's body stilled and his breathing grew ragged, but his lips continued to caress his wife's face; kissing her eyes, her cheeks, and her passion-laced lips. He could not seem to get enough of her. "You inflame me," he breathed as he gently let his fingers roam over her silky-soft golden hair.

Sabrina melted at the warmth of his words and caresses. She had scaled the very peaks of womanhood and had found delight with this man. He gave her substance, and he was hers. She smiled, her world seeming complete.

Chapter Seven

Sylvia turned about, agitated. She did not try to conceal her rage as she looked at the man she had wed, then hurriedly went back to her packing. "You promised that this would be the last of such traveling." She threw the words over her shoulder, not wanting to say too much but unable to keep her mouth shut, her temper being at the boiling point.

"Keep packing and keep your tone down. If the innkeeper gets wind of our leavetaking, you will be the one left behind to face him." Zaloe looked indulgently at Sylvia, and he wondered why he did not just leave her here in this small town and let her fend for herself. She had done little except plague him, thinking that as his wife she had the right to make demands on him. But he had quickly showed his little wife the way of things. A thin smile of remembrance came over his lips as he thought of the first night they had spent as man and wife. Feeling his blood run hot, he rose to his feet. This was not the time to reenact that night.

At the departure of the beautiful Sabrina, they had gone directly to the clergyman waiting at a nearby parish. After gold coins had been passed from Zaloe to the priest, the banns had been set aside and, with little fanfare, the ceremony had been performed.

Sylvia had thought her dreams had come true as she had stood next to her tall, darkly handsome lover and repeated her vows. She had forgotten the lustful way he had looked at her twin sister earlier that day, and she had forgotten the harshness of this man when all did not go exactly as he would wish. She knew only that she would be Mrs. Zaloe Tolliver, that the man she loved would be forever bound to her.

Zaloe had spoken the words after the priest, with little thought to what he was saying. He only wished the vows over so that they could be on their way. His driver was awaiting them, and he wished to make the next town by the lowering of the sun. He had made plans for this eve, and he did not wish to be detained.

Hurriedly Zaloe took hold of Sylvia's elbow and steered her out of the church, his other hand reaching out to grasp the marriage papers the priest held out to him. Then, with a swift nod of his dark head, he was through the doors and was helping his bride into the carriage.

He called to the driver, and they began the jostling trek back down the dirt road.

"Could we not have spent this night here in

this village?" Sylvia asked, her brown eyes gazing through the window at a small country inn set back on a lawn.

"Nay we cannot stay here. I have an appointment this eve in the next town." Zaloe looked at his wife as though awaiting her next words.

"But this is our wedding eve. You cannot leave me to some empty room while you keep an appointment. It is unheard of." Sylvia was truly scandalized. She had envisioned her wedding night, and now her husband of only moments was telling her that she was to be alone. She would not tolerate such treatment. Not even from Zaloe.

Knowing well what her reaction would be, Zaloe stretched out his long, thin legs, and let his eyes roam over the woman next to him, for a moment thinking of the one that had lain upon that seat this very morn. Her beauty was like this bride's but very different. Why could not this woman have been her twin, he thought a bit wishfully. "As my wife, Sylvia, he began, as though explaining something to a child, "you shall do as you are told and not question me about my business."

Sylvia, never one to hold her tongue, glared at her new husband. She had taken a lot from Zaloe in the past, feeling that she had little hold upon him but after the vows they'd taken this afternoon, she was not going to let him order her about or cheat her out of what was her due. And a wedding eve was most assuredly her due. Zaloe could attend to his business in the morning as any gentleman would. "As your wife I shall be treated with some respect." Her tone was haughty. "You shall not leave me alone on our wedding eve."

Without thinking, Zaloe reached out and grabbed hold of his lovely bride's dress, roughly pulling her to him, her trim body being draped across his lap and chest. "Do not try me, my flower, for in the end you are little match for my will. I have waited a time for the day when I would teach you who is the master in our home, but the time is finally at hand." With a light touch he caressed her jawline, feeling her tremble. Then, with a vicious movement, he squeezed hard. "You shall indeed receive your wedding night, my love. Yes indeed, I would not think of leaving you without first giving you what you deserve."

Sylvia shuddered as he released her, and she once again leaned back against the cushioned seat. Though Zaloe, had sometimes been harsh, never had she seen him so heartless. She had always felt he loved her, even when he had pinched her or handled her a bit roughly. But Sylvia now feared him, and sitting next to him she kept her thoughts to herself, not daring to utter a word that might provoke his anger. Perhaps he had only meant to frighten her and he would leave her alone this evening. Sylvia knew she would prefer that to what his cruel words had promised.

The rest of the trip was made in silence. Zaloe did not speak to his wife, and she said nothing, fearing to evoke her husband's anger. Her hands primly folded, she tried to figure out what had provoked such a cruel response from Zaloe.

The inn to which Zaloe took Sylvia on her wedding night was a simple one. Those sitting about it seemed cruder folk than Sylvia had ever been about, and as the innkeeper approached them, he spit a long stream of tobacco juice onto the plank flooring. He eyed Zaloe and then gave Sylvia a lecherous look. "Ye be wishing rooms?" he asked, again looking at Zaloe.

"One room will be sufficient, good sir," Zaloe responded smoothly, as though at ease in such an atmosphere.

"Ye be paying in advance?" The innkeeper could see by the cut of their clothing that they were not of the ilk that usually made their way to his establishment, but he had learned to be wary.

"Aye. You will be paid as son as I come down from my room after going through my trunk," Zaloe responded, looking the large, unkempt man in the eye.

"Be sure. I be watching fer ye." The innkeeper reached into the deep pocket of his dirty apron and withdrew a key.

As though he were the most considerate of husbands, Zaloe then took Sylvia's elbow and helped her up the stairs, the driver following close behind with their bags.

After entering the chamber Zaloe spoke a few words to the driver, who left; then he shut the door and eased the key into the lock. "What do you think of our accommodations, my lovely wife?" Zaloe looked about the ill-furnished chamber at the same time Sylvia did, taking in the lone bed against one wall and the small dresser opposite.

Sylvia spun about, her pride coming to the fore. "We cannot possibly stay here." At that moment a large spider made its way across the floor and scuttled under the bed. "There must be some mistake. You will have to go to the proprietor and speak to him. Surely he has a better chamber for us?" Sylvia had never in her life been in a room furnished as badly as this. Not able to believe that this was where she would be spending her first night as Zaloe's wife, she looked toward him with wide eyes.

"Come over here, Sylvia." Zaloe ignored her demands. "I promised you a wedding night, did I not?" His dark eyes held hers. But she stood as though rooted to the wood flooring, her mind going back to his earlier threat.

"Do not try me, wife!" The words struck out across the chamber. "Do as I say. Now!"

Not knowing what else to do, and thinking to soothe his mood somewhat, Sylvia slowly approached her husband.

"So you would have your wedding night, would you, my dear?" Without another word, Zaloe took hold of the gown she had worn for the wedding, and he tore it from neckline to waist.

Sylvia's abundant bosom spilled out over her torn chemise, and she gasped, never having been so handled. "Zaloe I . . ."

But he did not allow her to finish. He grasped those creamy molds of flesh, and his thin, hard lips slanted over her mouth as he pushed her to the floor.

Fear overcame Sylvia as she felt herself falling to the floor. As Zaloe wrapped his body about her own, she shut her eyes, feeling the sharp pain of his hurtful fingers upon her breasts.

"Is this what you desired, Mrs. Tolliver?" he taunted, as he finished tearing her clothing from her and left her bare to his gaze.

Of course this was not what Sylvia had had in mind for her wedding night. She had expected love words, flowers. "Nay, Zaloe, I did not mean . . ." She tried to reason with him for she felt very vulnerable.

"You will learn to keep your thoughts to yourself, and to do as I tell you." With these words, he swiftly unbuttoned his breeches, and without taking them from his slim frame, he plunged into her dry body, delighting in forcing this tense woman to be his tool.

Sylvia moaned aloud, hurt by his first entry, still not believing that he would treat her in such a manner. But as her body began to respond to his hands and his movements, all reason flew from her. This was what she had wanted—this man, his name now her own, and all that went with him. She had known of his cruel streak, she had to admit. It was similar to her own. Perhaps she had not expected such a forceful show of power, but this man did stimulate her. His hands alone drove her to a throbbing pulsing rhythm.

185

Though he was evil, he fed her passion, and she knew at this very moment that no other would ever do for her.

Zaloe felt her response and he smiled darkly down at her enraptured face. He had not expected this reaction to his hard caresses, but as her movements matched his own, he threw back his head and laughed aloud as he pounded down on his wife.

Sylvia wrapped her arms about his neck, and she undulated with his movements, her cries of passion pushing him ever onward until she felt the storm within burst into showering brilliants.

Zaloe wasted no thought on the woman beneath him. He just kept driving up and down, up and down until, with a large grunt of satisfaction, he spilled his seed. A few seconds later, he rose to his feet. His dark eyes looking down upon Sylvia with some disgust. He had known she was not a gentlewoman in fact, but he had not fully known the extent of her own cruel passion. It all but matched his own. In a woman, and especially in his own wife he had not expected as much. Straightening out his clothing and adjusting his doublet, he turned his back upon her and crossed to where she had dropped her small bead purse earlier. He drew from it a small cache of gold coins.

Slowly Sylvia sat up, reaching out to gather some of her dress about her and to cover her nakedness. "What are you about?" she asked as she saw Zaloe pick up her purse.

"The innkeeper demands payment in full this

eve. I shall go down and see that he gets his coin."

"But that is more than he needs." Sylvia had taken the small sack of gold from her uncle's desk that morning. It was all she had, and she had intended to keep these coins for herself in case an emergency arose. After all, wouldn't they live on Zaloe's money? "Why do you take my coins and not use your own?" She tried to pull herself up from the floor.

"You are my wife. What is yours is mine. Do not question me on such matters again."

Sylvia did not say anything further about the gold for she was becoming aware of the raw pain in one of her breasts. It had been badly bruised.

Zaloe also looked at his wife's breast and then at her torn clothing and disheveled hair. "Try to make yourself presentable. I care not to have a hag for a wife." He started toward the door, but turned and said, "Do not await me. I shall not be returning early." Without another word, he walked through the door, his mind already on the card game that he was sure to find downstairs in the common room of the inn.

That had been the first of many such inns. Always Zaloe played out his luck in each town or village, never gaining much and always venturing his winnings until his luck ran it's course and he had to try to stay a step before the authorities so as to not be pinched for running out on an innkeeper.

"I am tired of this life, Zaloe. Why can we not go to my mother now and tell her that we are married? I cannot go on living out of trunks and running at the slightest word from you." Sylvia threw the rest of her clothing into her bags quickly, knowing after only two weeks that Zaloe was not idly threatening to leave her to face the innkeeper.

"I thought that you desired nothing more than to be my loving wife?" Zaloe cocked a dark brow in his wife's direction.

Sylvia saw the trap in Zaloe's words, and responded softly, "I do not mean that I do not wish to be your wife. I mean only that I think it is time we approach Priscilla. Surely she will relent and allow us to live in London, and she will not see us live beneath our station." Sylvia now knew the extent of her husband's income. In days past she had not wondered how he had made his livelihood, but after evenings alone, his moods changing as quickly as his luck, she knew that at any given moment they could have barely enough coin to purchase their next meal.

Zaloe knew that the time had to be right when they approached Priscilla with the fact that Sylvia had not married Garrison McBride, but had instead run away and married him. He could not afford to underestimate Priscilla's reaction to such an announcement. "It is not yet time for us to approach her," he responded. "More time will be needed." He took hold of two of the bags, and looking back at Sylvia, he nodded to the other bags and motioned for her to follow him down the back stairs, hoping that neither the servants nor the innkeeper would see them making their escape. With the darkness of the hour and the busyness of the inn, Zaloe hoped that his luck would hold until they were out of this town.

He had been told about a fair in the next town, and all that day he had been making plans for himself and Sylvia. It is about time, he told himself, that my lovely little wife begins to earn her keep. He could well imagine her reaction when he told her of her part in their daily fight for coin. He would tell her tomorrow, when they reached the fair. And perhaps the following week or so, he would consider getting in touch with Priscilla. He wanted to live the idle life of a gentleman. He had married this woman so he could one day do as he pleased without worrying about how much he ventured upon a hand of cards. He could envision the day when he would go through a pile of coins without a second thought and then sign a note.

Chapter Eight

Awakening to the dawn's first light, Garrison stretched out full-length upon the massive bed. As his hard, muscular body came into contact with his wife's, a sense of well-being came over him and his light emerald eyes slowly went to the one who now shared his name. To him, Sabrina seemed even more beautiful in the quietness of sleep. Aye, he thought to himself, she is the kind of woman poets write about.

Her honey-gold curls cascaded over the satin pillow, and without a second thought he reached out and took one of the soft, clinging ringlets in his fingers, rubbing it gently and then bringing it to his nostrils so he could inhale her rose-delicate scent. His thoughts then turned to her heady attack on his senses the preceding night. She had more than surprised him, she had delighted him. She was all woman, soft, giving and loving. As he thought of how eager she had been to please him, how adept a pupil she had been he could feel his heartbeat accelerate.

As a strange name came from her petal-pink lips his eyes were drawn back to her tender features. Had she called out the name Zaloe? He wondered, but as sleep pulled her further into the realms of unconsciousness, he reasoned that he had been mistaken. If not, perhaps the man had been a friend of hers in London. Trying to cast the name from his thoughts, he again concentrated only upon her sweet body. Yet some small prickle of premonition nagged at him, presaging future pain and heartache. Deliberately, he pushed such thoughts aside, forcing himself to think only of a future with Sabrina always at hand and of the children they would surely create.

Only days ago he had thought his life was in order and that no woman could possibly change it. With a smile upon his strongly chiseled features, he thought of how he had planned to wed this woman and then live his life as he had in his past. Well, Sabrina had shown him much in a short time. She had shown him the true meaning of loving and caring.

Surely he could ask for no more than what this beautiful woman could bring to him. He wrapped his large body about her smaller frame and let his senses absorb the feel of her, the scent. Then he shut his eyes, and sleep once again overtook him. But before his mind dulled, he again remembered the name that had slipped from his lovely bride's lips, *Zaloe*. What kind of name was this, or had he been mistaken?

The day was proclaimed a holiday by Garrison when he and his lady descended the stairs to make their way through the main hall and toward the back of the house. Lusty laughter and deep-throated male voices assailed them, but at last Sabrina pushed open the door and stepped boldly into the kitchen, Katie's domain.

Several servants were arrayed about the large, stone kitchen, all involved in the preparation of food; some stirring pots, others cutting vegetables at a long, wood table. A small child sat off in the corner, turning a spit of meat over burning coals.

But what truly drew the couple's attention was Brian who sat with two of his men at the long work table along the wall. Katie stood near them, her thin features alive with amusement as they regaled her with tales of the antics of their cohorts on the preceding eve.

As Brian saw the newly wedded couple coming through the portal, his dark eyes came alight. "What say ye, lads?" He looked to his companions and then to Garrison and Sabrina. "Do you not think that perhaps Lord Garrison is looking a wee bit peaked this morn? Could it be that this marriage business sits not well with the fellow?"

The other two men grinned boldly at Garrison and nodded their heads. Garrison scowled darkly at them, quickly looking to Sabrina to be assured that she was not offended by their merrymaking. But seeing a small smile gently touch her lovely features, he began to relax. "Nay, lads, that is not the way of it. If I am looking a bit under the weather this fine morn, it is from all the noise that came up to my chamber as you and your friends played the night through."

The three at the table all began to nod their heads in agreement, their grins wide in remembrance of what had taken place. Then Brian, in a rare moment of joviality, slapped one of the men sitting closest to him heartily upon the back, and chortled with glee. "Dave here got lost and didn't show himself until only an hour past."

With a reddened face the one called Dave muttered into his steaming mug of brew, "It were the lass Maggy that kept me overlong. Aye, Maggy be a fine lass." He said the latter almost dreamily.

Even Sabrina joined in the loud laughter that filled the kitchen area, and seeing her radiant smile, Garrison grinned broadly. Taking hold of her hand, he then started out of the kitchen's back door, his other hand reaching out and capturing two of the sweets on a plate upon the long table. "Go about your duties, lads, as usual. That is, if your heads are not too enlarged." He laughed as Brian glared in his direction. Then he pulled Sabrina out into the fresh, cool air and the brilliant sunlight. "Would you care for a ride this morn, Lady McBride?" His eyes devoured her as his warm smile thrilled her.

Sabrina eyed him appreciatively, her thoughts on the hours spent in his strong arms. Then she nodded her golden head. "Whatever you desire, Lord McBride," she lightly rejoined, leaving Garrison to wonder about her play on words.

Not able to find a stableboy that was not still abed, Garrison roused the youth called Johnny, the lad he had set to work in the stable as punishment, and his large stallion and his lady's mare were quickly saddled.

With a gentle hand, Garrison helped his wife to mount, and within seconds they were riding from the keep.

They rode through a wooded area, and Sabrina sighed with pleasure. Greenery and foliage were about them as Garrison led her deeper into the dense stand of trees.

"As a lad I came here to hide away from everything," Garrison said. "There is a secret glade that no other knows about, or at least I would like to think that it is still my secret." He urged his beast onward, his eyes never leaving the face of his bride.

When he finally pulled his mighty black stallion to a halt, then helped Sabrina down from her mare, she looked about her and slowly nodded her golden head. "No other could know of this beauty and not return often. Surely you would know of intruders." Off to the side of the thicket was a small stream and the lulling noise from its waters touched lightly upon her ears, mingling with the sounds of the birds and the small creatures that frequented the place.

"You are the very first intruder," Garrison whispered against her hair, his nostrils inhaling her rose scent, his nearness to her rendering his wife incapable of thought or movement. A light wind gently tugged at her blouse and riding skirt, but the pair remained immobile, their senses attuned to one another.

With some strength of will Garrison took his arms from his lovely bride, and pulling a blanket from his saddle he led her toward the rumbling stream. "It is a wonderful place to wile away an afternoon. Do you not agree, love?" His warm gaze held hers. Not able to resist his winning smile, Sabrina nodded. As Garrison spread out the blanket, and drew her down upon it, fire raced through Sabrina's veins for she knew this was a prelude to his spellbinding lovemaking.

Without a word Garrison tenderly traced her heart-shaped face. Then his fingers lingered on the soft, creamy skin of her neck as he undid tiny buttons of her blouse.

Sabrina held her breath at this tender play, and her brown eyes glazed in wonderment. This man had such power over her. Tentatively, she reached out and touched her husband's handsome face, tracing his features, his cool lips, and then lightly brushing the tuft of hair that lay upon his collar. Her fingers quickly returned to his lips as though they were drawn to that most special spot.

At seeing the naked hunger in her husband's green eyes, Sabrina thought her heart stopped, but then quickly it began to hammer wildly as he slowly rose upon his elbows and looked deeply into her gentle brown gaze. He took her mouth then in a deep, penetrating kiss.

As their kiss deepened, Garrison entwined

himself about Sabrina, his clasping her tightly, molding her soft coolness to his angular heat. As his chest covered her breasts, he felt the rapid beating of her heart, which told him far better than words of her need for him.

Secluded deep within the glade, the young couple lay on the earth, the soft sun yielding warmth, the autumn breeze cooling them, the rich smells of dark earth and forest filling their senses. As the gentle stream played a wistful tune and the tall, majestic canopy of trees shadowed them, their passions were came to the fore.

Wifely instincts as old as time overcame Sabrina, and she reached out to caress her husband's hair-matted chest, her lips then boldly explored it after following a delightful path along his strongly corded neck. Her body was aflame as she sought release, the storm of desire ravaging her.

Garrison soared toward spiraling plateaus as his hands caressed her, molding her small waist and firm buttocks. The earthy scents about him, her soft, searching touch upon his body, and her softness beneath him sent him ever onward until he longed to give her womanly fulfillment.

"Garrison," Sabrina cried out in the moment when they were joined, losing all power of reason as he drew her deeper into their union. She felt his hardness, his strength, and she clasped him more tightly as she was whirled into a flaming vortex of pleasure.

With her velvet softness wrapped about him, Garrison looked down upon his beautiful wife whose lightly fringed eyelids were closed. Her passion-bruised lips parted and soft, throaty moans of pleasure escaped her. As her body arched toward his, he was lost in those moments. The sweet-savage pull of his insides sent him spiraling, and with thrust after thrust, he carried her toward complete satisfaction.

As she approached the peak of ecstasy Sabrina's senses were burning. Her husband's being was suffusing throughout her, leaving her ablaze yet enveloping her and sending her ever upward until she was swept along on the wings of bliss.

The couple hung together on the very edge of existence, the white heat of their passion encircling them. And as they returned to earth they clung together, binding each other in a hold that would last for an eternity.

Some moments later Sabrina gently spiraled back to reality as Garrison lay holding her tightly against his strong chest, his breathing ragged and sharp against her golden hair. She tasted total contentment as she nestled against his hard, loving body. Tilting her head, she looked into the emerald depths of his eyes and her heart hammered wildly. She loved this man. "Will it ever be thus?" she asked, as though speaking to herself.

A few weeks ago, Garrison would not have believed that he would answer this question honestly; but his heart had softened where this woman was concerned. "Aye, sweet," he responded, and he lightly kissed her soft brow, his finger tracing her fragile jawline. "I shall not allow it to be any other way." He brought his lips to her mouth, and leisurely partook of the delicious ambrosia that awaited him. "With you at my side I can conquer lands, build cities, and even cross vast seas." A small smile touched his handsome mouth. "I can do whatever you wish, and I have no fear of defeat." He kissed her again. This time his mouth was not as gentle but more hungry for her.

"You place great faith in my charms, my lord" Sabrina said softly as he eased his tight hold on her.

With a lustful grin Garrison nodded and remembering moments just passed, he answered, "Your charms thus far have proven quite formidable, my lady."

She smiled, and added, "I have little fear of anything in this life as long as you are at my side, your gentle gaze drawing me ever onward."

For the first time since becoming Garrison's wife, Sabrina thought of the game that had sent her to him. If he were to learn her identity, would he still hold her in such high regard? A frown creased her flawless features.

Seeing her mood change, Garrison wondered what had he said that could have wounded her so sharply? "What stings you into looking so thoughtful, my love?" His green eyes looked deeply into hers, wishing to impart strength and understanding, but when she shook her head and no answer was forthcoming, he held her tightly in his caring arms. "I have much strength, sweet. I can bear whatever it is that you would share with me." He still thought there had been another in her past. Though he had tasted of her innocence upon their marriage bed, still he was aware that there was something she was keeping from him. And being honorable and forthright, he thought it best to bring all out into the open at the start. He was winning her heart, and had little doubt that she would not dwell long on thoughts of another. But if she were to tell him of her past, perhaps with it out in the open she could more easily put old memories from her. "If thoughts of the past are besetting you, perhaps it would be best to bring them forth?" he said.

As though she knew his eyes were seeking access to her mind, Sabrina drew back somewhat and, gathering her clothing, stood and began to dress. "It is nothing, Garrison. I just do not wish ever to lose this moment." She settled the riding skirt about her trim hips, drew on her silk blouse, and began to do up its tiny silver buttons.

Standing now, and feeling the tension between them, Garrison smiled in an attempt to put his wife at ease. Deciding that he wished nothing to destroy their new-found closeness, he swept her tiny hands away from the buttons and began to fasten them, covering with material her beautiful breasts. That done, he swept Sabrina off her feet and swung her about in the air, his grin wide as he looked down upon her. "This has been the most glorious day of my life, wife," he boldly declared before setting her back on her feet. That brought a smile to her face.

It was late to the afternoon, and dusk was approaching when the couple returned to the keep, their glowing faces proclaiming that they had shared a wonderful day.

"We had thought to set out with a large group of men and to come looking for the pair of you." Brian laughed aloud as the pair strode through the large, double portals and into the main hall, arm in arm.

Garrison did not reply, but looked about the large manor hall, his eyes coming to rest on Craig who had just shouted out the greeting. Brian sat before the large, wall-length hearth, enjoying the heat of the blazing fire that the servants kept stoked at all times now that the coolness of winter was setting in. "Have you nothing better to do, Brian, than to warm your backside like an old man?" Garrison grinned at his lifelong friend, his words provoking loud guffaws of laughter from the men scattered about the hall.

"Nay. This day was given us to relax, Lord Garrison, and I intend to do no more than prop my feet up in the air or warm my hide." Brian responded good-naturedly.

Garrison knew that his men toiled hard at the keep and guarding the boundaries of his land, so he slapped his friend's large back and took a seat next to him. His eyes then went to his wife, and with ease, he pulled her down on to his hard sturdy lap.

The small group in the main hall took in the tender caring of the couple, their eyes not missing the gentle caress their lord bestowed upon his lady's arm as she easily accommodated herself to his lap.

But Sabrina, noting how quiet the men were in her presence, whereas usually they were loud and jovial, whispered quietly into Garrison's ear that she would go to their chambers and change for the evening meal. When he released her, she smiled toward his men and made her apologies for having to leave their fine company.

The hearty men jumped to their feet as she rose, and feeling her brown eyes upon them, they nodded their heads and one or two even reddened slightly and then bowed to her.

"You have truly gained a treasure in the lass." Brian spoke to Garrison as to a friend while he watched the younger man's light eyes linger upon the graceful curve of his wife's backside as she mounted the stairs.

"Aye, she is that and much more." Garrison sighed aloud. Though Sabrina was not now in his presence, his thoughts went back to what could be plaguing her. Perhaps it had to do with the strange name she had called out in her sleep. Zaloe was certainly an unusual name. It sounded like a man's name. But as Brian handed him a mug of warm cider, Garrison was again drawn into the group about him.

"Do you still plan to leave at the end of the month?" Brian asked his employer and friend.

Garrison had not thought much about the trip lately. It had been planned months ago. He was to be gone for only a few days, to purchase some horses at a farm outside of Edinburgh. But now he realized that to leave McBride keep, which he had hated to do in past days, would also mean leaving Sabrina. Realizing that his men's eyes were upon him and that he had little choice in the matter, he nodded his head in assent. The plans had been made, and the farmer would be awaiting them. And his men, though they sought out what pleasures could be found in the village on the McBride property, were looking forward to a few nights of merrymaking in a larger town. "The trip will be a short one," he said to Brian. His friend nodded, but Garrison sensed that Brian would have been unwilling to leave a young bride so quickly after the vows had been spoken.

Garrison remained in the company of his men until Sabrina returned to his side, her riding clothes discarded for a warm, rich green velvet evening dress with delicate, cream lace etching at the throat and wrist. Her beauty was breathtaking as she descended the stairs and started across the main hall toward her husband.

Garrison's eyes were immediately drawn to her, and the talk about the hearth stilled as each man viewed the woman approaching. As earlier, the men rose to their feet, to show their new mistress respect.

Quickly rising, Garrison took Sabrina's small hand in his much larger one, and excusing himself from the group, he said aloud so that all would hear, "Let us ask Katie what is delaying the evening repast." But privately, as they rounded the corner of the hallway leading to the kitchen, Garrison halted Sabrina. Turning her about and taking her within his arms, he drew her up, bringing her on tiptoes and leaving her breathlessly craving his lips.

His mouth found hers and then withdrew. She rested her golden head upon his strong, sturdy chest for a moment, delighting in the feel of this strong fortress encircling her. "You truly should be ashamed, Garrison. What if Katie or one of the other servants should venture in here and catch us in such a revealing situation?" She feigned annoyance, though she loved the feel of his arms about her.

"If any should dare to interrupt us I am quite sure it will be evident that the lord of McBride is deeply in love and has only stolen away for a moment to be alone with his bride. Surely an intruder would retreat to the kitchen." His smile was large and entrancing, and a tug at her heart told Sabrina of her strong feelings for this handsome man. Rising up on her toes, she placed a feather-light kiss upon his warm inviting lips. "Let us go see what could be keeping, Katie. I fear I am starving."

Garrison wholeheartedly agreed, and taking her small hand within his own, he started to the back of the large keep. It is amazing, he thought, how different my wife is now, though we have been wed only a day. She had seemed so shy only a short time ago, but with each hour that passed she was becoming more open. She is like a small bloom, slowly opening it's petals to the sun. In the right setting and with a gentle touch, it's beauty comes forth.

As the kitchen door swung wide, Sabrina greeted the servants and then turned to Katie. "What is keeping dinner?" she asked, adding, "I am truly famished." She went to a table littered with pies and cakes, and took a bite of a delicious spiced concoction.

Katie smiled at her new mistress, and then, in dignified tones, she assured her and Garrison that it would be only another moment or two before the serving girls would be taking the food into the main hall.

"It took me most of the afternoon to track down the servants after last evening's affairs," she declared, ladling the soup into a fine china tureen.

Garrison leaned back against the doorjamb, delighting in this domestic scene. Now that Sabrina had tasted several of the seets, she was going from pot to pot and looking within, her golden head nodding in approval of the culinary delights she was inspecting.

Even Katie, who usually ruled her kitchen with an iron hand, allowing few to trespass, was pleased by her mistress's curiosity about the meal she had spent the afternoon preparing.

When Sabrina went to the beef set out on a platter, she tasted of a small morsel, and her brown eyes went to Katie. "I would think this is in need of a bit more seasoning, Katie," she said softly. She did not wish the beef to be served at her husband's table as it now tasted.

205

"I have a delightful sauce cooking here, my lady. That will season it to perfection." Katie took the small pot and slowly poured the thick brew over the platter of meat, sending a delightful aroma about the large kitchen.

Sabrina felt no embarrassment over her mistake. She just watched Katie with quiet interest as the housekeeper bustled about the kitchen, getting the bowls and platters of food ready to be carried to the main hall. Sabrina had worked hard all her life, and she intended to help out wherever she could. Her husband would not find her to be a lazy chit, unwilling to lend a hand where it was needed. She would welcome some tasks to help her pass the days at the keep.

"Come, sweet." Garrison held out a hand to his bride. "Let us go into the main hall and await dinner with my men." Next, he thought admiringly, as he noted that his lovely wife was watching everything that Katie was doing, she will be wishing to help the servants with the serving of food.

Without delay, Sabrina did as he bid, feeling secure and loved as Garrison's sheltering arm came about her waist. Katie watched the pair leave the kitchen, and the housekeeper smiled before she hurried the girls who were to serve dinner.

Dinner was served as on each eve in the past, in the main hall of the castle, the lord of the keep presiding at the main table and his men sitting at the long tables in the hall. At the end of the delicious repast, the lord of McBride keep excused himself and his young wife, pleading tiredness after the day's activities. His men looked in his direction, grins on their faces, for Garrison had hurriedly eaten so that he could once again be alone with his young bride.

Once he and Sabrina had reached their chambers, Garrison lit the two small tallow candles nearest the bed. A fire had been started earlier by one of the servants, and its golden light lent a warm glow to the chamber.

"Ah, wife, I am alone with you at last," Garrison said. He took Sabrina in his arms and inhaled her rose scent.

A shudder went through her at his touch, and with a soft sigh, she molded her body to his, her smallness seeming to match perfectly to his large, hard frame.

Bending his head, Garrison gathered in her waiting lips, and with deliberate slowness, he gently caressed those sweet petals, leisurely plundering the inner crevices of her mouth with his heated tongue as he stoked the blazing fires within her soul. As his mouth became more demanding and searching, Sabrina eased her arms about his neck, let her fingers run through his sun-streaked hair.

Delighting in the feel of her hands upon him, Garrison brought his own hands up to do some exploring. Slowly, he traced the outline of her heartshaped face, running his hands over her delicate cheeks and down along her fragile jawline. And she trembled slightly, his fiery lips followed his fingers, kissing her silky skin and exploring the soft, delicious hollows of her neck. Finding his progress hindered by the cream lace trim of her gown, he turned back and his mouth once more devoured hers with tender urgency as his fingers began to unbutton the back of her gown.

Sabrina was powerless to do aught but hold to his strength, for she seemed to be drowning in him. Losing all reason and will, she allowed his hands and eyes to roam over her at will.

When her gown lay about her feet, a pool of velvet, she stood before her husband in her chemise and petticoats. Her breath caught and held as his fingers lightly caressed the swell of her bosom. She was so weak that she had to lean against him for support.

"Your skin is like satin," he breathed softly, as his lips found the hollow of her throat and then descended. He slowly eased her sheer chemise down, deftly unlacing its gathered ribbons, and then his emerald eyes devoured her womanly perfection before he lowered his lips to a rosy peak that seemed to be straining toward them.

As though she were shattering into a million pieces, Sabrina dug her hands into Garrison's strong back, gasping aloud as he gently suckled a taut mound while his hands eased the rest of her clothing from her.

Though only a few moments before, Sabrina had felt caught up and lost as she stood before her husband in naked splendor, as her heated gold-flecked orbs met his, she was again drawn into his passionate green eyes. Only this man was real to her now.

Garrison feasted his eyes upon her luscious curves, as though memorizing each curve and hollow of her body. Then, with an animal-like growl, he gathered her to him, carried her to his bed, and without taking his lips from hers, he quickly eased his own clothing from his towering frame.

Within seconds he was lying next to his bride, the proof of his manly passion throbbing against her satiny thigh.

Though this was her second night as his wife, Garrison lowered himself carefully onto Sabrina, for at the moment she seemed somewhat shy. But as his lips claimed hers and stoked the embers of her desire, a need for him was rapidly built in the center of her being.

Needing to ensure that Sabrina was completely his, with consummate skill, Garrison brought Sabrina to the heights of wanting. His hands and lips roaming over her body evoking passion, delving and delighting until she gasped aloud and writhed beneath his touch; but still he lingered, holding back until it was almost too painful to delay longer. "Tell me what it is that you want, Sabrina." He spoke softly, his mouth next to her ear.

Sabrina's passion-filled eyes met his as he held himself above her. "I want you to love me." The words came from the depths of her soul. "Oh, love me. Please love me," she cried aloud.

But still Garrison hesitated, though need and desire were plainly written upon her face. "Who is it that you desire, Sabrina? Tell me who." His hands burned her as they plundered the depths of her womanhood.

"You, Garrison . . . my husband. Only you!" she finally got out, and as though she had spoken the magic words his spear of love plunged into her woman's moistness.

Her need being so great, her desire bordering upon madness, at his entry Sabrina felt her insides erupt into a towering swell of passion. Then, with each move of his body, she seemed to lose a small bit of herself to his keeping, until, exploding, she clasped him to her, her mind and body lost to all but the sweet pleasure of his assault. She spiraled to an unreal sphere, held on to him as the brilliant rainbows glittered about them.

Garrison moved slowly at first, seeming to savor the feel of his wife's velvet giving, but feeling her response, he accelerated into wild, reckless rapturous thrusts that built in tempo. Finally with a last plunge, he let out a groan of pleasure, and he, too, was spiraled into silvery delights, to soar upward to the very stars and then to slowly, lingeringly, return to the softness of the bed and to the woman in his arms.

Sabrina was barely able to breathe when Garrison drew her head onto his shoulder, yet she knew contentment.

Garrison had assured himself that she was truly his, her heart and her body, and now he was happy. Had she not spoken his name in her need of him? He could not have been mistaken in that; there could be no ghost within his bed. Though he still believed that she was holding something back, he knew that it was not another man. "I love you, sweet Sabrina," he said softly.

It seemed to Sabrina that she had been awaiting these words. "And I love you, Garrison." The quick sting of her tears told her the full truth of her words. This man had drawn her out, had taught her what life was about. He had shown her what it meant to be cherished and loved. She could not contain her feelings.

"Does love for me bring about these tears?" Garrison felt the salty wetness upon his shoulder, and he turned to her.

"Nay, they are not tears of sorrow, but tears of love. It fills me and needs some escape. I fear that my heart is bursting and these tears are what is left over from my rejoicing."

Taking her lips tenderly, Garrison tasted these tears of love, and with a groan, he held her tightly against his long frame. "Never will I let you leave my side." he declared. "What is mine, I hold and you, my love . . . my wife, are my most treasured jewel."

Feeling at peace, loved and protected for the first time in her life, Sabrina closed out the past as she fell asleep in her husband's arms, certain that she would awaken to see his handsome, loving visage.

For a few lingering moments Garrison let his gaze feast on his wife's beauty. The light from the hearth revealed her peace and contentment as he positioned his body to better accommodate her sleeping form. Then, inhaling her fragrant scent, he allowed himself the pleasure of sleep.

Stretching out full-length upon the large, down mattress, Sabrina slowly opened her eyes to see sunlight filtering into the chamber. As she looked about she noticed that her husband's pillow was empty, but remembering last night's passion, she sighed deeply and then snuggled deeper into the soft coverlet.

She had been swept away last night, had fully tasted of the draught of love, and had given as good as she had received. How wonderful it all was, she thought.

But unbidden, a small voice from within said accusingly, "Surely you are deceiving yourself, Sabrina. Does this man that you claim to love know you are an impostor—a sham and a deceiver? Would he love you still if he knew all, or would he cast you from him, declaring that you had tricked him."

"No." Sabrina shut her eyes, trying to deny this inner voice. He loves me. He said as much last eve. Surely he is not a man who would easily give his love and then take it back?

Again that small voice responded. "But who is it he loves? Not the wife he speaks love words to. Is it the woman he was promised by Priscilla Buchanan?

At that moment Garrison strode into the bedchamber, bearing a tray of food, a wide grin on his face. His eyes lit as they fell on his bride. "I see that you are awake, my sweet." He set the tray across from her upon the bed and then sat down next to her, his head lowering and his lips descending to hers. "Good morning, love," he breathed as he was about to kiss her.

Though shamed by her duplicity, Sabrina could do naught but melt against him, her breath mingling with his in a soft sigh of love.

"I thought that you might be hungry this morn, so I went to fetch something for the two of us." He sat back and broke off a piece of the sweet roll that Katie had put upon the tray. Then he placed it between Sabrina's teeth.

"You should have awakened me, Garrison. I would have joined you downstairs to break the fast." Sabrina felt somewhat guilty for staying abed, and that, combined with her shame, made her blush.

"I wished to eat alone with you, here in our chambers, my love." Garrison's eyes devoured her, taking in her slight flush, and when she held the sheet up to her bosom he glimpsed the gentle swell of her breasts and felt a stirring in his loins.

But exerting control, he turned to the tray that contained their breakfast. "Hurry and eat, sweet, and then dress. For there is something I wish to show you."

Curious, Sabrina asked, "What is it, Garrison?" She took another bite of the sweet roll and then pulled herself into a sitting position.

"It is a surprise. After you finish."

He needed to say no more. Sabrina could not contain her curiosity, and pulling the sheet about her, she went to the wardrobe and pulled out a velvet day dress. Quickly pulling on chemise and petticoats, she donned the gown, then went to the dressing table. With the gold-handled brush, she began to stroke out her long golden tresses.

Longingly Garrison watched her dress, and as she brushed her hair, he rose, went to her side, reached out, and took the brush. "Let me do this for you, love."

Willingly, Sabrina stood before him as he ran the brush through her hair, her senses filled with the manly scent of tobacco and cologne.

"Your hair is beautiful," he declared, letting his fingers caress its silky strands. Then he drew her to him, breathing in her delicious fragrance. "You leave me stunned."

Sabrina shut her eyes, delighting in his iron-hard hold. But he kissed her atop the head and spun her about.

"Are you ready for the surprise?" He smiled.

When she nodded, he took up her cloak and, grasping her hand, started toward the door.

Seeing that he'd taken her cloak, Sabrina questioned, "The surprise is out of doors."

"Aye, but your cloak will keep the cold away. He pulled her behind him as he started down the hall.

He led Sabrina toward the back of the keep, to the stables, and pulled the great doors wide. "I only found them this morning, hidden behind some bales of hay."

Sabrina watched in wonder as Garrison led her to an empty stall. At the back, on a pile of hay, was a female dog with a litter of puppies. Sabrina's eyes came alive as they took in the sight before her. "Oh, Garrison, they're beautiful," she gasped. She started to reach out and scoop one up.

"Just a minute, love." He stilled her hand. "I am afraid their mother may be a bit nervous right now. She doesn't know you yet." He knelt down and petted the large mastiff. The dog looked up to him, complete trust in her doleful eyes, and he took up a tiny, brown and black puppy.

"Isn't he something?" Sabrina asked as Garrison handed the small creature to her.

"Aye, love, that he is," Garrison responded as he watched her coo over the small dog, her expression tender as she looked at the tiny life that had just come into being. When the puppy tried to suck upon Sabrina's finger, laughter bubbled from her, bringing a large grin to her husband's face.

"We must put him back with his mother, Garrison. I fear that we are disturbing his breakfast."

Placing the puppy back with its dam the couple stood arm in arm and watched the litter feast upon their mother's milk.

But a small noise drew their attention away from the puppies, and they both looked across the stable at young Johnny who was now working at the McBride stables.

"How is all going with you, Johnny?" Garrison called out to the lad who had a large broom in his hand.

With a start, the boy swung about, for the first time noticing the lord and his lady. But when he looked into Garrison's smiling face, he smiled. "All is fine, me lord. Me dad is back on his feet and able to do light work now and me mum says that it will be no time before he is his old self."

"I am glad to hear this, Johnny. And I hope that you are working hard and doing what Jamie tells you to do."

Jamie was the head groomsman, and since Johnny had come to work at the McBride stables he had diligently followed Jamie's instructions. Whatever that small man told him to do, he did without question, and he was now sweeping out the stalls. "Aye, me lord. I be doing all that I'm bid. Ye need not be worrying over me not making good on me payment that I be owing ye. I'll not slight ye none."

Garrison and Sabrina both grinned at the youth that stood before them. "I did not think you would, Johnny. And perhaps, with hard work, one day you will become the head groomsman."

As though nothing could have pleased the lad more, Johnny smiled broadly and then went back to sweeping out the stall. This time, though, his movements were surer, as though he now had a purpose.

With a soft chuckle, Garrison led Sabrina into

the yard, his arm about her waist. She was feeling the sharp bite of the cool wind despite her cloak, and was more than willing to return to the keep.

They spent most of this morning in the main hall, Sabrina sitting by Garrison as he talked with his men, sending them about their day's work about the castle and the village.

At midmorning it was announced that visitors were approaching the keep, and being in a genial, relaxed mood Garrison sat back with Sabrina at his side and awaited the arrival of their guests.

It was not long before Hugh Ferguson, along with two women and at least twelve retainers, entered the main hall of McBride castle.

"What say ye, Garrison me lad?" The large, red-haired and red-bearded man said as he stepped through the portal and saw the lord of the keep sitting before a fireplace.

Garrison's smile did not reach his eyes as he looked at his nearest neighbor, Hugh Ferguson, his wife, Dorothy, and her younger sister, Corinne. But as a good host he rose to his feet and, as the large man drew abreast of him, offered his hand.

"What brings you out on such a chill day, Hugh?" Garrison asked as he let his gaze go to Sabrina.

"Did ye be thinking that I'd not be coming to pay me respects to ye and yer lady. It be all over the country how ye have finally taken yerself a bride, Garrison lad."

For the first time since the large man had

entered the hall, Garrison allowed himself to relax. He had never known what to expect from this large Scotsman. At times he had felt strong resentment, almost hatred when in Hugh's presence. Knowing the man clung fiercely to Scots' ways, he was certain his animosity stemmed from a belief that Garrison was not the one who should preside over McBride castle and Garrison knew that if the chance presented itself, Hugh Ferguson would try to take over the keep. But Garrison would stand firm and protect what was his.

When outsiders had come onto McBride property, burning and looting, Garrison and his men had ridden them down and had quickly disposed of them, granting no quarter, so that all would know of his might and fierceness.

Now here was his neighbor, the one man Garrison wondered about most when there was trouble on his properties. Time and again he had thought that the nightly raids upon the crofts near the village had been caused by this large man, but having been unable to prove it, had not retaliated. He distributed this man's gesture of friendship, but he kept his own counsel.

"This is my bride, Hugh." He took Sabrina's hand and helped her to her feet. "Sabrina, may I present Hugh Ferguson, his wife Dorothy and her sister Corinne."

The two women looked at Sabrina coolly, their nods being the only signs of recognition.

"I am pleased to meet you all." Sabrina turned first to the large red-haired man and then to the women at his side.

"Garrison, I did not know that ye had planned to wed?" The seductive quality of Corinne's voice drew Sabrina's attention.

She is rather pretty, Sabrina thought as she took in the woman's dark hair and blue eyes, which at the moment were fixed on Garrison. And Corinne Ferguson's gown of shimmering green plainly outlined her enticing figure.

Feeling the hand he was holding tense, Garrison gave Corinne a smile as he replied, "My wedding had been planned for some time. The first moment my eyes viewed Sabrina's beauty, I was lost."

"Surely ye jest?" Corinne ventured, knowing Garrison had had numerous women in his life and in his bed. In fact the last time Corinne had visited his castle, it had been she who had filled his arms at night.

"Nay, never would I jest where my wife is concerned." Garrison knew what Corinne was up to, and he was determined that she would not hurt Sabrina.

"Dorothy I hope that you and Sabrina will become friends." He turned to the older woman, trying to put Corinne in her place.

With a thin smile, Hugh's wife slowly nodded her head. She had hoped that her sister and the handsome Garrison McBride would eventually make a match. Corinne had told her what had occurred the last time they were at McBride's keep, and Dorothy had been sure that, given a little time, the lord would ask for her sister's hand in marriage. But that had not worked out as she had expected, though even Hugh had thought that Corinne would win Garrison, and would have access to his lands and fortune.

"Let us share a mug of ale, Hugh, to my bride." Garrison was not about to let these two women cast a pall on the happiness he had found with his young bride.

Hearing his words, a servant hurried over with mugs and a pitcher of warmed ale, and poured out the brew as the women settled their skirts about them and relaxed near the fire.

Hugh's green eyes studied Sabrina so thoroughly that she felt a bit shaky. "Yer not from hereabouts?" He sipped from his mug.

"Nay. She is from London."

"However did ye meet her, Garrison? I did not know that ye had left for that fair town." Corinne's tone was still questioning.

"Needless to say we did meet." Garrison's emerald gaze was cool as he looked at her. It was not her business, or anyone else's, how he had come to meet his bride. It was sufficient to say that he had married Sabrina—that she was entitled to his name and his protection.

Seeing that she was making little headway with Garrison, Corinne tried a new tactic. "Tell me, Sabrina, how is it that ye are here at this keep? Do ye not find it lonely after yer life in London? Surely it is drab and most boring?"

"Nay," Sabrina responded. "My husband's home is far from boring." Thinking for a moment upon the eve just past, she turned her gold-flecked eyes on Garrison, and as though he also were reliving what had taken place within the confines of their chambers, he smiled fondly at her. "I assure you that I love it here, and do not in the slightest miss London."

Feeling somewhat miffed by the looks the pair were bestowing upon one another Corinne sat back, her mind searching for some way to draw Garrison's attention to her. Perhaps at dinner she would be able to lure him to her side, she thought. Then, with a smug smile, she sat quietly and listened as her brother-in-law spoke of what was taking place on his own lands, as always talking of the feud between the Ferguson's and the MacIvers. Always in the telling he spoke of the daring of his men and himself, leaving out the crofts burned and the farmers killed because of this stupid feud which meant they must constantly be on guard lest an arrow find its way through their protection.

It was an early dinner which turned out to be a feast Katie had prepared in honor of their guests. As the main hall filled with Garrison's men and Hugh Ferguson's retainers, the servants brought from the kitchens large platters of oysters, clams, roasted venison, grouse stuffed with herb-seasoned dressing, mutton pie, pigeons, capons, and bowls of fresh vegetables. Later ginger cakes were served with sweet cream.

Sabrina ate her fill and then sat back with a satisfied sigh. As she glanced down her husband's table she felt a touch of malice toward the woman at his side.

It had been plain to all within the hall that Corinne was trying to gain Garrison's full attention. She had forced herself into the seat next to him, which Garrison had expected Hugh to occupy, and her blue eyes were ever upon Garrison. She constantly questioned him about something, and lavished food upon his plate.

But Garrison had acted as though nothing were amiss when he had seated Sabrina and had helped her choose the choicest meats and the tenderest vegetables, leaving the woman at his other side seething. And before the evening was over it was plain to all within the hall that Lord McBride had found his true mate.

It was rather late when Garrison excused himself and his wife, assuring his guests that rooms had been readied and that whenever they desired servants would attend them.

Once they were alone in their bedchamber Garrison let out a long-held breath. "It would seem, my love, that this day has proven long and tiring." He pulled her to him and kissed her gently. "I have wanted to do that all this eve."

Sabrina relaxed in his arms, agreeing that she was pleased to be away from the main hall and the eyes that had been upon them.

As Garrison released her and bent near the hearth to stroke the coals and place more wood upon the embers, Sabrina watched him. It is no wonder, she thought that Mistress Corinne has tried to gain his attention. He is a man over whom many a woman would make a fool of herself. And she certainly did that, Sabrina thought. She laughed.

"What is it that so tickles you, my sweet?" Garrison stood to his full height and looked at his bride.

"I was but thinking of poor Mistress Corinne."

"Poor Mistress Corinne?" Garrison was stunned. "You call that scheming creature poor? I would venture to call the man poor who will one day be tied to her."

"Aye, you are right there. Though I think that she had set her cap upon you, my darling."

"Nay. That is not the way of things." Garrison thought for a moment that Sabrina was jealous and suspected that he might be unfaithful to her, but when he saw the glowing lights dancing in her gold-flecked eyes he realized that she was teasing. "I would surely have run for cover, my love. But now that I have you, there is little need for running. With you at my side to remind all that I am happily wed, I have no fear of those like Mistress Corinne." He left out the telling of how he had cornered Hugh alone for a few minutes, and had set him straight, explaining that Ferguson was welcome in the hall only so long as the members of his party showed Garrison's wife respect.

Hugh had turned so red that his face matched the color of his hair and beard. Garrison's soft words had had an underlying meaning that was not lost on the older man.

Garrison was now certain he could entertain

his wife alone in their chamber on the following morning, for Hugh Ferguson and his party would be gone from McBride castle. Perhaps Ferguson's ears would be burning, but better that than a taste of the sword, Garrison thought. He would allow no more slights to his wife.

Sabrina smiled at his easy bantering, and he started toward her. But his eyes fell upon the stack of papers on his desk, and she knew what he must be thinking.

"I could read for a time if you have matters to attend." She reached for the book of poetry she had ignored since her wedding.

Garrison looked at his young wife and at the book within her grasp; then he turned toward his desk and slowly nodded his head. "If that would be your pleasure for a short time, there are some papers that I must go over." For a moment he thought to those wasted moments without her in his arms, but it struck him that perhaps she truly wished to read for a time. Would he deprive her of this simple pleasure when he should be seeing to business of running his properties?

As though her mind were made up, Sabrina sat close to hearth, her book open to the page at which she had last stopped reading. But before Garrison settled down to his desk he had to taste her sweetness, and bending down next to her chair, he let his mouth settle over hers and drink of her honey lips.

As though wishing to hold back time, Garrison finally rose to his feet, sighing heavily. "Love, you would test the endurance of any man."

Seeing her gaze upon him and realizing she did not understand his words, he went on. "If possible I would only keep you in my arms, my lips on your own, your body held tightly to mine." His eyes looked deeply into her brown ones. "But, alas, I have some duties that I am unable to pass to another, though you do not know how much I would like to. I doubt that any of my men could keep the books of the manor."

"Do not stand about any longer, darling. Go to your work while I spend some time with my book." Sabrina smiled up at him, seeing that he was struggling to leave her side and see to his paperwork. They would be man and wife for a very long time, and she knew that they would have to settle into tending to the needs of the keep as well as their own needs.

Seeing her wisdom in dealing with this matter, Garrison lightly patted her shoulder and then went to his desk, sat back upon the cushioned, leather chair, and began to go over the estate books, his thoughts still littered with memories of the feel and smell of his young bride.

In the quiet of their chamber all thoughts of Hugh Ferguson and his sister-in-law fled Sabrina's mind, and she tried to concentrate on the page before her. But her eyes kept slipping from it to glance at the man that caused her heart to hammer so violently within her chest.

It had been several days since Garrison had looked at his desk and many records and bills needed his attention. At first he tried to concentrate on his work, but his mind kept straying back to his bride. Each time his eyes left the figures before him and went to Sabrina, he caught only her profile, and her eyes were on her book. So he forced himself to focus on the ledgers and finally became involved in the accounts.

Finding that she simply could no longer pretend to be interested in reading, Sabrina quietly went from her chair to the dressing screen across the chamber, and trying not to disturb her husband, she began to pull her gown from her body, then her underclothing. She reached out for the diaphanous, violet nightgown that Katie had set out for her and donned it, then stepped from behind the screen. She padded silently to the large bed in the middle of the chamber, and, pulling back the silk coverlet, climbed into its downy comfort.

Garrison, focused upon his work, did not hear his wife changing or getting into bed. Later, when he leaned back in his chair and rubbed at his tired eyes, he looked about the chamber, noticing for the first time that Sabrina was no longer before the hearth, reading. As his emerald eyes went to the bed and saw a soft mound beneath the coverlet, he smiled. She must have grown tired and, not wishing to disturb him, had quietly climbed into bed. His thoughts flew to what was awaiting him. Being a husband seemed to suit him well. Never in the past had he tended to his papers and then climbed into bed with a warm-blooded, beautiful woman. He had always had to leave the keep to find entertainment, but never had he found any woman that could rival his young bride. He rose and began to take the clothing from his large body, his eyes lingering on the visage of his sleeping wife.

When finished with undressing, he stood for a moment and looked down upon the woman he so loved. She seemed sweetly innocent, and he thought it was good fortune that had brought her to him. A new world had opened to him when Sabrina had entered his life. Suddenly remembering the plan he'd made months ago to leave the castle, he wondered if he dared to be parted from her for a few days. Would not he be tormented with each passing hour, picturing her in his mind? How could they be parted now when they had just found each other? Then it struck him. Why not take her with him? There was no reason to leave her behind. He could make the trip a holiday of sorts, for the both of them. They would sleep beneath the stars, and when they arrived in Edinburgh, he would rent a room at an inn. Was this not the answer to the dilemma plaguing him?

With a sigh, he gently lowered his large frame down beside Sabrina, and reaching out, he stroked the satiny smoothness of her arms. A hunger for her devastated him, but holding of himself in check, he pulled her into his arms. Her sleepy mind tried to surface to reality, yet she was quickly lost to the thrilling volley of sensations that played up and down her limbs. It was hard for her to draw breath because his curiously cool lips had found hers. And as his big hand bent to other sweet labors, tenderly sweeping over her from neck to thigh, thrilling her and awakening inner needs, her silky-soft arms went about his muscular back

It was as though a tormentingly sweet night vision encircled her, sending whispers of pleasure through her yielding, young body and bringing her to full awareness of the hard yearning desire of her husband. She kissed him heatedly and melted in his hungry embrace, responding eagerly to his heady assault on her innermost being.

Garrison drank deeply of the cup of her womanly essence, his hard body agonizing for release as it felt the fullness of her. As she pressed tightly against him, a torturous ache tormented him and he rose above her, his green eyes catching and holding her gold-flecked brown ones. Their bodies joined then, and spiraled upward to unknown regions of passion, where fulfillment lay in wait for them. Waves of delight crashed down upon them as they clung together, lips and bodies molded.

Soft, tender words were whispered in the chamber as the light from the hearth dimmed and the keep was given over to night's gentle hold. Finally silky caresses ceased, and sleep overpowered the couple, still forged together, fulfilled and in each other's arms.

Chapter Nine

Sabrina's delicate laughter filled the air as, from the low stone wall that enclosed the small paddock in the back pasture at McBride keep, she watched her husband and Brian try to halter the spirited colt that skittered away from them, always staying out of their reach.

Garrison had thrown doublet and jacket across the stone fence, and his shirt was soaked through with the sweat of his labor. Once more he circled the colt as Brian started to its side.

The sun shone warmly upon Sabrina on this cool morning as she watched her handsome husband attempt to capture the sorrel colt. She smiled as the wily young horse again slipped between the two men as though he were more intelligent than they.

"Can you not keep hold of him even for a minute?" Brian's patience was fleeing him as he pulled himself up from the ground and wiped at his breeches.

Still in good humor, Garrison laughed aloud, his emerald eyes going to his wife, who sat upon the stone wall, and with a call to Brian, once more he started toward the colt, this time holding a rope.

As though at last tiring of the game, the colt ran toward Garrison and the rope encircled its long, sleek neck. Garrison shouted as he pulled tightly on the other end of the rope, holding tightly to his prize. "Here you are, Brian. It is as easy as laying hold of a newborn babe."

Brian now laughed aloud along with his lord. "Remember his sire, Dandy Fellow, had this same spirit. This one will be worthy of him, I'd bet me life upon it."

Garrison nodded his head in full agreement as he walked toward the sorrel colt.

And with a wide grin Sabrina jumped from the stone wall and started to her husband's side. Her laughter joined his as he handed Brian the rope and then wrapped his arms about his young wife, exuberantly lifting her off her feet and swinging her about in the middle of the paddock.

On this day, as on all the others since Garrison had met Sabrina, he had found complete happiness with her at his side. She was all things to him—his hopes, his dreams, his very life. Never had he known such completeness. She was the part of him that he had been missing for years, not only his wife in name but a part of his heart.

Sabrina had never known such happiness either. Her days were filled with joy and her nights were filled with love. Though life at the convent had not prepared her for these days at McBride keep, she was learning her wifely duties, and she was delighting in each new pleasure she was experiencing. Garrison drew her out from her shyness, yet he made her feel at peace in his home and with his way of life. As he now set her on her feet their eyes locked in an age-old communication.

Brian, seeing their look, hastily took the colt into the barn to turn it over to the stableboy.

"You were wonderful, Garrison." Sabrina smiled, her eyes still fixed on her husband's.

Laughing aloud, Garrison took hold of her hand and then led her to the gate. He took up his jacket and doublet, his breathing still ragged from his exertions. "Wonderful?" One dark brow rose. "Well, I deem it a privilege that you think so, sweet." He lightly kissed her forehead as he began to pull his outer clothing back upon his large frame. "I will certainly let you view my efforts whenever you like." He decided that he did, indeed, enjoy the feel of her brown eyes upon him, for they revealed her love for him.

As they walked slowly, hand in hand, toward the castle Garrison thought this a good time to tell Sabrina of their departure on the following day. He had put off doing so, thinking that perhaps he would change his mind and decide not to take her upon this trip, and he had even had thoughts of remaining at the keep himself. These past weeks had been so pleasurable, with her ever at his side, that he had thought seriously about what option would be best.

Having determined the past eve that he would make the trip, his need for fine horses negating postponement, he had begun to envision Sabrina at his side on the way to Edinburgh. Thinking fondly of the long nights they would be sharing within his tent, he had awaited the right moment in which to tell her of his plans.

Now, with his lovely wife snuggled close to his side, her form molded tightly to his own, he looked down and tilted her face up to his own. His mouth descended and he drank of the sweet nectar of her lips. Then, turning her into his arms, he asked, "What would you think of coming with me to Edinburgh?" His light eyes rested upon her, desire evident in his warm gaze.

A small smile came to Sabrina's lips as she thought of going to a strange place. "Oh, Garrison, I would love to go with you. But when? I have heard nothing of such a trip." She envisioned sights she had only imagined.

With a wide grin, Garrison said softly, "We leave tomorrow morning at the break of day."

Upon hearing this, Sabrina ceased to smile. "Tomorrow?" she finally repeated aloud.

And as her husband slowly began to nod his

head, she began to worry. "I shall never be ready in so short a time." There were trunks to be packed, gowns to be pressed and prepared, and all manner of preparations to be made.

Garrison saw her quick look of concern. "Forget everything except that you will be by my side, love," he said. "We shall be going by horseback, spending our nights in my tent." His green eyes turned warm as he looked over the length of her, bringing a quick flush to Sabrina's delicate cheeks. "Whatever you shall be needing, we shall purchase in Edinburgh. It will be a pleasure trip for the two of us. Though I admit that my aim is to purchase horses, all I can now think of is showing the town of Edinburgh to my beautiful bride." As her mouth began to open to protest such haste, he kissed her.

With his lips upon hers, Sabrina gave in to her emotions, knowing that she would agree to anything this man proposed.

"Then all is settled?" Garrison withdrew slightly.

Sabrina felt his breath on her golden curls, and as soft prickles ran down her spine, she nodded her assent, then leaned heavily against his strong chest while she tried to regain her composure. But when she came to her senses she pulled away from him and started up he path leading toward the stone keep.

"Whatever is your rush, pet?" Garrison strode after his fleeing bride.

"If we are to leave in the morn, I must see to

some things. I certainly cannot be expected to travel without anything to wear." She looked up into his face, her expression serious.

"Why, surely you will only have to pack your riding clothing. I wish to purchase you gowns when we reach Edinburgh. I have been there on occasion and I know a fine dress shop. So do not pack much. Besides, we shall be unable to carry much. We can have what we purchase sent on ahead to the keep." For a moment he thought of the pleasure he would derive from helping to clothe his young bride. He had never imagined that he would be so pleased at the thought of spending his hard-earned coin, but as he looked down into Sabrina's beautiful face he knew that he would gladly give all that he would ever own to see her dressed befittingly.

Standing upon tiptoes, Sabrina lightly placed a kiss upon her husband's strong chin. "Thank you for being so good to me, Garrison." Quickly, she turned about and started once again down the path to the keep. "But I see no reason for telling me of this trip at such a late date. There is still so much to be done." She tossed the words over her shoulder as her husband hurried after her.

Garrison shook his head, realizing that this woman would have her way and that the next time he would, indeed, think before waiting so long to inform her of a trip.

The afternoon was spent preparing for their departure. Sabrina rushed about the keep as though possessed. She tried not to forget anything that she might possibly need while away from the castle. She had been only in the convent and at her husband's home, so she had little knowledge of what to take. Nonetheless, she was determined that she would not be lacking any items and that she would not embarrass her husband.

Garrison's mind was far from the trip they would be taking when he sought out his young bride in the privacy of their chambers as the sun lowered in the sky. He had left his men about the great hearth in the main hall. They were discussing the day's work.

But when Garrison made his way into his chambers, his eyes rested upon devastation. Gowns, riding habits, hats, gloves, and a variety of lacy undergarments were scattered over the large bed, the chairs, and the small settee before the hearth. He drew in a sharp breath. "Sabrina, what is all of this?" he asked, startling her and causing her to cease searching through a drawer.

Katie was rushing about the room, and having seen the lord enter the chamber and having viewed the impatient gleam in his eyes, she quickly sought to calm him before he could say anything that would hurt the young mistress.

"We are but sorting out a few of the mistress's finer things for her trip." Sabrina had told Katie that Lord Garrison had wished her only to take a few riding habits, and she and her mistress had agreed that men could be silly about matters such as packing for a trip. Indeed, they were going all the way to Edinburgh, yet Lord Garrison wanted his wife to take along only a few pieces of riding attire. Nonsense, the older woman thought as she stood before Garrison McBride. His wife would need gowns that would honor him and would befit her position as his wife.

"All of this is not necessary." He swept out his hand, indicating the clothing spread about the large chamber. "We are going to be riding horseback with my men, and will not have time for such frivolous apparel."

"But surely, Lord Garrison, you would not have the mistress be shamed when you arrive at your destination. You would not wish her to strut about the streets upon your arm, wearing only a drab riding habit?" Katie spoke up before Sabrina had to defend her actions. "Of course, a few extra things must be packed."

Garrison looked upon his housekeeper. She was right as usual. He had not been thinking clearly. It would take time for gowns to be made, and Sabrina would not be able to wear them while they were in Edinburgh. And had not it been his plan to show her the sights? He couldn't do this if she was wearing clothing that she was ashamed of."

But before he could speak Sabrina saw his confusion, and taking it for a touch of anger at her disobedience, she quickly tried to make amends. "Of course, it is silly of me to wish to take so much along. Katie, I will be needing no further help. I will but take these." She reached down and scooped up the riding clothes that were draped over the back of a chair. Then her glance went to her husband. "I am sorry, Garrison, for being so thoughtless." Before he could say a word she rushed on. "It is only that I have never been farther than your home here, and I did not know what I would be needing. I am sure that you know what is best." Sabrina looked directly at the man she loved and only wished to please, and when she smiled, a small grin slowly replaced his frown.

"It is I who have been foolish in this matter, sweet. Of a certainty you will be needing several gowns. I had not thought of the time it will take for a dressmaker to make ready the gowns that we order. Certainly you cannot be expected to walk about in naught but your riding habits; though I would not object, for anything that adorns your graceful form is honored by being worn by you." He boldly stepped to her and looked down at her sweetly innocent expression. "Lord, I am the luckiest of men," he muttered, before his lips sought hers.

On quiet feet Katie left the chambers of the loving couple, a small smile on her face. It was surely good for her old heart to view such unashamed devotion.

"You need not relent in this matter, Garrison. I was not thinking clearly. The excitement of going on a trip clouded my reason. I do not need all of this clothing. As long as you are at my side, I have no other need." Sabrina meant every word she said, for at the moment she was in her husband's arms and he was all that was important to her. He had changed her life and her thoughts since she had met him. Only Garrison mattered to her—his happiness with her and their life together. Clothing was of little concern.

With a deep chuckle, Garrison held her at arm's length. "You are a treasure, my love. If you had said these words this afternoon, I would willingly have agreed with you. But as Katie has so aptly pointed out, you surely cannot roam about the streets of Edinburgh in your riding clothes. Take whatever gowns you wish. A carriage can follow us. Perhaps this will be for the best after all. The trip may prove tiring for you, and you may wish to ride in the vehicle."

"Nay, Garrison, I will ride at your side." She did not wish him to think her weak and unwilling to abide by his wishes.

But her frailty and genteel manners were never more apparent to Garrison than at this moment. Nodding his head in agreement so as not to argue the matter further, he still thought the idea of the carriage a wise one. "Well, if you will finish with your packing I have a few papers to look over." Kissing her brow lightly, he turned to his desk, but after sitting down and looking at the stack of papers, his eyes rose and lingered for a moment on his wife. Sabrina had set about packing the trunk Katie had ordered brought to their chambers.

Their lovemaking that night was gently filled with caring and tenderness. His touch was soft and lingering, his lips were soothing, gently seeking. He caressed her breasts, his tongue aflame at it boldly encircled the taut crests, and after taking his fill, his tongue ran over the silky skin over her rib cage and her belly. Then, with a bolder play, he sought the triangle of her woman's jewel, bringing soft moans of passion from her lips, and she buried her fingers in his sunstreaked locks, her body aflame, he rose above her. Then in a searing brand of love, he joined with hers. Breast beating against breast, hard, unyielding thigh against soft, smooth thigh, lips joining and molding, they were one, male and female — man and wife — forged together.

The tenderness of her husband's love play drove Sabrina to wrap her sleek arms about his neck. Pulling him to her, she slipped into that world of feeling only he evoked, her very soul now in his keeping. And as desire welled in her, she was swept to the pinnacle of fulfillment, her body arching against his, her movements striving for release. She floated ever higher, all but touching the circling clouds; and then a shattering burst of pleasure left her breathless. Slowly she slipped downward.

Garrison joined Sabrina in those moments of ultimate release. Then, with breathless wonder he looked deep into her love-drawn features, her name coming to his lips.

In that slow return to reality, Garrison gathered Sabrina against his chest, his hands lightly caressing her silken flesh. "I love you beyond what words can express, my sweet. You are my very existence. You carry my heart about in your palm."

Sabrina sighed as she laid her head against his massive, firm chest, content in his love. For a moment she let her mind dwell upon the circumstances that had brought her into Garrison McBride's life. He was so trusting and giving, how could she ever tell him of her deceit? Raising her head, for a moment she considered bringing all out into the open, but as she looked into his eyes, she knew that she could not chance seeing hatred or accusation replace the love in them.

Garrison looked questioningly toward his young wife, seeing her worried look. Remembering that he had seen this same look in the past, he wondered what could be troubling her. He said softly, "What is it that plagues you so, sweet?"

"Oh, Garrison, hold me close," Sabrina whispered, tears coming to her eyes and then dropping onto the black hair matting his broad chest.

Garrison did as she desired, knowing that to pry any further would only cause her more distress. He wrapped his arms about her and drew her to him, hoping that she would learn to trust him more.

Far into the night, even after Garrison heard Sabrina breathing easily in sleep, he lay holding her tightly, his green eyes not able to shut because of the worry that she had caused him. What did she so fear that she would not share with him? Was it something from her past that so disturbed her at times? He tried to put it down to his imaginings, but something about the way in which she had looked into his eyes kept troubling him. Something was bothering his wife, but he knew it would do him no good to worry over it. He was powerless to help her until she trusted him enough to share it with him.

Chapter Ten

It seemed to Sabrina that she had hardly shut her brown eyes and fallen asleep when she was being kissed awake by her husband's impatient mouth.

"Love, we must dress and be about. The men are at the ready downstairs, filling their bellies with food in preparation for the day ahead." Garrison's gently nudged her, not allowing her to evade getting out of the soft warmth of their bed.

"Let me sleep only for a moment longer," she yawned, not opening her brown eyes, trying to burrow deeper within the silk coverlet and the pillow.

"Nay, love, time is awasting, and we must be about." Garrison gently pulled her from the covers, and grinning at her tiredness, he bent down and kissed her soft lips once again.

Seeing that she must, Sabrina opened her eyes and looked about the chamber, taking in the darkness of the room, the only light coming from the tallow candle upon the bedside table. "Are you sure that it is time?" she questioned as she rubbed at her sleepy eyes with the backs of her hands.

"Aye, sweet, it is time to go." Garrison felt some pity for his bride, but he knew they had to be off quickly so he went to the chair and brought her the riding habit that she had laid out the night before. "I shall help you dress, love." He reached out as she pulled the silky nightgown over her head, and though he knew the need for haste, his pulses raced at the beauty she displayed for his eyes alone. Forcing control on himself, he restrained his appetite for his young bride and quickly held out her underthings and the top of her riding outfit. When she had donned them, he found that he could relax somewhat.

"Why, you are already dressed," Sabrina exclaimed, now fully awake. "How long have you been up, Garrison?" she asked, feeling somewhat guilty for wishing to stay abed.

Garrison smiled into his wife's concerned face. "I have only been awake a short time. I dressed and made sure that Brian had everything under control before I came back to awaken you."

Sabrina smiled back at her handsome husband, and having dressed, she sat back and began to pull on her high kid boots. But with a brush of his hand, Garrison bent down and did this for her, his face clouding with a touch of passion as he felt the softness of her inner thigh.

Though he found it torture to resist his desire, when she rose to her feet, he drew her into his strong arms. "I love you, my beautiful, tempting wife." His lips descended and took hers, and for a full minute they remained together, lost to all about them, knowing only the sweet reality of their special touch, their bond.

It was Garrison who broke free from his wife's silken arms, knowing that in another moment he would be powerless to do aught but sample her treasures further. She was a fire in his veins, fuel to his desires, food for his very soul. But, with a small laugh, he stepped back from her. "My men await us, love." Though he saw desire in her brown eyes, he was determined not to be swept away by her gaze. But as he awaited for her to place a small saucy-looking hat upon her golden head, he admired the beautiful woman before him.

"I am ready now, Garrison," Sabrina finally announced as she started toward her husband who had gone to the door to place a distance between them.

In a short time Sabrina was sitting her horse and riding close beside her husband who was upon his mighty black stallion. The pair was followed closely by Garrison's men and by the carriage. The men, due to the earliness of the hour, were quiet and sullen, having been awakened early by Brian.

Husband and wife, though, appeared to be wide awake and enjoying the fresh coolness of the morning. Their eyes held and were filled with the tenderness they harbored for one another.

With such a beautiful start Sabrina thought that the entire trip would be a pleasure. The horses were walking at a leisurely pace, and though the coldness of early morning nipped at her cheeks, her velvet cloak lent her comfort. At her side was the man she adored.

But by early afternoon she found that her happiness in the trip had dissipated.

The sun, despite the time of the year, gleamed down upon the countryside, forcing Sabrina to remove her cloak and jacket. And the ride, though they still proceeded at a leisurely pace, had begun to tell upon her delicate backside. She now winced when her mount missed its footing. And though she had remained at her husband's side, his nearness was now a strain and she wished he were riding with his men. She did not want him to notice her condition, or to think that she would slow the party down. She had no desire to be a hindrance, but as the afternoon wore on her brown eyes often went past the men and lingered upon the comfortable-looking carriage.

Though Garrison noticed Sabrina's fatigue, he did not worry overly much about it because each time she caught him looking at her she gave him a radiant smile, seemingly to assure him that all was well. It was in the late afternoon, when the party rested for a time under the coolness of a large oak, that he noticed her grimace when he helped her from the back of her mount, and though she tried to hide her discomfort he could not help but perceive her awkward gait as she went to the cool, running stream that ran by their place of rest.

Garrison did not immediately follow his young bride, thinking to give her a few moments to herself to tend to any personal affairs, but with seeing that his men were all in high spirits, not being used to keep to such a leisurely pace, he smiled and went in search of his wife.

He went downstream a few yards, then saw her resting upon the grassy embankment. Her handkerchief, having been dipped into the cool water, was now resting upon her forehead. In that moment Garrison realized the extent of his wife's exhaustion. Thinking herself alone, she had let her guard slip, and he could plainly read her fatigue. He had not thought her so delicate, and he rebuked himself for not having more accurately judged her capacity. Being used to having men about him, he had not thought of the frailer condition of his wife. With this in mind, and knowing that she had, for some hours, been trying not to let him know her true state, he put on a smile and began to hum a lively ditty, drawing her attention to the path he was following.

Feeling somewhat refreshed by the cold water and the comfort her bottom was finding on the soft grass, Sabrina smiled sweetly in return, her brown eyes filling with warm adoration of her husband. "Oh, it is so beautiful here, Garrison," she called out.

"Your lovely visage is what truly makes it

beautiful. It seems a master painted you on the lush grass, your skirts stretched out and the stream flowing swiftly by. Though Garrison had wished to please her with these words, he at once saw their truth. Though tired and weary, his Sabrina was beautiful.

"You flatter me, Garrison." She blushed as his eyes traveled over her length. "Come and rest for a moment. My handkerchief makes a cooling cloth." She extended a delicate hand toward her husband.

Garrison was not one to linger overlong on his thoughts, being a man of action, and he quickly complied, seating his large form on the grass.

Sabrina dipped her handkerchief into the cold water once again. After wringing it out, she gently wiped her husband's forehead, and seeing his eyes glow with a rich love, she smiled into his tanned face for a moment before allowing her lips to touch upon his own.

The taste of her was ambrosia to Garrison, and he immediately drew her into his embrace, his arms cradling her. "You taste of the earth and the sun, wild and giving," he breathed out, as she rested her golden head upon his chest, being content at this moment just to know that he was with her.

"And you, Garrison, you taste of . . ." For a moment Sabrina did not speak; she sought the right words. "You taste of life . . . and love," she finally said, feeling the steady pounding of his heartbeat beneath her ear.

No further words were needed, and the pair

rested for a time, content to be in each other's arms and to be alone.

It was only a short reprieve, though, for Brian was not a man to linger about for long. Wishing to be on the move once again, he soon sought Garrison out. As he silently approached the couple, he thought at first that they were sleeping in each other's arms. So quiet and still were they, that he stood silently for a moment before he called out, hating to disturb them in this setting, but knowing that they still had some traveling to do before they could set up camp for the night.

At the call from his man, Garrison slowly rose to his feet, still holding Sabrina in his strong arms. "Go on ahead, Brian, and have the men mount. We shall be but a moment," he responded. As he did, he saw Brian's eyes glow with the remembrance of his own past love.

"Put me down, Garrison," Sabrina said, as he started toward the spot Brian had just left.

"Nay, love. I deem it an honor to carry you in my arms and next to my heart." Garrison smiled down into her beautiful face.

"But I am able to walk." Sabrina was feeling guilty about hiding her tiredness from her husband yet she did not wish him to know how sore and exhausted she really was. In fact she had to admit, but only to herself, that she did rather enjoy being carried by her husband. But she recalled that she didn't want to be a hindrance to him, and she knew that she should try to walk back to the horses.

"I love to feel your softness against me," Garrison said softly, and quickly he placed a featherlike kiss upon her lips, silencing any further arguments she would have offered.

As he passed by their horses, which were standing ready for their riders, and started toward the carriage, Sabrina looked questioningly up into his face.

"Let us enjoy the rest of the afternoon together in the privacy of the carriage, sweet," he said. As her brown eyes rested upon him, Sabrina wondered if he had seen some telltale signs of fatigue in her, but he added, "Then I can be close to you. The horses have a tendency to draw us apart."

Sabrina grinned now, in agreement. Nothing could be more pleasurable to her than sitting close to this man and enjoying his company for the rest of the afternoon.

And the following hours were idyllic for the young lovers. They sat close together upon the cushioned seat of the vehicle, leaving the opposite seat empty, and after a while Sabrina's eyelids became heavy. Garrison saw a small yawn overtake her, and when she tried to stifle it, he pulled her golden head onto his shoulder and whispered, "Let me be your pillow, madam, your place of rest for the time being."

Needing no further invitation, Sabrina let her eyes close, and within moments she was sound asleep.

Garrison delighted in the rose-scented fragrance and soft silken skin of his bride, his mind dwelling on the weeks she had been a part of his life. Never had he known such an abundance of happiness. Sabrina was the perfect wife for him. She had beauty and bearing, but it was her heart that had truly captured him. She was truly kind and sweet. With a small sigh, he placed a light kiss upon the top of her honey gold curls. What a treasure she was, and how thankful he was that she had come into his life.

The sun was setting when Garrison gently roused his wife from trouble-free sleep. The carriage had halted, and his men were quickly setting up camp, some making ready his tent while others were seeing to their own shelter for the night.

"Come, sweet. We should leave the carriage and find some food to sustain us. Then we will retire to our tent, where you can rest more comfortably." He kissed her brow as she tried to focus her eyes upon him and then to take in her surroundings.

"Oh, I am so sorry, Garrison. I did not mean to sleep so long." She could see for herself that the light was dim. She had only thought to rest for a short time, but she had been more tired than she had imagined.

"Do not be sorry, love. I enjoyed my gentle thoughts of you as I held you within my arms." Garrison smiled.

Not able to resist his cheerful visage, Sabrina smiled in return, then she looked out of the carriage, at the men busily putting up a small tent in the shelter of a group of trees, away from prying eyes. "How exciting!" she exclaimed.

Seeing Garrison's questioning eyes upon her, she added, "I have never before been within a real tent."

Garrison opened the carriage door and jumped out. He extended his hand to his young bride and helped Sabrina down. "Then let us not delay. I shall be your guide, madam." He tucked her arm within the crook of his elbow, and started to lead her toward the tent.

Sabrina was amazed at the spaciousness of the small shelter. There was a large pallet in the center, with pillows and coverlets to lend comfort to their night's sleep, and in one corner was a small wooden table that could be folded up to be carried atop the carriage, along with the two folding chairs set about.

"We shall take our meal here this eve." Garrison said to the man checking the ropes of the tent. Then his eyes fell upon his wife, who was walking with an uneasy gait about the small interior. He was certain that she was still sore from the morning's ride and he wished not to cause her any more discomfort. They could take their meal together in the privacy of this enclosure and then rest upon the pallet.

Sabrina did not say anything as her husband gave the instructions, but she was relieved. She felt weary, and her limbs and backside were sore.

At the completion of the meal, Garrison pushed his plate aside and then rose to his feet. Reaching out a hand he helped Sabrina to stand.

"Let us retire, sweet, and try to find some much-needed sleep." He, too, felt a bit weary from the day's journey. He had wished only to fill his belly and to be able to lie down and feel the softness of his wife next to him. But as he watched Sabrina go toward their pallet, a small frown creased his brow. He could see her pain, and he felt angry at himself for having allowed her to ride such a distance. Telling her that he was going to check with his men before retiring, he left the tent and sought out Brian. Having told him to post a guard about camp, Garrison made his way to his saddle and pulled from the saddlebags a small jar. He then started back to his tent.

Sabrina was pulling off her clothing when Garrison pulled back the flap of the tent and then bent to allow his frame through the passageway. His indrawn breath caused Sabrina to spin about. Frightened, she clasped her breasts, fearing an intruder. But when her brown orbs spied her husband, a smile eased the tension on her face.

Garrison stepped over to his wife, and with a frown, he told her to turn about. Without a word, she did as he bid her, and Garrison gasped as his emerald eyes took in the darkening yellow and blue bruises upon her backside.

For a moment Sabrina thought that she had somehow angered her husband, and not knowing what to do, she stood obediently before him, her hands at her sides, as he gazed at her naked form.

Tentatively, her husband caressed her soft

flesh. And though his touch was gentle Sabrina winced.

"Come, sweet. Lie down and let me tend you." Garrison looked at her with some pity, now knowing how extreme her pain was.

Lying down, on her stomach, upon the soft silken coverlet, Sabrina allowed her husband to administer the soothing salve to her backside, and with gentle, almost hesitant fingers, he slowly massaged the yellowish mixture onto her.

"I should be quite angry with you for your behavior, madam," Garrison scolded, his tone low but gentle to let his wife know that he was not only mad but concerned. "Do not be so foolish again, Sabrina, or I shall be the one to determine how long you will be allowed to travel on horseback in the future. I will not have you ailing like this again." Finished with his doctoring, he bent over her prone form and softly kissed her below a tender earlobe, loving the feel of that most delicate spot. Then he pulled up the silk sheet, and lay next to her.

Sabrina turned her head toward Garrison, her love-filled gaze holding him for a moment before she spoke. "It is almost worth the pain to gain such tender care from your loving hands, my lord."

"Have a care, my sweet. You need not allow such a thing to happen to your body to receive tender care. It truly hurts me to see such perfection marred. Do not allow it to occur again." His warning was given in a loving tone, but Sabrina knew its meaning. He was not jesting when he had told her that he would judge her abilities better than she had this morn if she wasn't more careful in the future.

"I shall not allow it to happen again, Garrison," she whispered softly.

Gently Garrison eased his body over to his wife's, his weight resting on the pallet, for he knew full well that this eve he must restrain his overpowering need for his wife's body. His mind's eye saw the bruises upon her satiny buttocks, and knowing that he would never do anything to cause her pain, he was content to hold her and to inhale her rose scent.

They traveled on at a leisurely pace. On the second day Sabrina rode in the carriage, and on the following days she was allowed to ride her mare only a short time to gain some fresh air and to have a respite from the confinement of the coach.

The days seemed to pass slowly but Sabrina was interested when they rode through villages or passed near country estates. Her brown eyes were filled with wonder, of life, for she had never seen anything but the confines of the convent walls and then McBride keep, but she was now making up for her days of imprisonment by filling her mind with all that it could hold. Garrison, delighted by her interest in all about them, smiled when her face became animated.

This morning Edinburgh was within the day's riding distance, and Sabrina was more alive and alert with each moment that passed. Her eyes looked intently along each road and over each hill, for she was impatient to see their destination.

At moments Garrison found her excitement almost childlike. And he thought that no one would believe this young woman had come from a large busy town such as London. Of course she was acquainted with that large city, but now she was anxiously looking forward to a small town like Edinburgh. That seemed strange to him, but, with a sigh, he realized that he had been surprised by this woman since he'd first met her.

Chapter Eleven

Edinburgh ... the mere name of the town evoked images of grandeur in Sabrina's mind, filling her thoughts with visions of a splendorous city, beautiful carriages, bejeweled ladies, and suave gentle man, but in reality it was a small town that still had her looking about in wonder as she rode down its dirt streets.

Never having been in a town, though she had lived on the outskirts of London in the convent, Sabrina had nonetheless heard many stories of cities and she had read about them. Now as she looked at the people passing by, who in turn watched the procession of which she was a part, she thought surely this town must not be their final destination.

Garrison intently watched his wife, seeing first her surprise as they rode into the town and then her curiosity. And as she studied a small woman holding a babe in her one arm and clutching a young lad with the other, Garrison laughed aloud.

His wife's face slowly rose to his own.

"I had the impression that we would be going to a large town, Garrison. Is there some mistake?" Her brown orbs once again went back to the street which they were riding down.

"No mistake, love. This is the fair town of Edinburgh." Seeing her disappointed look, he added. "You will find it much changed on the morrow. A fair of some sort shall be in town."

"A fair?" Sabrina's face now came alive as she thought of the sights and smells that she had only read about.

"Aye, sweetling, a town fair. They have it once a year here in Edinburgh. People come from quite a distance. We shall spend some time resting, but later I have to go out to the farmer's to take a look at the horses he promised me. It was only with some luck that I persuaded him not to try to get a better offer at the fair."

Sabrina was excited by the prospect of the fair and the adventure it would be to go with her husband to inspect his horses. She now looked about her with some enthusiasm, noting the shops lining the streets, and seeking out the one in which she would have her gowns made, she spied a small shop set back farther from the road than the rest. A small sign hung over the doorway: Sims Dress Shop—Ladies Apparel." This was most likely where she would have her gowns made, but she had little time to wonder about that, for Garrison and his men were reining in their mounts, having just turned a corner.

Sabrina looked at the imposing inn, which seemed to be the busiest place in the small town.

"Here we are, sweet." Garrison jumped from his stallion's back and came to his wife's side. Reaching up, he helped her dismount, and then, wrapping an arm about her waist, he started up the brick steps. He called over his shoulder to his men, telling them to take the horses to the stables out back and then to come to the common room for a hot meal.

Sabrina was excited as Brian opened the portal and she stepped into the coolness of a large room. All eyes turned in the direction of the threesome, but with the fair only a day away most of the inn's customers thought they had come to take part in it, though some men's eyes lingered on the beautiful woman with the two large men.

"Take Sabrina to a suitable table. I shall order a meal brought over and see to our rooms," Garrison told Brian, and then he left them.

This inn was much like the one in which Sabrina had met her husband. In the large common room tables and chairs were set about for those that were hungry or wished to visit with a friend. Along one wall was a mohogany bar. Men stood about it, drinking ale and talking companionably.

Sabrina felt relieved to have a comfortable chair to sit upon as Brian, acting the gentleman, pulled it back to allow her to be seated at the table. Then, pulling out his own chair, he sat down with a gruff sigh. "I must be getting old, my lady." When Sabrina's fine brows rose, he laughed. "This chair sure feels uncommonly good to my aching backside."

Knowing full what he meant, Sabrina smiled at the kindly man, nodding her head in agreement. "Do you know there's a fair tomorrow, Brian?" she asked, not able to get from her mind from thoughts of the morrow.

"Aye, lass. I have been to Edinburgh's fairs a time or two in the past." A twinkle in his eyes, he smiled at her. "It is a great time for the whole town. People see those they haven't met for a year. And strangers spend their coin as though there was no end to it. There are those that follow such events for their own gain and those that only seek a day's entertainment."

"It all sounds so exciting. I must confess I have never been to such an event."

The gleam in her eyes touched Brian's heart. "My lady, you shall have a grand time. I shall see to that." As Brian was giving her this assurance, Garrison returned.

"Our meals will be here shortly, and I have gotten our rooms. Perhaps you would like to rest this afternoon, Sabrina. These past days have been tiring for you, and I am sure that you are anxious to get some sleep." Garrison, as always, thought of the comfort of his lovely bride. Noting that she seemed to wilt before his very eyes, he sat down and took her small hand in his own. Bringing it to his lips, he said, "But if you already feel rested, I would wish you to ride with me and Brian to select the horses that I will purchase."

"Oh, Garrison, are you sure that you wish me to come along?" Her face began to gleam with joy once again. She had no thought of resting when there was so much to see. There would be plenty of time for sleep later, she told herself.

"Of course, sweet, I always wish you at my side, but I do not want you to tire yourself." He looked at her, love in his eyes as he tried to discern her condition, but seeing only happiness on her visage he settled back into his chair. It would be best for my peace of mind to have her along with me, he thought. Had she stayed behind, he would have posted several of his men outside her chamber door, to insure that no harm came to her while he was away from the inn. With so many strangers in Edinburgh, he was not about to chance leaving a lovely morsel such as his wife alone. She would be too tempting. "Perhaps you will help us to select the best of Amos Parly's steeds."

Brian nodded his head in agreement, for he, too, noticed how much Sabrina wanted to go with them. And for his part, he rather enjoyed the company of this beautiful woman.

Sabrina quickly finished the meal, the prospect of the day ahead of her. And Garrison, seeing her eagerness to be done and off, pushed his plate from him.

"If you two are ready, we can go out to the Parly farm now." He rose to his feet and drew back Sabrina's chair.

Both Sabrina and Brian rose, the pair of them

wishing to be out of the inn and to view the sights of the town.

The Parly farm was not overly large, but there were no finer horses than those Amos Parly raised. And as the short, frail man took Garrison and his companions out to the corral, Sabrina remained close beside her husband, her hand clutched tightly in his.

The business transaction was soon done, with Garrison telling Parly that he would stop by for the ten stallions and six mares he had purchased when he started back to the McBride keep, and arranging to pay board for the animals until then.

The farmer, grinning as Garrison handed him the payment in gold coin, nodded his gray head. "They be here when ye be ready ta get them." He shook Garrison McBride's hand in a friendly manner, inviting him to return the following year to see what horses he would desire.

Garrison nodded, indeed thinking of the next year and feeling sure that he would return. Parly was a fair man, not asking more than an animal's worth, and most of his beasts were fine ones.

Sabrina delighted in seeing the farmer and her husband conduct their business, her pride in Garrison growing as she heard the questions he put to Mr. Parly and noticed his knowledge of horseflesh. Garrison was everything to her, and each day her love for him grew deeper and stronger.

When they had returned to the inn, Garrison took Sabrina to their room, having ordered a meal to be sent upstairs. She was glad that her husband had suggested their meal be taken in their chamber, for the common room was filled to bursting upon their return. Men and women of all descriptions were standing and sitting about, most discussing their plans for the morrow when the fair would be in Edinburgh. Nonetheless, as the large, assured gentleman had protectively led the young beauty through the room and up the stairs, many pairs of eyes had followed their passage, more than one man hungering for the lass. Feeling eyes upon her, Sabrina did not look about but kept her eyes downcast. She was glad that Garrison was at her side. She felt secure in his strength. Once before he had rid her of an unwanted gentleman, and she had no doubt that he would do the same again.

Once they were within their chamber, Garrison pulled off his jacket and vest. Then, with a large sigh, he sat down on the upholstered wing chair near the small hearth. "Come here, love." He held out his arms to his wife as she stood looking about the chamber. "You seem to be filled with such curiosity about everything, one would never guess that you are from London and that you have ever known the best of life."

As Garrison said these words, Sabrina recalled her past, and guilt came over her once again.

Garrison saw the happy, animated features of his bride fall, and tears came to her limpid, dark eyes. He reached out and pulled her into the security of his arms. "What is it, sweet? I did not mean to upset you with my foolish talk."

Sabrina shook her honeyed head. Unable to tell him the truth, she was caught up in her lie. There seemed no way out for her. "It is nothing, Garrison. I was but touched with a small pain." Again she had lied to this man that she so loved, and the knowledge hurt her.

Garrison drew her head down upon his chest, and his cheek softly touched her rose-scented hair. His heart was beating very fast. Slowly and with one finger, he carefully traced a lone tear as it made it's way down her creamy cheek, his chest aching because she would not confide in him. "My love for you is great, Sabrina. There is more in my heart than words can touch upon. So great is my feeling for you that I would never allow anything to come between us or to harm what we now have."

His gentle words stilled her tears, but feeling her heart constrict, Sabrina looked him full in the face, knowing in that moment that she could tell him all. This man could handle any problem. He would come up with a solution that would set all aright; she had but to tell him the truth, to share all with him. His vow was not idly spoken. He loved to her.

But as she opened her mouth to reveal what was in her heart, a knock sounded, stilling her.

Garrison silently cursed whoever was beyond that door, for he knew his wife had been about to tell him what had been bothering her from the moment they had met. "I will be but a moment, sweet." He gently lifted her and then set her back on the chair, hoping that the moment of truthfulness had not been completely destroyed.

"Your bath water as you ordered, sir." A young girl with bright sandy-red hair stood outside the door, holding onto the ring of the wooden tub with one hand, while the other was laden with towels, soap, and bath salts. Behind her were several young boys carrying buckets of hot, steaming water.

Garrison looked back into the room at his wife for a moment, then he allowed the servants to enter the chamber. He had wanted to send them away and to let his wife make her declaration, but he had noticed that Sabrina was approaching him.

"Oh, Garrison, how wonderful—a bath." She smiled tenderly at him, and then turning to the young girl she directed her to set the tub before the hearth.

Garrison knew full well that the special moment was lost. He only hoped that later they would be able to recapture it, that Sabrina would again feel that she could trust him completely.

The servants were gone, the tub was filled with water, and a fragrant rose scent permeated the chamber, emanating from the bath salts that Sabrina had selected.

Spontaneously, Sabrina turned her back to her husband, to allow him to help her with the row of buttons that ran down the back of her outfit. When her clothing lay in a heap at her feet, with no concern for her nakedness, her only thought of the bath, which she had done without the past few days while traveling, she quickly stepped into the wooden tub. Her delight was plain as she leaned her head back against the edge and sighed contentedly.

Garrison smiled with joy at her pleasure. And with sure movements he also shed his clothing.

Sabrina was still, her brown eyes closed as she allowed the rose-scented water to soothe her tired limbs, but when she sensed that her husband was standing next to her, she opened her eyes and saw him step into the bath. "What are you about, Garrison? There is little room for two." She looked to him, wonder upon her features.

Her confusion was short-lived, however, for her husband smiled and then bent and scooped her up into his arms. Before she could feel the chill of the room, he sat back down with her on his lap.

Their lovemaking on this eve was wild and carefree. Never had Sabrina known anything like Garrison McBride; he had stormed into her life and her thoughts, and had turned all her reasoning upside down with a single glance. His hands and mouth played dreamily, sensually, upon her flesh, leaving her breathing raggedly. The silken water added a certain exoticism to their love play, and Sabrina had never before experienced such lovemaking.

Her body gleamed golden in the water, the only light coming from the hearth, and she noted her husband's bronzed magnificence as his arms encircled her. His manhood throbbed against her thigh as he drove her toward a heady delight.

Their lovemaking was a wild surging of passion. Garrison stormed her body and mind, opening wide the floodgates of her desire, and Sabrina entered another world in which only she and her handsome husband existed.

Their bodies joined, their cravings mounting, the pair pursued their goal, and with each stroke Sabrina held her husband more tightly, relishing the feel of his strong back, his male scent, and the feelings he evoked in her. She lost all sense of reality, letting herself be carried away by the rapture of the moment.

When she had achieved ultimate pleasure, Garrison eased her from the tub and carried her to the large bed in the center of the room. There, their bodies naked covered with droplets of water, he made tender, all-consuming love to her.

Finally, their breaths mingling, they slept, even in their dreams holding one another.

Sabrina awoke as the first light of morning streamed through the open window of the chamber, to the gentle kisses of her husband who was leaning over her, propped on an elbow.

"I love to watch you while you sleep," he said softly, then took her lips in a gentle kiss. "You inspire in me a longing to create poetry."

Sabrina laughed aloud. "I did not know that I had married a poet."

"Indeed you did not, madam. However, I but think of your beauty while you sleep and my mind is filled with flowery phrases. To bring them to fruit is yet another story. I rather enjoy keeping my delightful thoughts to myself."

With a silken arm, Sabrina pulled her husband's head down and she drank in the gentle love that he offered.

For a moment Garrison thought of the eve before, when she had been about to share with him what ailed her at odd times. He considered trying to pry it out of her, but seeing her mood was so high, he hated to make her sad. There will be other times, he told himself. The right moment would present itself once again, and when it did, he would allow no interruption.

Sabrina's thoughts were far removed from her husband's. Upon awakening she remembered this was the day of the fair, and as her excitement grew, she happily kissed Garrison.

A knocking at the door made him think of strangling the person behind that wood barrier, but instead he sat up upon the bed, propped a pillow behind his back, and called for the intruder to enter.

Seeing Brian carrying a large tray, Sabrina quickly pulled the sheet up under her chin and then squirmed lower into the mattress to hide herself from his eyes.

Garrison smiled lovingly at his bride and, wrapping an arm about her waist, pulled her naked form tightly against his side. "Thank you, Brian. Have the men eaten?" Garrison questioned as his friend set the tray on a small table across the room. Brian's eyes lingered for a second upon the tub half-filled with water—evidence of last eve's love play, for water still lay in puddles about the floor.

Sabrina saw where the older man's glance fell, and her face flamed when his eyes returned to the pair upon the bed. But she could only hope that Brian would not notice her discomfiture.

"Aye, Lord Garrison, all have eaten. And some of the men have already set off to see what mischief they will be able to get into."

Garrison laughed aloud, knowing full well the way of his men. He himself had been like them before he had met Sabrina, only thinking of finding a woman and drinking. "As soon as Sabrina and I have eaten and dressed we shall come downstairs."

"I shall be awaiting ye then." Brian turned about and left the couple to the privacy of their chamber.

After one last, lingering kiss, Garrison drew Sabrina from the depths of the bed, placing her robe about her shoulders as though he were in some rare form of pain. "If you do not cover yourself, pet, we shall be spending the day here in this chamber." He winked boldly at her and then playfully patted her shapely bottom.

"Nay, Garrison, not this day." Sabrina tied the sash to her robe, knowing well what was on his mind. At any other time she would have preferred to remain in the room with her husband, but on this day there was a fair and she did not intend to miss a moment of it.

The town of Edinburgh seemed to have been transformed while Sabrina had slept. The streets were no longer dusty, lone paths; everywhere that one chanced to look, there were bright colors and laughing faces.

The common room of the inn was packed to capacity that morn as Garrison led his young wife down the stairs, his eyes seeking Brian or some of his men. But with the throng of people standing about, even with his great height, it was impossible for him to espy those he sought.

With glowing eyes, Sabrina watched men and women rush about the inn, their loud talk and laughter making such a commotion all thought was blocked out. Some of the people present were from the town; others were visitors who'd come for a day of fun and excitement.

"Wait here for a moment, sweet." Garrison steered his bride to a table and helped her to sit down. "I must find Brian and then we shall be off."

Sabrina smiled and nodded as her husband left her side. She had never before seen so many people in one place, and as her eyes traveled about the large room she drank in the life throbbing about her, her blood pounding fiercely.

"What we be having here, Pete? A wee bit of a thing sitting all by herself?" A tall, thin man approached Sabrina, with another man almost as tall at his side. "Be ye all alone, miss?" he asked, and seeing Sabrina's delicate features turn pink, he grinned to his companion. "Didn't I be telling ye, Pete, that this were the right place ta be finding a gal?" Both men's eyes seemed to devour the long flowing golden curls which Sabrina had let hang free. Their eyes then roamed over her ice pink gown and the silver-gray cloak that she held, dwelling overlong on the sheer lace of her bodice, which was low in cut. Sabrina felt herself blush under their stares.

Pulling her gaze from the two, she thought if she ignored them they would leave her to herself, but hoping to have this beauty to themselves for the day ahead, they did not budge from her side. "Come with us, pretty girly, and me and old Pete here will be showing ye a grand old time. We be having some coins in our pockets and we'll spend the day pleasantly enough."

Not knowing what to do, Sabrina looked about for Garrison. Upon seeing him across the room at the long bar, talking with Brian, she began to feel real panic when the boldest of the young men reached down and took hold of her arm.

"Don't ye be shy now, miss. Today is fair day, a day for all to enjoy. Come with us." The young man was so smitten by her beauty he had but one thought, and that was of walking about the town of Edinburgh with this lovely young thing upon his arm.

But at that moment Garrison glanced across the room to his wife. And when he saw her fright and the two men at her side, one with his hand upon her upper arm, he froze for a second, then uttered a loud growl of rage.

For a split second Brian looked at his lord, not understanding what had come over the young man. Only in battle had he glimpsed such fury in his friend. But as he watched Garrison stride

271

angrily across the large room, his fists clenched tightly at his sides, he quickly realized the cause of his anger, and he hurried after him, determined that his lord's lady would not be harmed.

The young man that held Sabrina's arm never knew what hit him. He sailed across the large common room, finally coming to a halt when he struck the wood paneling of the room. The other young man was not as fortunate as his friend, and as he took in the feral gleam in the cold emerald eyes of the man standing commandingly before him, he cowered and his hands came up as though to protect his face.

"I-I did not mean to offend the lady, sir," he stammered quickly. "My friend here but thought that she was all alone and would care to join us for fair day." He slowly backed away from the fearsome figure threatening him.

Garrison's rage was evident as he glared at the man, but when Brian came to his side and bent to see that Sabrina was unharmed, he took hold of Garrison's arm.

"Let him be, lad. Your lady is not hurt, and I doubt that these two will again be so foolish." He felt tense anger course through Garrison's body and his grip tightened upon his lord's arm. "See to your lady, Lord Garrison. I will tend to these young yokels."

Garrison's mind was clouded by anger. He shook himself, but all that he could see was the man touching his Sabrina. Taking a deep breath of air, he nodded his head toward Brian, then turned to Sabrina. Seeing that she was still afraid, he bent down next to her, taking her tiny hand within his own. "Are you all right, sweet?" he asked softly, trying not to let her know the full extent of the rage that consumed him. And as he looked about, he saw that all within the inn had stopped talking and moving, and all eyes were directed toward them.

Sabrina now feared her husband as much as she had feared the two men. She had never witnessed such raw, fury before. Garrison had been without a care for his own safety when he had hurled the young man who had held her across the inn, had then stood before the other. "Garrison, there surely was no need ..."

Garrison saw her fright, and looking across the room at the young man still lying prone upon the floor, he surely could not blame her. He, too, had frightened her. He loved her so that it blinded him at times. "I am sorry, love, but I could not help it. When I saw that man with his hand upon you ..."

For a moment Sabrina looked into her husband's now-calm features, reading in his face the full strength and extent of his love for her. He had only wished to protect her. "It would seem that you are once again my hero, my lord," she said sweetly.

Instantly Garrison recalled the Boar's Head Inn and how he had chased away an unwanted man from her side. "Aye, it seems ever my job to see that you are well protected, my lady." Garrison smiled, for he saw that his wife was no longer upset.

"The young man does apologize to your lady and to yourself, Lord Garrison. It would appear that the pair are from a farm of small worth and have come to town for the fair. Your lady's lovely looks deprived them their good sense for a few moments is all." Brian grinned at Garrison and then at Sabrina.

Garrison nodded his head, not caring for any excuses, only caring that Sabrina had not been harmed, that he was once again at her side, and that she was not angry with him for the way he had protected her. "Let us be out of this inn and see the sights that Edinburgh has to offer us on this fine day." Garrison rose to his full height. His green eyes devoured his bride for a moment before he extended a hand to help her to her feet. Casually, his long fingers pulled her cloak together.

Brian went before the couple, clearing a path to the door. His large frame pushed some of the crowd out of the way, and his purposeful look caused others to step aside.

The morning wore on, with Garrison staying at his wife's side, his angry glare discouraging any man who dared to cast a second glance at his young bride. He felt very protective of this woman at his side, and though he cautioned himself that he was being foolish, he could not help his behavior.

Brian was on the opposite side of Sabrina, and following the threesome were two of Garrison's men, heavily armed, their eyes ever watchful for some form of an attack upon their lord and his lady. Sabrina's excitement was evident as she strolled up and down the streets of Edinburgh, her arm linked tightly to that of the man at her side, her warm, brown eyes taking in all of the happenings about her.

Masses of people crowded the streets. Vendors were shouting, extolling their wares or calling to passers-by to take a moment to taste a tempting morsel or to try their hands at a game of chance. And there were those who had come out this fine day to trade, barter, or buy. Fruit peddlers openly displayed their ripe, delicious produce, and walking about and drawing attraction to their baked goods were several women and young girls. Games were set up in small booths or wooden planks so those passing by might be tempted to risk their coin.

Sabrina's gaze devoured everything in her path. At one booth she stopped to touch a fine bolt of cloth, her fingers lingering upon its satin texture, at another she was drawn to a fine gold hairbrush with a matching mirror. But she did not dally long at any one spot, her excitement being at such a pitch that she could not stand still.

When her eyes touched upon an article or her hand reached out to one, usually one of the men at her side, or on occasion one of the two that followed, pulled out the necessary coin and purchased the item that had attracted their lady, with each purchase receiving a radiant smile from the one they so wished to please.

Garrison watched his bride lovingly, thinking

her much like a child in her enthusiasm. She filled his heart with gentle pain whenever she glanced his way, her features so happy and care-free. He wished only to please her and to keep her this joyful forever.

It was midafternoon when the horse auction began, and along with the men at her side, Sabrina wanted to be among those watching this event.

There were several fine animals for sale, though as Garrison looked each one over, he realized that the farmer from whom he had made his purchases had a far better selection. Still, as a small dapple-gray mare was led forward, some-thing about her fine disposition and the toss of her head attracted Garrison. "What would you think, Sabrina, of a beauty such as she?" He watched her intently as she studied the animal with a critical eye.

"She is much prettier than my own mount, Garrison, but do you think she would sit well?"

Not one to place his wife in any danger, Garri-son again looked over the mare, but seeing only a gentle demeanor as she stood still while the auctioneer rubbed her flanks and pointed out her mane as a virtue, Garrison knew that the beast would be a good mount for Sabrina.

When the bidding began, he was among the first to call out an offer. The men in his group looked over the mare and he saw approval on their faces.

The bidding was rather lengthy, for another gentleman was also of a mind to claim the mare.

But once Garrison's mind was made up he did not draw back, and finally the gavel was struck and the grinning auctioneer shouted, "Sold to the large gentleman there in the back with the beautiful lady at his side." The circle of onlookers nodded their heads as their eyes went to Garrison and his wife.

After giving instructions to one of his men to take the mare to the stables at the inn and to make sure she was well tended, Garrison again took hold of his bride's elbow and steered her from the group at the auction. "Let us find some other entertainment, sweet." He had no wish to let her stand about and become bored. This was her day, and he did not wish it to be dimmed.

Turning a corner, the small group halted once again, for they were on a roped-off street on which a horse race was in full progress. A black stallion was coming into the lead, his long neck straining as he tried to outdistance a fine-looking roan. Sabrina clasped her hands together and then began to shout to the young man upon the black. Fascinated, she watched him slowly pull away toward the finish line.

"Oh, Garrison, does he not look similar to your Apollo?" she shouted to her husband above the din. "I do so hope that he will win."

"I think there will be little chance of his losing now, my sweet." Garrison shouted back to her. He also was caught up in the race they were viewing.

And as the black stallion broke through the ribbons that had been lightly laced across the street, Sabrina called out joyously, "I knew he could do it." She smiled at Garrison.

"My lady, had I known that you would watch the horse races so enthusiastically, I would have brought more coin with which to place you a bet." Garrison laughed aloud, delighted that she had been caught up in the race.

"Oh no, Garrison. I would not wish to place money upon the winner or loser." For a moment her tone turned serious as she watched the men about them. Some were shouting and waving fistfuls of money in the air, others were standing about sullenly, indicating that they were indeed the losers. "I would not care to lose even a small bit of gold by taking a chance such as this."

Garrison and Brian both laughed aloud at her serious manner. "Some derive great pleasure in making such a bid. For they think they may have more gold in their pocket when the horses are at the finish." Her husband tucked her hand within the crook of his elbow as he told her this.

"But I would ever keep within my mind that I might be losing what I have already gained through hard work."

Brian nodded his head in agreement, for he was of the same mind as she. It had ever disturbed him when he had been coaxed into placing a bet. For a man such as he, money was hard to come by. And at times his very life had been staked on the gold that lined his pockets.

"Come along, sweet. Let us see what other adventures we can find. Perhaps you would care for something to eat. I am fairly starving, and al.

278

these smells assailing my nostrils are making my belly growl."

Nodding their heads in agreement, Sabrina and her husband's men followed the lord toward the first booth that sold foodstuff, and within a short time they were all sitting about a small table laden with an assortment of appetizing viands.

"I cannot remember ever having had such a fine day." Sabrina bit into a piping hot hand-size pigeon pie, small bits of the ingredients sticking to the corners of her lips.

Feeling his chest swell with love, Garrison took out his handkerchief and gently dabbed at the food upon his wife's face, his eyes holding hers and speaking of his joy in her.

"It surely has been a fine morning, me lady." Brian declared. "But it ain't done by half yet. Why, the afternoon is just begun."

Nodding her golden head in agreement, Sabrina hurriedly ate the rest of her pie and then drank thirstily of the sweet mint drink that Garrison had purchased for her.

The small group finished their meal quickly, not about to be left behind by Sabrina, and they surveyed several booths before they came to one with a bold sign. Madam Knows All was printed above the entry. And upon the outside of the booth was a portrait of a woman draped in dark hangings.

"Come, Sabrina, let us go inside and see what the good madam has to tell you of the years ahead. Perhaps she will be able to predict years of happiness for us." Garrison drew upon his wife's hand, trying to get her to enter the booth of the fortuneteller.

"Nay, Garrison. I believe not in such as this madam."

Garrison grinned at his lovely wife, and still pulling upon her hand, he laughed aloud. "It is not of a real nature. I am sure the woman within tells everyone almost the same thing. By pleasing their ears, she gains shiny coins. Come, sweet, it will be great fun and you will be able to tell Katie about visiting a fortuneteller."

Feeling very reluctant, Sabrina nonetheless let herself be led by Garrison. Brian and the other two men followed, and when the drape which served as a door was pulled aside, the small group entered a tiny booth, Sabrina holding tightly to her husband's hand.

Her brown eyes settled upon a woman seated at a small table in the center of the room, and she immediately began to feel a sense of doom.

With a husky, raspy voice the woman at the table addressed them. "Come in. Take this chair," she said to Sabrina as the men pushed her ahead of them. Madam's dark eyes watched the young girl's every movement, noticing her nervousness and reluctance.

"Do not fear me." The raspy, almost false tone of this woman's voice had the opposite effect. It struck fear into Sabrina.

"What is it that you would wish to know? Is it a lover you seek? Or perhaps you are with child and would know its sex?" The madam tilted her

280

head, and though she was completely covered, both hair and face, only her dark eyes visible to those in the booth, she seemed to possess a power that frightened Sabrina.

"There is nothing. I am a married woman and have no child." She answered, desiring only to be allowed to leave this booth, to flee the dark, probing eyes before her. There was something sinister about this woman, and Sabrina was haunted by fear of whoever was concealed behind all that dark draped material.

With a quick movement, the madam took hold of Sabrina's soft, white hand, and she slowly went over the lines upon her palm as though studying them thoughtfully. Sabrina could only look at the hands that were now holding her own.

"You are indeed a married woman. To the tall one standing here beside you?" The madam looked up from Sabrina's hand and gazed at the large, handsome man behind her. As Sabrina slowly nodded, the madam continued. "I see here that you have known much solitude in your limited past. And here"—the madam's slim finger went over a tiny line in Sabrina's palm—"here I see something quite strange. It would appear that you are but half of an identical whole!"

Sabrina froze. Then, pulling her hand sharply from the woman's grasp, she looked hard at the madam, trying to peer within the folds covering her face. How could this woman know of her past? Yet she had spoken of her as one-half of an identical whole. What had she meant? Did she know Sabrina's terrible secret, or was it written within her palm that she had a twin sister?

It was Garrison who broke the quiet as the two women stared hard at each other, dark eyes holding dark eyes, one pair revealing fear and confusion, the other haughtiness as though that woman knew all that life had to offer and only waited for the right moment to impart her knowledge.

"Come, sweet, it is time that we take our leave and make our way back to the inn." Garrison took Sabrina's elbow and helped her to her feet. His hand going to his pocket, he pulled out a gold coin and tossed it upon the table. As he did so, he again looked at the woman who was just sitting and watching his wife.

He had seen others like her in the past, women making a living by inventing stories that would entertain their customers. But this one did seem a bit odd. The things she had told his wife had made little sense to him, but they had inspired fear in Sabrina. It was best that he pay the woman for her time and then take his wife to the inn so she might rest for a while.

As though dazed by a nightmare, Sabrina let her husband lead her out of the booth and into the coolness of the afternoon.

"Half of an identical whole." The words drummed over and over in Sabrina's mind, leaving her trembling as she tried to gather her wits and make her way to the inn. Had that dreadful woman truly read her past in her hand? Had she seen into her life, noted the lies and deceit? She had mentioned solitude. Had she not meant the seclusion of the convent? With a soft moan Sabrina brought her hand up to her head. A pain throbbed behind her brow as she tried to figure out what was happening. Her husband had said that the madam would only make a good show of knowing all. Yet surely there was more here than a good guess. The woman had acted sure, and she had seemed to know all that had ever happened to her. The half of one identical whole had to be her twin sister, Sylvia. But no other woman except her sister knew of this.

Garrison heard his wife's moan softly, and he watched as she brought her hand to her forehead. "Are you all right, my love?" His concern was genuine for she was pale and had a fearful glaze to her brown eyes.

Sabrina did not even hear her husband's words, so wrapped up was she in dread.

Brian and the other two men that made up their small party looked at her and then at Garrison, sensing that something was wrong but not understanding what it could be. The madam's words had certainly upset their lady, but they did not know what to do for her.

Garrison, feeling the slight trembling of his wife's limbs, quickly made a decision. She had become ill or was overtired from the long day's activities, he surmised, and halting, he took Sabrina up into his arms, her form fitting snugly against his massive chest.

That brought Sabrina back to the moment. "Garrison, put me down." She looked about desperately, not wishing for anyone passing to see her in the arms of a man. Even though he was her husband, few in this town were aware of this fact. Besides, a lady did not let herself be carried about in the arms of a gentleman.

"Nay, sweet. You are trembling and ill. The inn is only a few more steps, and I shall get you to bed and then see that a doctor is brought to you."

"I do not need a doctor, Garrison," she responded. But the set of his jaw and the tone he had used told her there would be no changing his mind so she let her head fall to his chest. She felt some measure of security while in his arms, her ear picking up his strong heartbeat.

As the small group slowly made its way down the street, dark eyes watched their progress for a moment before the curtains of the booth were drawn together. The madam then went out of the back of the booth, dark shawl draped tightly about her as she searched the booths until she found the one she sought. A card game was going on within, and she went directly to a small table at which four men were seated, then bent and whispered something into a dark-haired man's ear. His dark eyes glistened as he listened to all that she had to report.

"I have this hand to finish. Go back to your booth and await me there." His words were low so that none nearby could hear, but they held a strong measure of command.

"But, Zaloe, could you not come now? We must plan what would be best to do. I cannot believe it was them . . . and the fine rich clothing."

An angry glare came over the man's features, and without another word, the woman backed away from the table and left the booth. Her fear would have been plain for any to see if she had not worn the dark shawl, but as her hand fingered the gold coin in her pocket, a small thin smile came to her lips. Zaloe, no matter how cruel, could always be counted upon to come up with a plan to further their interests. She had learnt much in the time she'd been married to this man, and the main thing was that he always concocted some schemes, whatever came up.

True to his word Garrison sent Brian to find a doctor as soon as they arrived at the inn. He then put Sabrina to bed, and had a cup of tea sent up. His concern for his wife's condition was uppermost in his thoughts for she was still pale and quiet. He helped her to undress and then tucked the covers about her.

"I am fine Garrison," Sabrina declared. "I truly do not need to see a doctor." Her protest was feeble for she could only think of those cold dark eyes that had stared at her and of the madam's raspy voice telling her of her past. What could all of this mean? she wondered. Was she to be forever tortured for her part in this horrible game of changing identities? With a sigh she closed her eyes, wanting to shut out the horror of this day.

Garrison stoked the fire within the hearth, filling the chamber with warmth, and then he paced the chamber floor, his glance constantly going to the bed. Aware of his wife's distress, he was powerless to help her. All of his attempts had thus far proven futile. He knew that there was something wrong with her, and he could only pray that a doctor would be able to find out what it was.

When the doctor arrived, Garrison was quickly ushered out of the chamber and a speedy examination was made, though under protest. Sabrina believed that nothing was ailing her, that it was her thoughts that were tormenting her.

When he had finished the elderly man looked through wire-framed spectacles at the young woman lying upon the soft bed. Nodding his bald head, he let his eyes roam from her to her husband who had just been permitted to come back into the room.

"Perhaps you would care to step into the hall for a moment, Lord McBride?" Doctor Wales said as he started toward the door.

Sabrina gave little thought to this, for she knew that the doctor could not truly help her with her dilemma. Only she could set all aright, and she was not even sure that she could do it. The game had gone too far. How would her husband react to such news? How would he respond when he learned that he had been deceived by his wife of only a couple of months? As the pair left the chamber, she thought to the eve past. She had almost told Garrison all while sitting upon his lap, and now she knew that she was glad the maid had interrupted them. Surely he would not view her in the same way once he discovered that she had lied and had betrayed him. He would surely cast her from his side. His pride and honor, being wounded, would demand that he do so.

The portly Doctor Wales was a man of few words. He came straight to the point, and Garrison stood before him, wide-eyed.

"My examination led me to conclude but one thing, sir." With each word that he spoke, the spectacles slid lower on the older man's nose, causing Garrison to watch them rather than his expression. "Your wife is in the first stages of being with child. She shall need to rest, not to tire herself as she has just done. It is not so unusual that a woman in the first stages of pregnancy should wear herself thin. I suggest a good night's rest. She shall be fine in the morn. This fair has put many out of sorts."

Garrison could not speak. He was not sure that he had heard the doctor correctly. Had the man said that his Sabrina was to bear a child? But how could this be when they had been married so short a time? He desired children, but they had not even talked about such a happy occurrence. What would Sabrina's reaction to this news be? Would she be happy or would she think it was too soon? These questions came to Garrison's mind as he stood before the doctor, not knowing how to react or what to say. It struck him then that he would have to be the one to tell his bride that they were to have a babe, yet he was still in a daze.

Taking in Garrison McBride's expression, which seemed to change with each new thought, the doctor patted his large shoulder. "The idea of a babe will sink in quickly, Lord McBride. The reaction is always the same with the first."

Pulling himself quickly from the stupor, Garrison began to smile, slowly at first; then his lips seemed to split with happiness. What could be more right than for Sabrina to have his child growing within her body? A being created out of their binding love. "Thank you, Doctor." He reached out and shook the older man's hand before paying him his fee.

Doctor Wales was pleased as he took his leave. There were too few such happy occurences in his line of work. And Lord McBride certainly had seemed pleased enough after the initial shock had worn off.

Garrison went back into the chamber, but seeing that Sabrina's eyes were closed as though she were resting, he silently made his way to the side of the bed.

Sabrina felt his presence before she opened her brown eyes to look into his loving face. "The doctor told you that I was fine? I must have been a bit tired 'tis all." She smiled to reassure her husband that she was well, and she hoped that he would not press her about what the madam had said that had upset her. She could never tell anyone that.

Garrison sat lightly upon the coverlet, and took her hand within his own. He could not seem to voice his feelings, so he let his emerald eyes feast on her beauty, imagining how she would look holding their child. She would make a beautiful mother for the babe.

Something deep within Garrison's eyes unsettled Sabrina, leaving her chilled.

"Sabrina, have you felt well these last few weeks?"

Wondering if a disaster was about to befall her, Sabrina slowly shook her head, thinking that the doctor must have told her husband something dreadful. What could be the matter? Had some horrible malady beset her?

Seeing her fright, Garrison leaned over and gently kissed her forehead, hoping to reassure her. "Nay, sweet. The doctor's news was not unwelcome."

"What then, Garrison?" Sabrina was very concerned now, for by his manner she knew there was something that she must be told.

"He told me that you were with child." Garrison watched as disbelief clouded her features and terror appeared in the depths of her gold-flecked eyes.

All the terrible stories Sabrina had heard at the convent crowded into her mind at this moment. How is this possible? she thought. Perhaps the doctor was mistaken. Why would fortune deal her such a horrible blow? Was this to be her punishment? The mother superior had often told her that no wrong she committed would go unpunished. Perhaps this was the means God had chosen to remind her of deception. Was her body going to be torn asunder in childbirth?

Noting her pallor, Garrison truly began to

worry. "What is it, love? Doesn't the news that a babe is to be born of our love please you?" His tone was soft and gentle, for he wished to convey the depth of his feeling to this woman.

Pulling herself from her dreadful thoughts, Sabrina looked at her husband, seeing his love and concern. Of a sudden she realized it would be a pleasure to hold and love a tiny being born of their union. Would she not pay any price to have Garrison's child? she asked herself. Was not this the man she loved? A lone tear escaped and ran down her cheek as she now looked with some wonder at the man that had so changed her life. A child, she thought. A tiny boy much like this man sitting next to her. "Oh, Garrison, are you sure?" she finally whispered aloud, feeling excitement build in her at this news that he had brought.

Running a hand through his sun-streaked hair, Garrison softly repeated what the doctor had said to him. And as a glowing smile replaced the fear Sabrina had shown him, he also began to smile and his large hand went to her slim belly as though he were already anxious to feel the proof of the doctor's words.

"A babe." Sabrina sighed, then lay back once again upon the pillows.

"Aye, sweet, a child. Does the idea please you?" Garrison again looked concerned.

When Sabrina slowly nodded her head, he pulled her into his arms, and kissed her brow, then her eyelids, her small pert nose, and finally her petal-soft lips, sampling the sweet taste of her. At that moment Garrison McBride felt that life was truly complete. He had Sabrina—no other could ever be a fit mate for him—and he was to have a child, an heir to McBride keep. Or perhaps this first child would be a little girl with her mother's looks. He knew that would please him beyond all measure.

Sabrina sensed his thoughts as she clung to him, knowing fulfillment only in his embrace. He was her life and they had created the new being in her womb. Whatever the outcome their bond would always be a special one. But for a moment she thought of her sister and of the trick that had been played upon her husband, and drew him to her even more tightly. Feeling his warmth, she reasoned that there would be time to tell him all later. After the babe was born, she would share with Garrison what she should have made clear from the beginning. With his babe in her arms, he would never be able to send her from him. He would find a way to straighten out the situation. She loved Garrison and wanted him to know it, so she whispered, "I love you. No matter what happens I shall always love you."

Chapter Twelve

Garrison planned to stay in Edinburgh for at least another week, thinking to allow Sabrina time to rest before they made the long, arduous trip back to McBride keep. He wished he had known of her condition before they had left the castle. He would have sent Brian on to Edinburgh, and he and Sabrina would have remained at the keep. The thought of endangering her or the babe filled him with dread, so he had postponed the return trip, and now spent his days and evenings at his wife's side.

Sabrina found that the news of her pregnancy had made her husband even more patient and loving. He always seemed ready to help her, to hold out a wrap or cloak, to place a hand on her elbow when she was on the stairs, to help her dress. He was always gentle, as though he wished to assure her that he, too, was a part of what they had created and that he would share in all aspects of her time with child. Though Sabrina had never thought that it would be possible, she was actually enjoying her condition, and with each passing day, she was growing more fond of the idea that she was with child. With a husband such as Garrison, she knew that all would come out aright. He would be at her side, and would let no evil befall her.

Each morning after they had breakfast in the common room, Garrison would take Sabrina for a stroll. Not allowing her to grow weary, but knowing the importance of fresh air and exercise, he would soon escort her back to their chambers.

Though he had at first thought to take her to the dressmaker's to be fitted for the promised gowns, he now had a better idea, but thinking that the ordeal might tire his wife out unnecessarily, he had the tiny woman called Melanie close up her shop for a time in the afternoons and come to the inn. She brought with her two assistants and bolt after bolt of materials, along with sketches of gowns.

The first afternoon the small woman came, Garrison remained in the chamber, his eyes watchful lest Sabrina became weary, but after he told the dressmaker about his wife's delicate condition, warning her that he did not want Sabrina overtired, he noticed that Melanie frequently directed Sabrina to a chair while her assistants hurried about doing what was necessary.

Garrison sat at his wife's side as she was shown a large stack of sketches. Melanie could make gowns of every description, and as she set out the sketches, Sabrina lowered her small frame onto the carpet, her brown eyes scanning each design and then turning to Garrison.

"Pick those that you would have, love," Garrison lightly chided, seeing her indecision, perhaps because of the amount the gowns would cost or because she did not know which he preferred.

Still Sabrina hesitated as Melanie pulled forth more sketches. Finally Garrison picked up a sketch of a sprigged muslin day dress, and turning to the dressmaker he said, "This one, in a light heather color would be fine. Perhaps, though, we could do without the bows upon the sides. The style is long and graceful, and would look well upon my wife, but I think that she could well do without these adornments."

The small middle-aged dressmaker nodded her head. She was in full agreement with Lord Garrison's choice, thinking that she herself would not have been able to have done better. "Your husband has excellent taste, madam," she said softly to Sabrina, as she set out more of the drawings for inspection.

Sabrina had to agree. Garrison had ordered her dress with confidence, knowing that she would not care to have the bows at the sides. Among his many talents was an ability to dress a lady beautifully. She sat back against his knee, more than glad to leave the choices to him.

Garrison ordered the gowns that caught his

eye, wishing to dress his wife in what he would have her wear. He chose well as he pointed out a full dozen outfits. Then he started to order material for her underclothing. "Aye, this sheer lace will go very well with the white satin evening gown. And this light violet will make a perfect chemise for the heather day dress." And so it went, Sabrina sitting back in amazement at the amount of clothing he was ordering. Besides the gowns and underthings, he specified hats, slippers, and wraps among these an ice blue cloak of shimmering satin lined with velvet – fans, gloves, and even stockings.

How could I ever desire more? Sabrina wondered as the busy little dressmaker attached swatches of material to each sketch chosen and then wrote down the other items. Skillfully she gave directions to her two helpers who bustled about doing as she bid.

At the end of the day's work Melanie said that she would return the following afternoon and would keep her girls working far into the night since Lord McBride and his lovely wife were leaving Edinburgh in a short time. Garrison, in a congenial mood, then showed the three women to the door.

"I hope that you did not mind my choices of clothing, my love." he said to Sabrina who was still sitting upon the floor.

"Nay, Garrison. I could not have chosen better. I am but stunned at your knowledge of women's apparel," she murmured as he stood before her.

"Only where you are concerned am I interested in such matters." He reached down and helped her to her feet delighting in the feel of her as he drew her into his embrace. "I but knew what I would wish to see upon your lovely body."

"Thank you so much for all that you have given me." Sabrina was overwhelmed by the generosity of her husband.

"I would gladly spend every penny I own to see you well clothed, madam. Would I have my wife and the mother of my child go about in a beggarly fashion?" He grinned before taking her sweet, tempting lips with his own.

"Oh, Garrison," she sighed as she leaned against his sturdy chest. "I love you so."

"And that, madam, is payment enough for me." His hands gently went over her shapely backside, and molding against him, he breathed into her golden curls, "Let us send for a tray of supper and eat in our chambers. I wish only to have you next to me this eve."

Nodding her head in assent, Sabrina knew that she would always give in to whatever this man wanted. His love held her fast.

Sabrina soon found that the dressmaker was a friendly woman. The next afternoon she returned as she had promised, her two assistants following close behind her, their arms filled with cut-out gowns and bolts of material. And as the girls set about sewing and pinning, Melanie visited with Sabrina and sipped a cup of tea.

Meanwhile Garrison, now certain that the seamstress would not overtire his wife, sought out some of his men and rode off with them, seeking much-needed release for his pent-up nerves. They headed toward the Parly farm to check on his horses.

The following days passed quickly until only one day remained before their departure from Edinburgh.

"What say you, sweet? Shall we have our dinner downstairs this eve in the common room?" Garrison called across the chamber as he pulled his jacket over his broad shoulders. This past week they had spent many an evening in this room, content to lock out the outside world.

But since this eve was the last they would share in Edinburgh, Sabrina smiled and nodded. She felt that sharing the meal with Brian and some of Garrison's men would be fun. "That will be fine, Garrison, I shall look forward to it."

Going to her side, Garrison pulled his tiny wife to him, hand going under her chin and tilting her delicate jaw up toward him. For a moment their eyes locked and held, his green ones capturing her gold-flecked gaze. Then slowly his lips lowered to hers, and he tasted the sweet nectar of her as his tongue circled and played with her mouth.

Both became lost to all about them, but it was Sabrina who finally broke the magical spell. "This is the last of the fittings. Melanie promises that all will be ready in the morning just before we plan to set out for home."

Placing a light, last kiss upon her pink lips, Garrison smiled with feigned relief. "I did not think that having you clothed would be such an ordeal. I hope that you have not tired yourself." His emerald eyes ran over her, seeing the fitness of her young body and doubting that she had been pushed beyond her limits. Still, he wanted to be certain she did naught that would harm her.

Sabrina giggled behind her small hand. "Indeed I have done little. Melanie and I do no more than sip tea and talk while her girls are busy with the sewing. I must confess I shall miss Melanie when we leave this place. I have grown quite fond of her."

"Perhaps we shall return again. In a year or two Amos Parly will have more horses to show me." Seeing Sabrina's eyes come alight, he added, "And we can come at this same time so that we are here for the fair. You will not be so tired and weary, and will be able to enjoy yourself more."

A dark shadow fell across Sabrina's delicate brow at the remembrance of that day they had walked the streets of Edinburgh. The madam in the fortunetelling booth came to her mind and once again she heard her words: *"One half of an identical whole.*"

Garrison saw his wife pale, and wishing to chase away any dire thoughts, though he knew not what it was that could be troubling her, he again pulled her into his embrace. "Have I told you this day, madam, how much I adore you?"

"Nay, my lord, not this day." Sabrina smiled. She was unable to think of anything while in his arms except the feel of his strong, virile frame. Her heart hammered in her chest as his warm breath caressed her ear.

"Well then, let me set all aright. I love you with my heart and soul. You are the woman of my life, my wife, the mother of my child. I cherish you."

How wonderful he is, Sabrina thought, a small tear trickling down her cheek. "And I love you, Garrison."

Before more could be said, there was a slight knock upon the portal.

"That must be Melanie." Sabrina stepped back from her husband, straightening her gown and patting her curls back into place.

Garrison was quick to smile at her reaction. "I may be later than usual, sweet. We shall be bringing the horses near to town so that we have but to gather them up and be on our way in the morn. I will have several men stand watch over them during the night."

Sabrina nodded her head, knowing that he would be no longer than necessary. Usually he returned before Melanie and her assistants had departed. Perhaps Melanie would be able to visit longer with her if he was delayed today.

"Do not forget that we shall have our dinner downstairs this eve," he reminded her. Then he gave her a last lingering kiss before going to the door and opening it for the seamstress.

The fitting went rather slowly at this last session, and by the time Melanie and her assistants had left, Sabrina desired a few moments' rest. She wiped her brow with a cool damp cloth and lay down on the bed, intending to rest for a time before Garrison returned to the inn.

Feeling slightly disappointed when a gentle knock sounded upon the door, and thinking it to be Melanie or one of her assistants, Sabrina quickly went to the door, opening it wide. Horrified, she stepped back as she viewed the man at her door. Zaloe Tolliver stood brazenly before her, and for a full moment Sabrina remained frozen, her eyes wide with disbelief.

Zaloe let his dark gaze drink deeply of her tender beauty. Though she was the exact image of her twin sister, her gentleness drew him to her. "How have you been, Sabrina?" he finally said as he stepped into the chamber and shut the door.

Sabrina could but shake her golden head, for she was not able to believe that this man was standing before her. "How did you —"

He did not let her finish, but took a step toward her. "I was informed that you were in

Edinburgh and have come to you with information about your family."

Feeling uneasy with this man in her bedchamber, Sabrina went to the chair nearest the hearth, hoping to put this piece of furniture between the two of them. The first time that she had met her sister's friend she had been naïve about the ways of men. Now she knew how some of them dealt with women, and she was not about to let her guard down while in this man's presence. Zaloe Tolliver's eyes frightened her. There seemed more in his dark gaze than he was willing to let one read. "What kind of information do you have? Is it about Sylvia?" As she spoke the name of her twin, her brown eyes roamed back to the portal, and her thoughts going to her husband, she silently prayed that he would not come to their chambers until after this man had left.

"Sylvia is waiting to tell you the good news herself. She is down the hallway in our own chambers." Zaloe again took a step toward her, as though he would, indeed, take her by the arm, but seeing her fear-filled gaze he stopped in midstride. He could not afford to have her cry out. Someone might hear. "It is about your mother. You must hurry, though, for we are to leave on this very eve for London."

"My mother?" Sabrina could not think straight with this man standing before her. "What is the matter with her? Is there news that she has relented in her decision and now wishes to acknowledge both Sylvia and myself?"

In response he shook his dark head, and she knew she would get no information from him. Slowly Sabrina nodded, agreeing to follow him, for if his room was down the hallway she would only be gone for a few moments. Besides, she had to talk with Sylvia—tell her she had married Garrison and that she had not as yet told her husband of the game that had been played upon him. She could not afford to have Garrison view her twin before she told him all. Sabrina promised herself that the moment Garrison returned to their chamber she would tell him everything. Who could have expected that she would find her sister and this man in Edinburgh? No. She must deceive her husband no longer. She had delayed telling him all for far too long.

Zaloe stepped aside as he opened the door, allowing Sabrina to precede him. He then escorted her to the end of the long hallway, unlocked a door, and let her step into a chamber.

Sabrina looked about, and sitting on a straight-backed chair was the woman she had met the day of the fair. The frightful madam from the fortune telling booth. The woman rose, her dark shawl drawn about her as it had been that day at the fair. But as her slim fingers slowly unbound it, letting it slip to the carpeted floor, Sabrina stood immobile.

She was reminded of another time when this woman had stood before her in a tiny room at

Roundtree Convent. "You? You are the madam that told my fortune that day?" the words echoed softly in the chamber.

"Yes, it was I, dear sister. Who else would have been able to read so clearly your past?" Sylvia Buchanan Tolliver slowly started toward her twin, her brown eyes so like Sabrina's, taking in her paleness. "It would appear that you have done quite well for yourself, my dear sister." She reached out and felt Sabrina's gown, and her anger mounted as she realized that she lacked such fine treasures. She had had such things at her aunt's home, but with Zaloe she was lucky to have the barest of necessities.

"All did not turn out as you and Mr. Tolliver planned, Sylvia," Sabrina declared. "I tried to do as you had directed, but Garrison would not be swayed in his decision to wed and shortly after my arrival at his castle we fell in love." As her twin merely stared at her, she continued, "You met him at your booth, Sylvia." A small smile came to Sabrina's lips as she started to tell her sister of her husband. "He is the most wonderful of men, so strong and loving."

"And rich. Let us not forget that. He is indeed very wealthy, dear sister, and he lives in a castle."

Sabrina heard the venom in Sylvia's voice, and she flinched as though stabbed. "I do not think of his wealth. I love him with all of my heart, and he loves me."

"And does he know that it was I he was to

304

ed? Or did you forget to tell him that small act?" Sylvia and Zaloe held their breath while waiting her answer. They both knew that she could not lie to them.

"Nay, I have not as yet found the right time to approach him with the story of how I came to wed him instead of you. But this very day I shall tell him the full truth." Sabrina, having spoken, felt that something was not right with these two, and for a second she thought of turning about and fleeing down the hall to the safety of her husband's chamber. But exerting self-control, she reminded herself that the woman before her was her twin sister so nothing would happen to her here.

"Then he knows not I am your twin sister?" Sylvia asked. At the slow shaking of her twin's head she began to smile calculatingly. Her gaze went from Sabrina to Zaloe. "Did I not tell you, my love, that she would not be so stupid as to give herself away. Why with this Garrison McBride so wealthy she would have been a fool to chance that he would put her away from him." Her words were directed to Zaloe and he nodded his dark head knowingly.

"I am sure that Garrison will understand and all of this can be set aright. He knows I did not wed him for his holdings but because I love him." Sabrina did not fully understand what was going on between these two. "My husband will be back shortly, and then I will speak to him. I am sure that he will desire to meet you both."

"Come and have a seat." It was Zaloe wh‐
spoke, and taking hold of Sabrina's arm he le‐
her to the chair that Sylvia had vacated.

For a moment Sabrina, gripped by panic, trie‐
to free herself, but his grip was strong and sh‐
had little choice but to do as he bid.

Sylvia quickly went to the door and turned th‐
key in the lock. Returning to stand before he‐
sister, she ordered, "Take off that gown and you‐
shoes."

Sabrina had noticed how her sister's gaze ha‐
dwelled on her clothing, but she found this re‐
quest ridiculous. Her chin jutted out as sh‐
looked at the woman who was her sister. "If yo‐
desire gowns, Sylvia, I will be happy to shar‐
with you all that I own." She could not under‐
stand why her sister would desire her clothing‐
for surely Sylvia must have many such fin‐
gowns. "Mr. Tolliver spoke of news of our mothe‐
when he first came to my husband's chambers‐
Is there something amiss?" she tried to diver‐
Sylvia from the subject of her clothing.

With a grunt of displeasure, Sylvia glared a‐
her twin. "Priscilla Buchanan is dead." When sh‐
saw pain fill Sabrina's eyes even though their
mother had discarded her, she said, "She cared
only about herself and received what she de‐
served. Her lover's carriage overturned and sent
both of them to early graves."

"Oh, how horrible," Sabrina exclaimed, tears

coming to her eyes for she had never met the woman that had given her birth.

"What is horrible is that she left me and my husband completely penniless. Her will was drawn up before I could tell her of my marriage to Zaloe, so all her lands and her wealth go to Garrison McBride and his heirs."

Sabrina swayed as she felt the full measure of her twin's venomous anger. It surely was a strange twist of fate that her mother, who had done nothing for her in the past, was now making up for that in death, though actually she had left Sabrina nothing. "I shall talk with Garrison. He will surely—"

"You will do nothing. I will get all that is my due myself. You took my husband and my wealth, but I shall get it back."

"But you were the one who planned to switch identities. You and Mr. Tolliver came to the convent and sent me far away, knowing that I would be forced to marry a man though I had not seen him and did not desire to wed. And now that you have already married, what is it that you would do?" Sabrina shook her golden head, not understanding yet what these two could possibly be plotting.

"Well, dear sister, we switched placed so easily once, surely we can do it once again?"

Sabrina looked at the woman across from her. They were so alike in their appearance that she could see no difference. "But I do not understand." Then, slowly, it dawned on her. Clutching her hands together, she gazed from the woman to the man, seeing in him the same look of purpose. "You surely cannot think to get away with such a farce. Garrison will know that something is not right, and I refuse to go along with your plans this time, no matter what reason you give me."

"But will your wealthy husband know, dear sister?" Sylvia asked, her expression catlike.

"But you cannot." Sabrina was about to say that she was with child so that her sister could not possibly take her place, but before she could do so, Zaloe tied a piece of material about her mouth. With hurried movements, he then tied her wrists together at her back and attached her bonds to the chair.

Sylvia smiled at her sister's panic, caring only for her own gain. "See that you take care of her as we planned, Zaloe. We cannot afford to allow her to be seen by anyone at the inn. I shall meet you in the village when the time is right." As Sabrina thrashed about trying to free herself, Sylvia took off her gown and slippers, leaving her in her chemise and stockings. "Here, throw this robe over her for the time being." she said, taking a threadbare silk robe from the bed and tossing it to Zaloe, who hurriedly pulled it about the woman tied within the chair.

Sylvia was enjoying this part of the abduction. Since she had married Zaloe, he had treated her much differently than he had while she had lived in her aunt's home and he had sought her favor. He was not averse to striking her at the slightest instigation. In fact, she had to admit that her life as this man's wife had thus far been an unhappy one. He had forced her to play the part of a fortuneteller as he had dealt cards to country yokels, taking their coin or whatever else they had to risk in a game of chance. For the past few weeks, they had traveled with the fair from one town to another until Sabrina and her rich husband had come into Sylvia's booth.

Now fortune offered them a different hand to play. She would replace her twin, and when the time was right, Zaloe planned to do away with the fine Lord McBride and his wife. Sylvia had given little thought to this thus far. She would see how all turned out before committing herself to the crime of murder. Garrison McBride had seemed loving, considerate, and handsome that afternoon in her booth. She had learned weeks ago that her own husband was not. She had considered staying with McBride, as the rich lord's wife. Zaloe would be able to do little if she decided to play her hand this way. But surely she was letting her thoughts run too far ahead, she reminded herself. First she had to look like her twin. She gazed into the mirror upon the bureau—the only one the chamber had to offer—and she found to her amazement that the woman staring back at her was surely the woman who had stepped into the chamber a short time ago with Zaloe. She saw no difference now that she had on her sister's clothing. And as she stroked out her own honey-colored hair, she went to Sabrina, pulled the pink ribbon from her curls, and placed it in her own.

Zaloe stood back and looked his wife over critically, from head to foot, seeing for himself the exact likeness. But he knew what Sylvia was truly like underneath her beauty. Sabrina did not have such a cold gaze. And he knew his wife was a shrew, a woman that cared only for herself and what she could gain. But surely she would not show this side of her nature to Lord McBride until he was powerless to go against her. She was a woman much like her mother, vicious and purposeful.

Drawing her up into his embrace, he took her lips coolly this one last time, showing her the power he had over her before setting her from him and watching her go out the chamber door. Then his eyes went back to her sister who was tied to the chair.

Sabrina looked at the man before her, not knowing what he intended to do with her but certain that she must get free to warn Garrison of her twin sister's intent. Surely Sylvia will not harm him, she thought as she again tried to pull her hands free of their bindings. Obviously her twin only wished to gain the wealth that Priscilla had left to Garrison. That was all Sylvia had had on her mind when she had again switched identities.

But it was futile to struggle against the ropes that held her to the chair. Zaloe had made sure they were secure, and now he even went behind her to check on them. Having done so, he let one long finger run the length of her jawline. "In the end, my dove, you shall be mine. I have waited since that first day at the convent for you to belong to me, and I shall have you."

Sabrina's eyes were wide with terror as she stared at him, not comprehending what he was talking about, only certain that she must gain her freedom to warn her husband and to save herself.

When Garrison returned from bringing in the horses, he stepped into the chamber and his eyes settled upon his young bride. She was sitting primly on the chair before the hearth, a small fire having been started earlier by one of the inn's servants.

With a smile of greeting, he went to her side, noticing the richness of the gown she had chosen to wear and then remembering that he had planned to take her downstairs for their meal to celebrate their last eve in Edinburgh.

When the door had opened and Garrison McBride had entered the chamber, Sylvia had been aware of the harsh beating of her heart. She had clutched her hands together on her lap, hoping that they would not shake. These first moments were surely the most important. If she could fool him now, all would go as she had planned. As his steps brought him closer to her, her brown eyes rose to meet his green ones, and she saw that he was thus far unaware of her true identity. With any luck at all, he would stay within the folds of darkness until she wished otherwise.

"Good evening, love." Garrison bent, but when he would have taken her lips, Sylvia turned her head somewhat, leaving him only her cheek. With a small grin, he placed a gentle kiss on that most tender spot. "I trust that you did not tire yourself overmuch with your afternoon fittings?" He looked at her with a touch of concern.

Sylvia smiled up at her "husband," hoping that she was acting as her simpering sister would in this situation. Was Sabrina so delicate that this man had to ask about her health after a fitting? she wondered. "I feel in the best of health, Garrison," she answered lightly and then rose to her feet. "Though I am rather hungry." She felt the best course of action for the time being was to be downstairs in the company of others, so he would not have time to contemplate her every move.

"I shall be only a moment, sweet. I have but to wash up and change my shirt." Garrison looked at Sabrina with a critical eye, sensing something odd about her. She was usually so bubbly when he returned in the afternoon, talking about the gowns that were being made up and about Melanie and her assistants. Perhaps she was overly tired, he reasoned as he splashed water onto his face. His wife had already proved that she was not one to complain. It would be up to him to watch out for her health, and to see that she did not overexert herself in any way. And as soon as he got her back to his castle where they could be to themselves, that was exactly what he intended to do.

As he pulled his silk shirt over his head and began to tuck it into his dove gray trousers his gaze settled upon her once again. She did seem a touch paler to him this eve, her cheeks were not glowing with their usual healthy touch of pink. He would see that dinner was a short affair and then bring her back to their chamber for a good night's sleep. They would be leaving in the early morn and he did not want her to become ill.

As the couple made their way downstairs, Brian came to meet them. "Your table is ready, and some of the men have a desire to dine with ye this eve, Lord Garrison." Brian looked first to Garrison and then to his lady, quickly noticing how drawn and pale she looked.

Before Garrison could respond to his friend's request, Sylvia spoke up. "Surely we shall dine alone this eve, Garrison." And clinging to his arm, she left him little room to misunderstand her meaning.

Garrison McBride looked with surprise at the woman on his arm, as did Brian. Never in the past had Sabrina seemed so cool and insensitive. "Certainly, if that is your desire, Sabrina. I had thought that this being our last eve at the inn, we would make it a gay affair and dine in the company of my men."

"I am rather tired and would prefer a more quiet meal." Sylvia tried to soften her manner when she felt the eyes of both men upon her. She would not give in and eat with servants, be they Garrison McBride's men at arms or nay, but she knew that she would have to curb her coolness to these louts for the time being.

Garrison, after a moment's hesitation, smiled down upon his young bride, remembering her delicate condition and thinking that her strange manner was due to this. "Lead us to the table, Brian, and have the men served a round of drinks. Explain to them that I desire to be alone with my bride on this eve," he said. Then he took his wife's arm.

Brian did as he was bid, his own surprise at this woman's behavior not so easily settled. He had never known the lass to be so hard, and though he knew her to be with child, he had not expected her to change so drastically—and overnight. His eyes studied her for a moment as he pulled out her chair and her husband helped her to sit down. She seems as lovely as ever, he told himself. Perhaps this is but a passing fancy and she will be herself upon the morrow.

Consuming her dinner in silence, Sylvia studied the large man that was her sister's husband while he sat across from her, thinking her to be the woman he had wed. Sylvia suspected that she had truly made a horrible mistake by sending her twin to him in her stead. This Garrison McBride seemed more than willing to do anything his wife desired, he was very good to look upon, and he was wealthy. Thus far all was going along as planned. He thought her to be Sabrina, and he would go on thinking so until she decided that she did not need him any longer.

Garrison also remained quiet during most of the meal, his thoughts on Sabrina's strange behavior. But by the completion of the fine repast, he had attributed it to her condition and to tiredness.

When they were once again in their chamber, Sylvia went behind the dressing screen. As she began to undress Garrison came to her side and, as he had in the past, offered to help with the unbuttoning of her gown. Sylvia stiffened at his warm touch.

No other had ever touched her so intimately except Zaloe, and though he had been hurtful to her at times and had treated her cruelly, she still loved him. Something about him attracted her as though she were a moth and he were a burning candle. He was in her blood, and she knew it would take time for her to adjust to another's touch. "I can manage by myself, thank you," she said and she turned her cool brown gaze upon the man who was supposed to be her husband.

With a quizzical look Garrison slowly dropped his hands to his sides, wondering if he had said or done something to offend his bride. "Sabrina, if there is aught that I have done to displease you, please forgive me," he stated, but she quickly cut him off.

"You have done nothing. I am overtired and only desire a much-needed moment's privacy."

Her abruptness caused Garrison to step from behind the dressing screen and then to begin to undress himself. He wondered about this mood that had beset her.

Once she lay within the confines of the large bed, Sylvia turned her back to him and moved to the far side, hoping that this man would leave her to herself, that he would believe she was tired and in need of rest.

Garrison desired to hold his love in his arms the night through as he had since their marriage, but when he settled his large frame upon the bed, seeing her back turned coldly toward him, he felt a hard lump form in the pit of his stomach. Knowing that he would be awake the night through if he did not at least receive a kiss from her, he carefully approached her, his hands encircling her trim waist as he thought of the day when it would be expanded with his child. Her scent filled his nostrils as his lips touched her honey-colored hair, and for a moment he pulled back. The rose fragrance which always clung to her was absent, and instead a soft musk scent came to him.

When his arms went around her, Sylvia drew away, her body stiffening. "Please, Garrison, I am very tired," she pleaded, hoping that he would leave her to herself.

Garrison needed no other urging. He shifted to his side of the bed. The nightmare was finally becoming reality. His loving, giving wife was turning into a cold, uncaring woman. He hoped that her pregnancy was not the reason, yet he also hoped it was the cause of her changed behavior. He would not be able to bear living with a woman who did not want his attentions.

Long into the night Garrison laid awake, his arms folded behind his head as he thought over the strange evening. If he could not see that it was Sabrina beside him, he would swear that this was not the same woman he had fallen in love with and wed. Even the rose scent he had loved so well was no longer a part of her. In one afternoon she seemed totally changed, and at the moment he was not even sure that he liked the woman she had become.

Chapter Thirteen

The morning the carriage rolled up the long
drive to McBride keep, Garrison released a ragged sigh of relief.

Life with his fair wife had not been easy these
past few days, not for him or for any of his men.
At every turn Sabrina voiced some new com-
plaint. Either the carriage driver was deliberately going over too many bumps or her meals
were not cooked to her taste. And as the long
nights approached Garrison was finding that he
much preferred the company of Brian and his
men to being with his bride in the confines of his
small tent.

On the trip to Edinburgh she had seemed so
pleased by everything about her—even the tent
had delighted her—but on the trip homeward she
had not been able to sleep upon the thick pallet,
had claimed it was far too lumpy, and she had
hated having to bathe with cold water. As on the

last night at the inn, during the ones that followed Garrison was shown only his wife's back. She had suddenly became a screeching, nagging shrew who seemed to delight in ordering Garrison's men about or in being cruel to him for no apparent reason.

On her part, Sylvia was glad when the castle came into view. She had had all she could endure of this trip and the horrible way in which she had been forced to travel – sleeping in a tent instead of finding a soft, warm bed at an inn and having to eat the horrible food that Garrison's cook had fixed for them. Never had she spent a more horrible few days. She could not wait to soak her body in a warm bath, and to lie in a bed she had all to herself.

She hoped that her sister had not shared a chamber with this beast of a man. She had, at first, thought Garrison McBride would be the type of man she could eventually care for. If not, at least she could have tried to favor him for his gold. But she had quickly learned that she could barely abide the man. He was forever deferring to his men as though they were his equals. They even ate the very same food he and his wife were served. And he considered the large man called Brian a valued friend. Though this man was no more than a hired servant, Garrison conferred with him on almost every matter. Sylvia was fast beginning to loathe Garrison McBride and all those about him. And now, as the days passed, more often than not she found herself missing Zaloe.

His allure well suited her own inner needs. Indeed, his manner was much like her own, their wants and preferences a match. But this life as lady to Lord McBride was not at all to her liking. She would have to move, and quickly, she told herself for the tenth time since leaving the inn at Edinburgh.

Zaloe should have arrived in the village near the McBride keep, and she was sure that he would not be hard to find when the appointed time came. She had but to await the right moment when she and Garrison were alone. She would make certain that what happened to the lord of McBride would be an accident and that she – his "wife" – would be entitled to all that he possessed. And even if there were some error and she could lay claim to all that he owned, at least she would be entitled to what her mother had left in his hands.

Garrison opened the door to the carriage and offered to help his bride step down. He hoped that once she was back at the keep her mood would change for the better. He missed the tender moments they had shared, and he missed the soft concern that used to fill her warm, gold-flecked brown eyes. All caring seemed to have fled her a few days after she had learned of her pregnancy.

Katie met the lord and lady at the front stoop, and she held open the portals to the main hall of the castle. Her smile enfolded Garrison and then Sylvia, but as her eyes went to her mistress, her smile slowly began to fade from her kindly features. "What is it, child?" She looked into Sylvia's eyes and quickly noted the coolness of her gaze.

"I am tired and wish only to be taken to my chambers." The younger woman swept past the housekeeper, pulling back her skirts, her head held in a haughty manner. She was unable to pretend to be on kindly terms with a servant.

Katie stared after her and then looked to Lord McBride, but when he raised his broad shoulders, she knew that he had no more of an answer to his wife's behavior than she had. "Of course, my lady," she responded. "I will go right up and stoke the fire. We had not expected ye until this eve. Yer travel must have been made under fair conditions." The older woman made her way to Sylvia's side, hoping that she could spark some of the old Sabrina in her. She could not believe that this was indeed the same sweet-natured young woman who had left only two weeks earlier. So changed of manner was she that Katie could not believe her eyes. Her lady's coolness of speech and her actions implied that something was amiss.

"I will follow you right up" was the only response the housekeeper received from Sylvia. Never had she wasted her breath on a servant and she was not about to do so now.

Casting a look in Garrison's direction, Katie started through the main hall and then went up the stairway, Sylvia following close upon her heels.

And as the housekeeper opened the door to the

master's chambers Sylvia needed only one look to ascertain that Garrison McBride did indeed use these rooms. Standing fast at the door, she shook her honey-colored head. "Nay. Another room will suit me well this eve."

Katie looked hard at the young woman. What is she about? she wondered as she tried to read some meaning in the young woman's face. Her lady had slept within these chambers since the night she and Lord Garrison had wed, and never in the past had she complained about the comfort of these rooms. Had something drastic happened since they had left the castle? Were they no longer sleeping together as man and wife. "But, my lady, yer things are in this chamber," she responded, trying to reason with her mistress.

"Then move them to another. And be quick about it. I do not wish to stand here the day through and argue with you about my wishes."

"Yes, my lady." Katie was beginning to become quite annoyed with this slip of a girl. Perhaps she was angry with Garrison, but that certainly was no reason for her to act in such a manner. She had thought that she and Sabrina had become good friends, but now she was not so sure. The woman before her acted spoiled and arrogant. If she did not soon change her attitude, Katie would send another to see to her needs. As Katie started down the hall to the chamber Sabrina had used when she had first arrived at the keep, she began to suspect that perhaps the strain between the young couple was caused by Sabrina's being with child. She knew from long talks with the girl that Sabrina had a fear of what pregnancy would entail. "My lady, if ye wish to talk with me about yer problems, I would be more than glad to give ye an ear. Is it over children that ye and Lord Garrison are having problems?" Katie knew how greatly Garrison wanted heirs to his keep, and if this were the problem she would talk to the young man and convince him that he should not push Sabrina further on this matter. When she was ready there would be time enough.

As Sylvia walked about the chamber, her brown eyes taking it in, she quickly pulled the cloak from her shoulders. "It is of none of your business what goes on between myself and Lord Garrison, nor does it concern any of the servants in this castle. And as for children—ha! I will hear no more on such a subject," Sylvia commanded.

Katie's face flamed at this direct insult. She had been at the castle for more years than she could remember, and never had anyone spoken to her as this woman was now doing. "If that will be all, my lady?" She spun about, not waiting to hear if there was something the young woman desired. She was determined to seek out Lord Garrison and to find out what was happening between the pair.

Sylvia felt no remorse over the way she had talked to the older woman. She had been raised to believe that servants were to take orders and to keep to themselves, and she would have it no other way in her own home, which this castle would be. If not with Lord McBride then upon his death.

Katie found Garrison in his study, pouring himself a liberal snifter of brandy. She was surprised that he would do so at such an hour, but she soon saw the strain on his haggard features and decided he needed something strong to buoy his spirits. "Lord Garrison, may I be so bold as to question ye about what has happened between ye and yer lady?"

Garrison eased his large bulk onto the leather-cushioned chair behind his desk and with thumb and forefinger he rubbed at his eyes. "I am completely at a loss, Katie. At one moment she was as you remember her. Then, upon leaving her for only a short time one afternoon, I returned and was greeted the woman you have just seen."

"But was there an argument between ye two which left her with this cold and hard manner?" There had to be some explanation as to why such a sweet, kind girl had turned into such a one as she had just shown to her chamber.

Garrison shook his head as he brought the brandy to his lips and drank thirstily. "All I can think to blame for her new manner is the child she now carries within her body."

At first Katie thought she had not heard her lord right, "The child she now carries?" She watched him intently as he nodded his head.

"Aye, she became quite ill while we were in Edinburgh, one afternoon after going to the fair, and of course I called in a doctor. He found her to be with child."

"And how did Sabrina receive this news, my lord?" Katie asked. Something was not ringing true. The way the woman upstairs had responded to her only moments ago, she would have sworn that a child was the farthest thing from her mind.

"She was afraid at first, I do admit. I attributed it to stories she had heard from evil tongues while she was growing up. She did not say as much, but I assumed that this was the case when fear filled her upon receiving this joyous news. But I truly thought we had chased away her terror." He recalled holding Sabrina in his arms, recalled how they had spoken of the child they had created out of their love. "I had thought all was well between us, perhaps even more so than in the first weeks of our marriage. But then one afternoon, for no reason that was apparent to me, she became as she now is. Not even my men wish to be about her any longer. I can only hope that the cause is the babe and that once it is delivered she will again be the Sabrina that I so loved."

Katie heard raw pain in her lord's voice, and her heart went out to him. How could it be that a woman could change so easily only because she was with child? Had she been fooling all of them from the start? Was this her true nature? But that did not explain that the woman upstairs seemed not to desire any child. All was not right here. Katie heaved a large, impotent sigh, for she could not bear to watch Garrison be torn asunder by the woman who was his wife.

"Do as she asks," Garrison instructed his housekeeper. "I do not wish her to be distressed, nor do I want any hurt to come to the babe she is carrying." He thought that, if Sabrina remained as she now was, he would at least have the babe one day to bring him comfort. It was made from the love they had shared. He was so confused at this moment that he did not know which way to turn.

"She has taken the room down the hall. The one she had when she first arrived at the castle." Katie spoke these words softly, not wishing to be the one to bring this man any further pain.

"That is all right," he responded, then took another sip of the amber brew in his glass. "Lord knows there has been little between us of late."

For a moment Katie felt a stinging at the backs of her eyes. How could one be so in love at one moment and then change in the next? It all rang false to her.

"The men should be in the hall shortly. I imagine that they will be craving a good meal. I pushed them these last miles, not even letting cook prepare breakfast. My only desire was to get to the castle and to be in familiar surroundings." He had thought his life complete when he had met Sabrina, but now all seemed to be tumbling about him and he was powerless to do aught but to watch it.

Katie hated to leave him in this sorrowful condition, but she knew that he was right. She could already hear the loud commotion his men were making in the main hall. And perhaps she could also get some more information from Brian. Mayhap he would know what had truly changed her mistress.

But she was disappointed to find that she was to learn nothing from the large, red haired man. Indeed, his thoughts about the mistress were not very pleasant. To him she had changed overnight into the worse kind of nagging viper. "She be as though I had never before met her. So ill of temper and waspish of tongue was she upon the trip that I and the others went out of our way to stay out of her path. Hardly can I remember the sweet, innocent woman that Lord Garrison married."

Katie shook her head, not understanding what could have come over Sabrina. But she quickly determined to get to the bottom of what had become of the kind and loving girl that had left for Edinburgh.

Garrison spent the rest of the morning going over his books and tending to business he had forsaken while in Edinburgh, but as he tried to keep his mind upon the papers upon his desk, his thoughts frequently returned to his wife.

She had moved to other chambers, thus telling him the true extent of her changed feelings for him. Why could he not figure out what had come over her to cause her to act so strangely? Could it be only that she was with child? He wished that he could believe that, but something nagged at him, telling him there had to be another reason.

His thoughts ran in this vein till it was late afternoon and then he sat back and stretched, letting some of the tension out of his large body. He thought back to his first meeting with Sabrina. She had seemed so young and innocent that day when he had glanced across the common room of the Boar's Head. And as he thought back, he also remembered her simple joy in the small gift of a white rose. He envisioned her deep in her sleep, her slim, white hand holding the fragile flower.

Quickly he rose to his feet, and a small smile came to his lips. Perhaps she needed only rest. After being home awhile, she would become her old self. He would have a vase of white roses placed by her bed so she would see them when she awoke from her nap.

Whistling a jaunty tune, his spirits lightened by the idea that his bride would awake to see his gift and would be reminded of the time when he had left a single white rose upon the carriage seat, he set off for the gardens. He himself would oversee the cutting of each delicate flower, making sure that all were perfect.

When Garrison returned with the roses, he searched for Katie. Going into the kitchen, he requested that she find him a vase and put the lovely blooms into water. He then hurried up the stairs, hoping that Sabrina had not yet awakened and that his gift would be the first thing her gaze touched upon.

Sylvia had not stirred from sleep since she had stretched out upon the soft coverlet that morning, and as Garrison arranged the white roses upon the bedside table he looked lingeringly at his bride's face and form.

He remembered that eve only months ago when he had stood beside this bed and had looked upon her as she slept. That had been when he had determined that he would win her. Now there was a harder look upon her face, and even though she slept, he could see that she was not truly content. As his emerald eyes roamed over her form, resting briefly upon her slim belly, his thoughts went to the time when his child would blossom and push out her frail figure with its growth. He felt little of the joy he'd experienced upon receiving the news that he was to become a father. Sabrina had all but shattered his happiness this past week.

Still, now that they were back at his keep, perhaps they could settle into the life they had shared in the earlier months of their marriage. He would do anything in his power to recreate the happy days they had once shared.

Sylvia awoke to a nagging headache. Her brown eyes went about the large bedchamber, and for a second she could not remember where she was. But all to quickly it flooded back to her. As she stretched, she thought of how it had been since she'd left her aunt's home. That was the first time since her departure that she had awakened to such a well-appointed bedchamber.

She had always enjoyed luxury, and she had hated each day of her life with Zaloe, but she reasoned that he was not to blame. It was not his fault that they had not gotten back to London before her mother had been killed in that carriage accident. And surely he would have given her anything she desired if he had been able to. She put from her mind the days when Zaloe had struck her because she had dared to complain about their plight, deliberately forgot the hardness of his manner whenever he had conversed with her since their marriage vows had been spoken. Nor did she dwell upon how he had forced her to become the dreadful madam in the fortunetelling booth, having to accept a few coins so she could furnish him with more money to gamble and drink. No, now that she was away from Zaloe she thought of him with love and adoration, and was barely able to wait until she could once again be held in his arms.

Speculating on what it would be like when they had all the money they would need, she let her brown eyes fall upon the vase of white roses and, wrinkling her pert nose, rose from the bed. She did not remember such flowers being beside her when she had lain down that morning. Someone must have come into the chamber and placed them there to please her. Probably the housekeeper, she thought with some distaste. How utterly mistaken the woman had been. Roses had always reminded Sylvia of death, their thick scent bringing a nauseous feeling in the pit of her stomach.

Just then Katie came to Sylvia's chambers, several servants following her and bearing a large wood tub and pots of steaming water. As she opened the chamber door, she quickly noticed that the young woman had just risen. "I trust that you rested well, my lady." The housekeeper smiled, not knowing what to expect from the girl, but hoping that the rest had soothed her temper.

"Take these flowers from my chambers at once," Sylvia fairly shouted as Katie began to set about helping the servants prepare her mistress's bath.

Katie looked across the room at these words, and seeing the flowers that Garrison had brought to his wife's chambers, she frowned. "They do not please you?" Perhaps it is the vase, she thought, trying to find some reason for Sabrina's odd behavior.

"I hate roses. They make me ill, so just do as you are told," Sylvia ordered, anticipation of a bath bringing her from the bed to the hearth, near which the servants were laying out towels and fragrances for her inspection.

"But, my lady, I do not understand. You hate roses?" Katie could not believe her ears. Sabrina had loved roses when she had come to the keep. Then it hit her, perhaps the flowers ill-suited her mistress when she was in a delicate condition. She knew that some women became very ill when exposed to certain smells while they were with child. Perhaps this was the case with the white roses. "Of course, I shall remove them at once," she stated. She started across the chamber, leaving the girls to finish preparing the bath.

As she started down the stairs with the vase of beautiful flowers, she encountered Garrison who was coming from the back portion of the keep. When he caught sight of her carrying the roses, his brows rose, but before he could question Katie, she spoke up. "The mistress wished them removed. Their scent seems to bother her because of her condition."

Garrison had not thought of this, and for a moment he thought he should have been more attentive. Perhaps his wife had stopped using the rose scent he loved to inhale for the same reason. "If you would like, please keep them in your own chambers, Katie." Garrison smiled at the kindly woman he had grown to love as though she were a part of his family.

Katie blushed with true pleasure at receiving such a gift. "I had thought to put them in the front parlor, Lord Garrison."

"Nay. Enjoy them yourself. Anyway the mistress might go into that room, and I would not wish her to feel any distress."

Katie nodded in full agreement, her smile broad as she thanked him for his kindness.

"I will go up and see if Sabrina would care to share the evening meal with me." He spoke haltingly, as though he already feared the answer.

Katie did not know what she could do to soften the hurt he faced. It was something only Sabrina could alleviate.

As Katie started toward the back portion of the keep, Garrison went up to his wife's room. He stood outside the portal for a few moments, bracing himself for the confrontation that was about to take place. He did not know what her mood would be, but he was sure that the gift of white roses had not softened her heart.

Not able to linger any longer in the hall without feeling a fool, he gently pushed the door open, saw his young, beauiful wife in her bath, her body submerged in the warm liquid that gently lapped about her breasts as she washed her shapely legs.

When her eyes fixed upon him, he started across the chamber. As he did so, she sank deeper into the water, until all but her chin and face were hidden from his hungry gaze.

Seeing that she was trying to hinder his view of her, Garrison became irritated. Lately she had acted as though she were not his wife. What harm was there in a husband seeing his bride in her bath? "Sabrina, I want to know if you would share the evening meal with me in the main hall?"

Sylvia looked at this man who had once again intruded upon her, not seeing his concern but viewing him as someone she was fast becoming annoyed with. He always seemed to want something of her, to force his presence upon her. "Nay, my head is throbbing. I think I shall have a light tray brought up to my chambers this eve." She held no desire to join him for dinner. She knew, from bits of conversation she had heard on the trip to the keep, that his men also dined in the main hall, and she certainly had no wish to watch them while they gobbled down their food like starved animals. A slight shudder went over her at this thought.

"Perhaps I could join you in your chambers?" Garrison was willing to do anything that would please her. She had but to say the word.

Slowly shaking her head, Sylvia frowned at him. "I would prefer to be alone. I will retire shortly after dining, and I do not wish to impose my illness upon you," she lied, not wishing to be around him more than necessary.

"As you will have it." Garrison was beginning to become quite angry, but he did not want to say anything he would regret afterward. If she did not desire his company, he would dine with his men. These past few days had proven to him just how much he still needed the companionship of those that served him.

Sylvia did not say anything else, but she watched Garrison leave her chamber, then smiled as she laid her head back against the rim of the wooded tub. She would have to plan Garrison McBride's accident. She was growing rather bored with his constant attention. How her sister had endured him was a mystery to her.

Perhaps tomorrow she would be rested enough to formulate a plan. Mayhap a hunting accident, or while they were out riding she could hit him with some hard object and then say that he had fallen from his mount. With a large sigh she thought of all that she had to do—and soon. Tomorrow I will begin, she told herself as she again began to lather rich, creamy soap on her sponge, she brought up a slim leg and delighted in the sensual feel of the sponge upon her soft skin.

For the next week Garrison hardly saw his wife. She always found an excuse to avoid him, taking her meals within the quiet privacy of her chambers and pleading a headache whenever he suggested that they spend any time in each other's company.

By the week's end Garrison was like a wounded animal. The slightest infraction committed by those around him easily set off roaring anger, and he would shout at and abuse the unlucky offender. Even Katie was not immune to his quick temper.

One morning, while pouring him a mug of warmed cider, she looked across the table to find one of the serving girls flirting outrageously with one of Lord Garrison's men, and she accidentally spilt some of the warm brew upon the table. When a few drops of it fell onto his trousers, causing him to jump to his feet, he bellowed and cursed her clumsiness.

The housekeeper was deeply hurt, but the moment Garrison had said those words, he had regretted them. Seeing her eyes tearing, he quickly said, "I am sorry, Katie." Then, seeing that all within the hall were looking in his direction, shock on their faces, he turned about and hurried to his study, now cursing himself for being a cruel oaf.

A short time later Katie, carrying a mug of warmed cider, silently approached the master's study. Lightly knocking upon the portal, she slowly went within. "I thought you might be wishing for something to drink." She set the mug upon his desk, her face touched with worry and pity.

"Thank you, Katie. I do not know what has come over me lately. It is as though I am beset by some terrible anger."

Katie was witness to his deep pain at this moment, and she felt her heart begin to break for this man she had loved as though he were her own son. "You must set this right soon, my lord. It cannot go on as it is now. I know that your lady has not been in the best of health, but I think it is time that the two of you settle whatever is wrong between you." There, Katie thought. I have said what I have wanted to say for the past week.

Garrison looked at her as though she had suggested something he had never considered. Of course. She was absolutely right. He would confront Sabrina, ask her what was plaguing her and have all out in the open once and for all. There had to be more to her strange actions than the fact that she was with child. Why they had not even talked of the babe since they had been in Edinburgh. "Thank you, Katie. I shall certainly take your advice." He smiled for the first time that week, for he thought that perhaps he would have the answer to his torment shortly.

As Garrison made his way from his study a short time later, he was met upon the stairs by Sabrina. Her smile warmed him, and for a moment he thought of the happy days he had shared with this woman.

"Garrison, I thought that perhaps we could go for a ride together. It is such a pleasant day." Sylvia spoke softly, and her eyes were warm. The man before her stared at her as though he were completely bewitched.

The day was rather cold, and Garrison had planned to stay within the warm walls of the keep, but such thoughts instantly fled him. This was the first time his wife had offered him a kind word in over two weeks, and he was not about to put any obstacle between them. "Do you think it is wise for you to ride? Perhaps we could go for a long walk instead?" He was thinking of her delicate condition, for he knew in past days she had not considered her health. But when he saw Sabrina's face begin to redden with anger, he quickly nodded his head in agreement, reasoning that she would never do anything that would endanger herself or the child. A short ride would in no way cause her any upset. "I will have the stableboy saddle our horses," he said. Before he left her side he reached out and brought one of her soft hands to his lips.

Sylvia grimaced at this leavetaking. She had decided on how best to subdue this man, and after considering poisoning his wine, she had thought it best to overtake him at an unexpected moment while out riding. She had endured all that she could here in the wilds of McBride keep. The sooner the deed was done, the sooner she could return to London—and to Zaloe. As she walked toward the hearth she let her eyes roam about the now-empty hall. This was a dreary place to her thinking, and she did not understand how her twin could have remained here. But enough of Sabrina, she told herself as her booted foot kicked out at a piece of wood that had fallen from the fireplace onto the hearth. Zaloe would have taken care of her. She would not again have to look at the beauty that was so like her own.

Katie stood back in the shadow of the stairwell. Having seen Garrison and Sabrina upon the staircase, she had not wanted to disturb their private moment. She hoped they had settled some of their differences when she saw her lord take the young woman's hand and tenderly place a kiss upon it, and a small smile broke over her aging features. But when Garrison left the main hall and Sabrina turned toward the hearth, for some reason Katie stood and watched her mistress's movements. She saw the lovely young woman's face turn sour, and as Sabrina glared into the flames, she heard a small curse come from her lips.

"You should have been more wise, fair Sabrina. It would have been better for you had you stayed tucked away within the walls of your convent. Safer for you and for the one that calls himself your husband," Sylvia murmured, feeling no guilt at causing her own sister's death. She was now thinking only of dealing with Garrison McBride.

Katie's face paled as she listened to this woman who thought the main hall was empty. The young woman had called another Sabrina, and had spoken of a convent. And what had she meant when she'd referred to Lord Garrison in such a vengeful manner? What sort of game was being played upon the lord of McBride? On silent feet Katie slipped away from the stairwell and headed toward the back of the keep, intending to find Lord Garrison at the stables and to tell him what she had overheard. Even if the lady were only rambling, he should be aware of what she had said. A small prickle of fear stirred in Katie for a moment, and her feet fairly flew down the path. She would advise Garrison to take along a few trusted men. If this woman planned to harm him he should be prepared.

Their ride was made in silence as Garrison led his wife across the McBride property, his destination the secret glade to which he had brought Sabrina on the day they had been wed. He had listened to what his housekeeper had overheard, not fully understanding the meaning of what his wife had said, but he was determined that he would learn her meaning on this very afternoon. He would take her back to the glade where they had made such wondrous love and see her reaction to that place.

Sylvia followed closely behind him, the foliage so dense in some areas that she almost called out to him several times. But thinking that would serve her purpose, she let him lead her on. She had thought they would ride toward the village, out in the open, but this seemed a better spot for her foul work. She only wished that Zaloe had arranged to meet her. Then she could have lured this man to where he was awaiting them. But they had not thought so far ahead, and now it was entirely up to her.

As Garrison pulled his black stallion to a halt within the glade, the gentle sound of the stream came to his ears, and he turned in the saddle to look full into his wife's face. What he viewed there turned his blood to ice. This could not be the same woman that had lain with him upon a grassy embankment one wonderful afternoon in the seclusion of this glade. The woman on horseback next to him was not the one who had softly asked; love in her warm, brown eyes, *Will it ever be thus?*

For a moment Garrison was lost to that moment, recalling his own words as he had held Sabrina so close to him. *Aye, sweet,* he had promised, *I shall not allow it to be any way but as now.* As though his soul were being branded by a scorching flame, he came to his senses and at that moment he saw the quick flash of something coming down toward his head.

Sylvia had been waiting for her chance, and seeing Garrison falling into a dreamy state, she

341

had quickly taken advantage of that moment. Pulling a hanging branch from a tree, she had swung her arm upward and had urged her mare toward the stallion. Then, with all of her might, she had brought the wood down.

Having been well trained to ward off an attack, Garrison shot his large arm outward, catching hold of the branch, and with a vicious jerk, he tore it from Sylvia's grasp.

Quickly seeing her folly as fierce anger surfaced on Garrison's face, Sylvia kicked at her horse's sides, hoping to flee before he could lay a hand on her.

But her attempt was futile. Garrison took hold of her reins and, with a jerk of his wrist, halted her mount.

Let loose of my horse you loathesome blackguard!" Sylvia screamed, her anger matching his own now that her plan had failed.

Even though she had tried to club him, a part of Garrison still thought of this woman as his wife. But as venom came from her lips, he began to fully realize her deception. However, thinking that he must be certain, he clamped a fine hold upon his fury. "Dear wife, why do you wish me ill? Am I not the man who is the father of your unborn child?"

For a moment Sylvia was stunned. She thought of the day in the fortunetelling booth. She had said that perhaps Sabrina would care to know the sex of an unborn child, but her twin had not wanted such knowledge. This man must be trying to trick her. He knew that his wife was not with child. "You lie. I will never bear your seed," she declared.

Garrison was suddenly struck by the truth. This woman was not the one he had wed and loved. He lunged was off his horse and seized Sylvia in a tight grip, his large hands encircling her throat, his eyes a deadly jade.

Sylvia knew full well that her plan had failed, and as Garrison shook her by the neck, the fear of death came upon her.

"Where is my wife?" His angry words filled her ears as they boomed about the rich glade. "I will snap your neck unless you speak this very moment."

Sylvia knew that he meant that, her brown eyes widened. Slowly she nodded her head, agreeing to tell him all. Her life was all that she had left and she was not about to lose that, too.

"Where is Sabrina?" Garrison eased his hold upon her throat somewhat when he saw that she was willing to tell him what he wished to hear.

Chapter Fourteen

The day that Sylvia had left her sister in the hands of Zaloe Tolliver was one Sabrina would long remember.

After her twin left the chamber in which she was held, Sabrina had strained against her bindings, determined that somehow she would free herself and prevent harm from coming to Garrison.

But Zaloe's dark eyes had watched her every move, his gaze fixed upon her as though he still did not believe that she was truly his wife's twin. And in those moments he swore to himself that he would have it all. He would claim the McBride estate and he would also have this beautiful, gentle woman. He was obsessed with wanting his wife's sister. She was so much like Sylvia on the surface but so unlike her within.

He was fed up with Sylvia's foul temper and tantrums, and he silenced her with his fists when shouts and verbal abuse did not do the job. The woman had been raised as a spoiled darling of the rich, and upon marrying him and being forced do without luxuries, she had become a vicious, complaining nag. His dark eyes warmed as he looked over the woman who looked so much like his wife. He knew with a certainty that her temperament was different. If she had been his bride, she would have endured hardships with a gentle smile. Though he was a hard and, at times, a cruel man, something deep within him was stirred by this woman.

Going to the valise that lay open upon the bed, Zaloe eased out a small vial containing some of the liquid he had given to Sabrina long ago at the convent, and as her gold-flecked gaze met his, he saw a silent plea in the depths of her eyes as she silently begged him to have mercy upon her and to release her.

"Nay, my beauty. You shall be mine." He pulled the gag from her mouth and before she could scream out for help or voice a plea, he began to pour the liquid down her throat. "Sylvia would have me put an end to such perfection, but I have a better plan in mind for you."

He drew back, and within seconds, Sabrina felt herself slipping into unconsciousness. Her last thoughts were of Garrison.

Sabrina lost all track of time. Each day and night seemed to run into the next. At one time she thought that she had awakened in a carriage, but as her eyelids had fluttered open she had felt arms upon her, her head had been tilted back, and something cool and sweet had been poured into her mouth.

At other times she awakened to a fuzzy sphere of unreality and upon these few occasions she was vaguely aware that someone was feeding her. She tried to focus her thoughts, but would only imagine that she was ill at her husband's castle and that dear Katie were tending her. Upon occasion she called out to the one feeding her, but soon she lapsed back into unconsciousness.

A week had passed before Zaloe thought that he would let Sabrina regain some of her wits. He knew that the liquid he was feeding her could not harm her, but to stay healthy she needed to be up and about, getting some fresh air and eating more than the soup and broths he spooned into her mouth. Besides which he was beginning to tire of the whole affair. He still had had no word from Sylvia, and hating the seclusion of the cottage that was set well back from the rest of the village, he wished for some company.

The only time he dared to leave his prisoner was in the evening after he had dosed her with the potion and had tied her securely to the bedposts. And then he only went to the tavern of the small village, to play a hand or two of cards and to treat himself to a few drinks. His eyes always watched for Sylvia to enter the smoke-filled room and bring news of her sister's husband's death.

But after a week, when no such announcement was forthcoming, he wanted to spend some time with the gentle Sabrina. And so late in the evening, when he usually administered the brew that put Sabrina to sleep, he gently stroked her cheeks to draw her from her deep slumber.

Sabrina came to her senses rather groggily, her eyes not immediately adjusting to the dim lighting of the small one-room cottage. But as her brown orbs settled upon Zaloe Tolliver, who was sitting next to her upon the bed, they instantly filled with terror when the remembrance of his cruelty flooded back to her. "Where am I?" she asked, trying to bring some reason to her jumbled thoughts. She took in the small dwelling. It appeared that the only furnishing was the small cot on which she was lying upon.

"We are where no one will ever find you, my beauty."

The sinister reply chilled her. "But where is my husband? Where is Sylvia?"

"Do not worry yourself about either of them. I alone will care for you." Zaloe reached out a hand and tenderly, though there was little tenderness in his nature, caressed a tendril of her honey-colored hair.

Sabrina tried to draw away from his hated touch, but when she did, Zaloe became more forceful and placed a hand against each side of her face.

"You will learn to accept my touch as easily as you did McBride's."

"Never," Sabrina whispered, her brown eyes revealing her utter loathing of this man.

"Aye. One day soon, my beauty." His words

held a threatening promise.

Sabrina became aware that ropes tied her hands at either side, and when she tried to sit up, felt too weak.

Seeing that she was wishing to fight off her sluggishness, Zaloe rose to his feet, allowing her to rise to a sitting position. "That is right, Sabrina. Try to regain your strength." He started to untie her hands.

Sabrina just sat for a few moments, letting her head spin, before she slowly tried to stand. On wobbly legs she made her way to the window at the front of the cottage, but when she tried to look about to see where this man was keeping her, she saw only a forest. "Where have you brought me?" She quickly turned about, painfully aware of her imprisonment.

"You shall never escape me. And when Sylvia brings word of your husband's death I will take care of her and then you and I will be together forever."

Sabrina shuddered, and the horror of his words made her tremble. They planned to kill Garrison! But what had he meant by saying he would take care of her twin sister. Sylvia was this man's wife. Her head was still foggy from the potion he had been giving her, but she had one thought — escape. She ran to the door and turned the knob, but the portal was locked. "You cannot do this to me," she declared, and slowly slipped to the floor, feeling helpless and defeated.

Zaloe thought that perhaps he had been too hasty in letting her up from the bed, and he hurried to her side. Easily lifted her, he carried her back to the bed. Placing her upon the small cot, he again tied her hands at her sides, his dark gaze taking in her misery.

"I shall be back later. Try to get some rest," he said, but she did not seem to respond and he thought it likely that the mixture that he had given her was still affecting her. In time the effects would wear off, and then she would be more than willing to respond to him. But now he needed a drink, and he had promised a farmer that he would meet him at the tavern for a hand of cards.

Tormented, Sabrina heard the door slam. As she tried to pull upon the restraints on her wrist, tears coursed down her cheeks. She was too weak to do more than make a feeble attempt to release herself before her eyes fluttered closed. Her last thought was that she would sleep only a short time and when she awoke she would try to get away from this cottage and from her sister's cruel husband.

The small cottage was in total darkness when Zaloe finally stumbled through the door. He tried to light a fire in the fireplace when the cold penetrated his half-drunken stupor.

As a small blaze caught, throwing light about the small room, he straightened and his black eyes went to the cot. "Beauty," he mumbled. Picturing Sabrina awakening that afternoon, Zaloe slowly made his way over to her. What would be the harm in sampling her charms? he wondered drunkenly. What did it matter if he did tonight or on some other night?

At this thought, he fumbled with his clothing, his fingers ineptly trying to unbutton the buttons on his breeches.

Within the dull recesses of her troubled dreams, Sabrina sensed a deeper menace, and she forced her eyes to open. To her horror, Zaloe was standing over her, a cruel, twisted leer upon his face as he tried to shed his clothing. "No!" she gasped aloud, the sound filling the empty room.

"You are mine, beauty," he said lecherously, his words stabbing Sabrina.

"You cannot do this. What of Sylvia?" Frantic, Sabrina tried to discourage him and she bucked up on the cot, trying to pull free of the bindings that held firm.

For a moment Zaloe stood still, his dark eyes caressing every tiny curve and inch of the woman before him. "What need have I of Sylvia when I have you? You have the beauty that first drew me to her, but you have more. You possess something your fair twin will never have." And with this Zaloe lay full-length beside Sabrina.

As mounting terror beset her, Sabrina tried to pull away from him; his liquored breath was making her nauseous. But he pressed himself upon her, his mouth fiercely descending on hers and choking off the very air she breathed.

Turning her head from side to side, Sabrina pulled back and whimpered aloud. No other had

351

ever kissed her besides Garrison. And this man's lips were not tender and giving like her husband's. They were rough and demanding, seemingly free of any feeling except his need to dominate.

The drunken Zaloe thought his assault was welcomed, and he pursued the lips that shied away from his own. He would have her — and she would enjoy it. How could any woman resist him? He had always gotten what he wanted, and this woman would be no different.

Sabrina thought of the child within her body, and she feared the rough handling she was receiving might harm it. She tried to break the bindings, but they did not give.

Zaloe began to tear at her clothing. The black dress she had worn since leaving Edinburgh came apart under his rough handling.

"Noooooo!" Sabrina screamed, only too aware of her impotence as this man lost all control. "My baby," she sobbed aloud, little knowing that she was saying these words into his ear.

In a far corner of Zaloe's brain, her cry registered. Had she said that she was with child? Had he heard her right? With a fierce, black look on his face, he rose and viewed her tear-stained and terrified face. Was he to receive only McBride's leavings?

Harshly flinging himself from the cot, he stood over her, glaring down upon her disheveled state. Never! He could have plenty of women. He did not have to take another's.

Sabrina wept aloud, her sobs filling the tiny

cottage as she turned her face into the pillow.

Oh, I will have her all right, Zaloe told himself, still feeling desire rise in him like a raging tide. But he decided he would have her when she was totally at his mercy, when Garrison McBride no longer stood between them.

Crossing the room, he threw his drunken body down on a pallet near the hearth. As soon as she whelped the brat, he would get rid of it and then nothing would stand between them. Revulsion welled up in him because he had almost taken her while she was carrying McBride's seed. Perhaps he would not have thought twice about taking another woman, but Sabrina was his. She would be his from this day forth, and he did not want to feel that he had taken what Garrison McBride had left.

As Sylvia nodded her head, Garrison eased his fierce hold about her neck and she took a deep breath of air, knowing that she had barely escaped with her life.

"Where is Sabrina?" Garrison did not fully relinquish his hold upon this woman standing before him, knowing that he could not trust her in the slightest. "Tell me now!" He shook her by her frail shoulders, which were so like his wife's.

"All right," Sylvia responded, angrily at having been caught in her misdeed. "Sabrina was with my husband, Zaloe Tolliver."

"You say she was? What do you mean by this? What underhandedness is afoot here?" Garrison

353

looked upon Sylvia with contempt.

"Sabrina is my twin sister. Zaloe and I had thought to gain the money that my mother, Priscilla Buchanan, left to the McBride estate and its heirs."

"What are you talking about?" Garrison shook his head in disbelief. All that she had said made little sense to his baffled mind. "You say that my wife is your twin, but why did she not tell me of this?"

Since she had started to tell him the story, Sylvia saw little reason not confess all. In the end he would still be made to pay. For surely by this time Zaloe had taken care of the fair Sabrina. "My mother sent us away from her at birth. I went to my aunt's house and Sabrina went to a convent on the outskirts and of London, to be raised by the nuns. When Priscilla announced that I was to come to this horrible place and wed you"—here Sylvia showed her total distaste for the man who still held her—"needless to say I found out that I had a twin sister living within convent walls. At the time I was in love with Zaloe Tolliver and refused to be separated from him. So he and I went to the convent and convinced Sabrina to change places with me, to come here as your future bride."

Garrison now understood his wife's reluctance and concern when he had first met her. So many things that had seemed odd at the time now fit into place. But he could not understand why Sabrina had not trusted him enough to tell him all. Why have you come into our lives? Why did you and this Zaloe"—he remembered another time when he had pondered on this same name—"why did you not leave your sister alone and go about your own lives?"

"We would have if Priscilla had not gotten herself killed before I could tell her about my marriage to Zaloe. I would have convinced her to accept us."

"Priscilla Buchanan is dead?" Garrison was dumbfounded. This woman's mother when he had last seen her had seemed in the best of health.

"Yes. She was killed in a carriage accident, along with her lover." Sylvia seemed to derive some satisfaction from the telling of this cruel tale. "And when Zaloe intercepted the messenger that was to take the word to McBride castle, he found that her will stated that all she owned would go to you and your heirs, leaving me without a farthing."

"So you and your husband thought to kidnap my wife. Then you were to pose as Sabrina and lure me out here so that you could kill me and take what I own." It seemed clear now, and he wondered how he could ever have been fooled by this woman.

Sylvia did not answer him. He had already figured out everything except where his precious Sabrina was. As a venomous smile came to her lips, she felt his grip on her tighten.

"Where is my wife?" The words came from deep within Garrison's broad chest, and left little doubt in Sylvia's mind that he wanted an answer

355

at once.

"I do not know." She tried to pull herself away from him.

"You will tell me this moment." Garrison again wrapped his hands about her throat. Furious because of what this woman had done to his family, he began to squeeze, but when her face turned pale and she clawed frantically his hands; he came to his senses.

"She is dead!" the words came from her lips in gasps.

Garrison felt the full impact of what she had said. Then his eyes narrowed. "You are lying. Tell me where Sabrina is."

"I am not lying. Zaloe was to kill her and then meet me after I had taken care of you." Sylvia felt no guilt as she said this, only anger at being caught in her crime.

"Where are you to meet this Zaloe, your husband?" Garrison would not allow himself to believe that Sabrina had been killed. He told himself that she had to be with this woman's husband.

For a moment Sylvia did not speak, but knowing that it would be futile to hold anything from this large, angry man, she finally whispered. "He is in a small cottage outside the village. It is hidden by the forest."

"Then he is not far. You shall come along, in case you have been not telling me the truth. I am the law here, and you and your husband will surely pay dearly for this deception. Sabrina had best be unharmed."

Sylvia knew that there was no sense in arguing with him, and she thought, if she went along, perhaps she and her husband could overpower this big oaf that her sister had wed. All might still come out as they had planned. She climbed atop her mare, allowing Garrison to take hold of the reins and to lead her behind his large, black stallion.

Garrison kicked at his steed's sides, urging him through the trees and foliage that a short time ago had appeared so beautiful to him. Now he barely saw it. His mind was frantically going over what this conniving woman had told him. She was Sabrina's twin, yet she and her husband had taken his wife captive in order to accomplish their dastardly deed. He would not let himself think about her statement that his wife was already dead. She could not be, for he would have felt her death in his heart. He concentrated on getting to the cottage in which Sylvia had said her husband awaited her. Sabrina must still be with this man, he thought. And when he found her Zaloe Tolliver would pay dearly for daring to lay a hand on her.

Thinking only of the need for haste, Garrison pushed his stallion harder, leading the mare on as he did so, and causing Sylvia to hold on to the saddle horn.

Zaloe awakened at midmorning with a head-ache. His eyes went to Sabrina, who was still lying upon the cot, her dress torn and her sobs filling the tiny room.

Rising, he kicked out fiercely at the pallet that lay upon the dirty floor, his anger returning as he thought of the events of the past eve. Her words seemed branded in his memory—*my baby*.

He glared in Sabrina's direction. His head throbbed each time a pitiful moan came from her lips. He splashed some water over his face and then went to her side. Seeing the vile of amber brew next to her he sat upon the cot, took hold of her head, and with a sardonic glare, forced her lips open. The liquid slowly flowed into her mouth.

He had only given her a few drops when his ears pricked up. Horses were approaching the cabin. It must surely be Sylvia, he thought, and he set Sabrina's golden head back upon the pillow. Due to her exhaustion from the past night and her lack of sleep, the drops of the potion had already made her eyes dim.

As he gazed down at her one last time, taking in her delicate beauty, he pulled a revolver from his jacket, checked to see that it was fully loaded, and then smiled with satisfaction. He would settle things quickly. There was no longer any need to keep his wife about. He could finish with her here in the forest, and none would be the wiser.

Stepping to the window he saw that there were two riders coming down the path, and he recognized the large man in the lead; Garrison McBride had been pointed out to him at the inn in Edinburgh. Zaloe cursed his wife soundly for being a clumsy fool. She had botched up their plan, and had told Garrison of his whereabouts. Intending to give her what she deserved after he had taken care of McBride, he went out the back door of the cottage.

Garrison looked over the cottage. The only sign of life was the small stream of smoke coming out of the chimney. He did not see any movement, nor was there a horse tethered outside. He glanced at Sylvia, and the moment he looked at her, he knew that she had played him false. Her brown eyes were gloating and this could only mean she felt that she and her husband would still win out.

Garrison jumped from the back of his stallion and ran to the cabin. He pushed the door open, and his eyes went over the small room, then settled upon the woman lying quietly upon the small cot. Sabrina, he cried out. Her sister had lied to him. She was not dead. He wanted to rush to her side and hold her, but his experience in battle had taught him to do otherwise.

His wife lay still upon the cot as his eyes searched each corner and then went to the back door which was ajar. He knew that his adversary had heard his approach and had run out the back way. As he was about to step farther into the cabin, he heard the cold click of a pistol hammer being pulled back.

"That is quite far enough, my lord," a deep voice called from the front doorway.

Garrison slowly spun about. A tall, dark man was holding a gun on him, and his wife's twin sister was at the man's side. Again Garrison's eyes went to Sabrina to make sure that she was safe and out of harm's way for the moment. "You are the one called Zaloe who dared to take my wife by force?"

His voice had a chilling quality, and for a second the couple before him stood in silent awe. But Zaloe quickly shook himself from his stupor, remembering that it was he who held the pistol. The large muscular man before him was unarmed.

As Sylvia looked at Garrison out of the corner of one eye she saw a movement. Turning to the small cot across the room, she stared with disbelief at her sister who was trying to sit up. "What is she doing here?" she asked her husband, her anger mounting. Why had Zaloe kept her twin with him? They had planned to dispose of her as soon as they left Edinburgh.

"Shut up!" Zaloe glared at Sylvia. He had certainly not missed her sharp tongue this past week. She had become a thorn in his side, and he would be well off without her.

"But I thought you were going to get rid of her? Why have you brought her all the way to this cottage?" Sylvia was slowly beginning to understand her husband's reason for doing so, and her cheeks flamed. "You had no intention of killing her. I remember well the way you looked at her when she rode in the carriage with you from the convent. You wanted the twit that day and you still do!" Sylvia shouted out the horrible realization.

"I told you to shut up." Zaloe drove the butt of the pistol into her cheek, sending her to her knees. "You saw well my desire that day long ago, wife. Compared to you, your sister Sabrina is sweet wine, a delicate flower. You, though you look the same, are a bitter brew, a bramble."

"But you are my husband," Sylvia cried out from her lowly position upon the floor.

"Perhaps, but not for long. As soon as I tend to this one"—he pointed the gun barrel toward Garrison—"I shall deal with you. And none shall be the wiser when I claim McBride's widow as my wife."

Garrison had learned all that he wished to know from this insane pair. As a small moan came from the bed, his eyes went to Zaloe.

Zaloe had also heard Sabrina moan, and for an instant he took his gaze from his opponent. That was a fatal mistake. Garrison was waiting for such an opportunity, and he lunged toward the man near the door, his long arms striking out.

At that moment Zaloe tried to fire the gun, but quick as a lunging cat, Garrison drove a fist down onto his arm and the bullet struck the dirt floor of the cottage.

Zaloe thought all lost when Garrison flung him across the room. As he landed against the wall, pain flared in his chest and a stunned glaze came over his dark eyes. His hands went to his chest, and as he drew them away, he viewed a dark red stain—his own blood. His dark eyes went from his blood to Garrison, who stood looking down at him as though not knowing what had happened,

361

then they went to his wife. She slowly dropped the pistol onto the dirt.

Quickly pulling himself together, Garrison went to Zaloe, and bending down, he heard his last ragged, drawn-out breath. Then Zaloe Tolliver was still.

"He never truly loved me, but at least we shall be together in hell." Garrison heard the soft words of the dying woman. "I did all for him, and he did not care." Sylvia's small frame collapsed.

Going to her side, Garrison saw that Zaloe had accidentally shot his own wife, killing her as she, in turn, had killed him.

But he had little time to dwell upon the evil couple that had come into his life. He had to see to Sabrina. With quick steps, he rushed to the side of the cot. Seeing her glazed eyes and her absent look, he feared that she had been harmed in the fighting.

But a closer inspection showed him that she had suffered no physical abuse. Taking the small vial left opened by the cot, he tucked it into his jacket and gently reached out to his wife.

"Sweet love, keeper of my heart," he whispered softly as he brought her up against his chest, the delicate scent he loved so well filling his nostrils.

Sabrina tried to surface to reality. "Garrison," she whispered and then fell silent. Crystal tears sparkled in her brown eyes as she felt the gentle, loving pressure of his lips.

"I must get you to a doctor, sweet," Garrison said softly, and without a backward glance at the two lying upon the cabin floor he went outside and set Sabrina on his horse. Then he mounted and held her in his arms, her cheek pressed against his sturdy chest.

Seeming to collapse, Sabrina remained still as her husband pushed his mount toward the village, fears for her health and that of their unborn child in the forefront of his mind.

After a short wait in the doctor's front parlor, the physician came from his examination room with the news that Sabrina would be fine. "The potion in the vial is a concoction that I have seen in the past. It will not harm your wife or your child, my lord. At times it is used to put to sleep those who have trouble getting rest." The doctor smiled. "Your wife will have no problem when it has worn off."

Garrison shook the good man's hand and then hurried off to his wife, his heart soaring because once again Sabrina was in his keeping.

His bride's warm, brown eyes turned to him as he entered the small room, and her smile drew him to her. She had such a radiance about her, even in her condition, that Garrison could not help but desire to hold her soft, yielding body in his arms.

"You will be all right, love." He pulled her into his embrace, aware of his good fortune.

"And the babe?" Sabrina's fear that something would be wrong with her unborn child caused a chill to course through her.

Garrison smiled into her sweet face. "Our child

is perfectly safe." He lightly patted her belly as though trying to communicate with the one buried in her warmth.

Sighing, Sabrina rested her head on her husband's sturdy chest.

"I should be quite angry with you, madam, for not trusting me with the story of your twin," Garrison chided softly, not wishing to cause her distress but needing all to be in the open.

"I did not mean to keep it from you, Garrison. Truly. I was just so afraid that you would put me from you, thinking that I had so dreadfully deceived you." When he looked wounded, she went on. "I tried to put off the marriage when we first met, because I knew I could not live with such a deception. But after a few days of knowing you, it was too late. I had fallen in love with you, and there seemed no way but to play the game to the finish. You must believe me, though, when I say that I would have told you. I almost did that day at the inn in Edinburgh, but when the serving girl interrupted us, I again put off the tale, fearing that your sense of honor would make you set all aright and that I would lose you." Large crystal tears glistened in her gold-flecked brown eyes and then rolled down her creamy cheeks.

Garrison's heart went out to his bride, and with a gentle finger, he lovingly wiped away the tears. "Love, you need never think that I would set you from me. Though pride and honor may carry me far, without you I would surely be nothing. When I thought I had lost you, I was as one dead. You are my reason for existence, my life, my very soul. You shall always be at my side, no matter what forces come against us. Never doubt that."

Sabrina knew that her love for this man, like his for her, was total and complete. It was a bridge that would connect them throughout eternity. She would never doubt the strength of his love again. "Hold me, Garrison," she said. Only in his arms did she feel completely safe.

Wrapping his strong arms about her, Garrison whispered into her ear, "For all time shall I hold you . . . my love."

ZEBRA HAS THE SUPERSTARS
OF PASSIONATE ROMANCE!

CRIMSON OBSESSION (2272, $3.95)
by Deana James

Cassandra MacDaermond was determined to make the handsome gambling hall owner Edward Sandron pay for the fortune he had stolen from her father. But she never counted on being struck speechless by his seductive gaze. And soon Cassandra was sneaking into Sandron's room, more intent on sharing his rapture than causing his ruin!

TEXAS CAPTIVE (2251, $3.95)
by Wanda Owen

Ever since two outlaws had killed her ma, Talleha had been suspicious of all men. But one glimpse of virile Victor Maurier standing by the lake in the Texas Blacklands and the half-Indian princess was helpless before the sensual tide that swept her in its wake!

TEXAS STAR (2088, $3.95)
by Deana James

Star Garner was a wanted woman—and Chris Gillard was determined to collect the generous bounty being offered for her capture. But when the beautiful outlaw made love to him as if her life depended on it, Gillard's firm resolve melted away, replaced with a raging obsession for his fiery TEXAS STAR.

MOONLIT SPLENDOR (2008, $3.95)
by Wanda Owen

When the handsome stranger emerged from the shadows and pulled Charmaine Lamoureux into his strong embrace, she sighed with pleasure at his seductive caresses. Tomorrow she would be wed against her will—so tonight she would take whatever exhilarating happiness she could!

TEXAS TEMPEST (1906, $3.95)
by Deana James

Sensuous Eugenia Leahy had an iron will that intimidated even the most powerful of men. But after rescuing her from a bad fall, the virile stranger MacPherson resolved to take the steel-hearted beauty whether she consented or not!

Available wherever paperbacks are sold, or order direct from the Publisher. Send cover price plus 50¢ per copy for mailing and handling to Zebra Books, Dept. 2269, 475 Park Avenue South, New York, N.Y. 10016. Residents of New York, New Jersey and Pennsylvania must include sales tax. DO NOT SEND CASH.

A TENDER WOOING

The voice she had heard earlier had been cut from crystals of ice. Now there was a different tone to it, a husky gentling, yet Sabrina could not seem to respond to the change as she stood close to him outside her chamber door, her gold-flecked brown eyes looking up into his green ones as she drowned in his gaze.

She stood as though in a trance as his handsome face slowly descended. She could do naught but hold her breath as his mouth approached and captured her petal-soft lips.

She was lost. Never had any man made such an assault on her senses. Silky-soft bursts of pleasure went through her as her arms went about his neck, pulling him closer . . .